T0340202

Togani

MODERN KOREAN FICTION

Bruce Fulton, General Editor

TREES ON A SLOPE
Hwang Sun-wŏn

THE DWARF
Cho Se-hŭi

THE RED ROOM: STORIES OF TRAUMA
IN CONTEMPORARY KOREA
Bruce and Ju-Chan Fulton, translators

I MET LOH KIWAN
Cho Haejin

TOGANI
Gong Ji-young

Gong Ji-young

TOGANI

Translated by Bruce and Ju-Chan Fulton

University of Hawai'i Press

Honolulu

This book is published with the support of the
Literature Translation Institute of Korea (LTI Korea).

도가니 *Togani*
© 2009 by Ji-young Gong
First published in Korea by Changbi Publishers Inc.
All rights reserved
English translation © 2023 University of Hawai'i Press
English edition is published by arrangement with the author
    and KL Management, Seoul, Korea

Library of Congress Cataloging-in-Publication Data

Names: Kong, Chi-yǒng. | Fulton, Bruce, translator. |
    Fulton, Ju-Chan, translator.
Title: Togani / Gong Ji-young ; translated by Bruce Fulton and Ju-Chan
    Fulton.
Other titles: Togani. | Modern Korean fiction.
Description: Honolulu : University of Hawai'i Press, [2023] | Series:
    Modern Korean fiction
Identifiers: LCCN 2022058110 (print) | LCCN 2022058111 (ebook) | ISBN
    9780824894870 (trade paperback) | ISBN 9780824895242 (epub) | ISBN
    9780824895259 (kindle edition) | ISBN 9780824895235 (pdf)
Subjects: LCSH: Deaf children—Abuse of—Korea (South)—Fiction. | Child
    sexual abuse by teachers—Korea (South)—Fiction. | LCGFT: Novels of
    manners.
Classification: LCC PL992.425.C48 T6413 2023 (print) | LCC PL992.425.C48
    (ebook) | DDC 895.73/5—dc23/eng/20230222
LC record available at https://lccn.loc.gov/2022058110
LC ebook record available at https://lccn.loc.gov/2022058111

Cover photograph: Janis Baiks/Shutterstock.com

Contents

Togani

I

As Kang Inho was loading his car with a meager set of belongings and setting out from Seoul, the maritime fog began its
creep into the city of Mujin. Rising from the sea like a huge,
colorless beast, it advanced onto the mainland, a damp, dense
landfall moving forward, ever forward. The objects in its
path, like soldiers sensing imminent defeat, surrendered to
the vapor, which absorbed their amorphous shapes into its
bosom. Among the swallowed structures was a four-story
building of stone perched on a bluff overlooking the sea—the
Home of Benevolence. As the mist engulfed the building, the
light escaping through the window of the dining hall on the
first floor turned the color of mayonnaise. Elsewhere a church
bell began to toll, calling the faithful to the Sabbath worship.
The tolling reverberated in the distance, the only sound to
penetrate the fog.

⤳

Along the railroad tracks near the Home of Benevolence
walked a boy. And as he walked, the fog lowered like the fine
mesh of a net, effacing everything it met. Beside the tracks
were beds of cosmos that had blossomed early for the season;

they paled and trembled as the fog trapped them in its fine weave.

The boy was twelve, but if you were to stand him next to other boys his age, you would see how absurdly short he was, how withered and bony he looked. The boy's striped T-shirt, the color of bleached sky, was wet with mist.

Something wasn't right with the boy—he walked with a limp—but you couldn't have made out his expression, which was masked by the advancing fog. And soon the rest of him was sucked in. But his feet on the crossties could feel the faint tremor, its measured pulsations.

⌒

The Sunday worship at the First Church of God's Glory, in the Mujin city center, commenced at 10 a.m. The fog had already encroached on the church parking lot, and you might have heard an occasional muffled bump as latecomers attempted to squeeze in, high beams helpless to prevent the nudge of fender against fender. The fog devoured the headlights and everything else in its path, in defiance of the scripture then being read in the sanctuary: "The light shines in the darkness, and the darkness has not overcome it." The church custodian, helping to park the cars, dropped his key ring. He bent over and located it only with difficulty. "Damn thick," he muttered. His voice was lost in the swell of the organ accompanying the choir.

⌒

The tracks began to rattle. The boy looked back to where the railroad made a wide bend. The train was coming. He held out his arms as if to embrace it. Was that a smile on his face—or a grimace? The next moment his lips rounded in an outcry. But the sound he produced was eerie and inarticulate: no vowel or consonant could have been distinguished. The locomotive blared a warning, then tossed the boy aside like a kernel of popcorn. The boy's blood streamed along the ground. The billowing fog covered the blood, the train continued on its way, and the surroundings grew still—underwater still. The boy's eyelids fluttered one last time before his eyes came to rest on the milky void.

~

No sooner had Kang pulled into the service area than his cell phone beeped. It was his wife. Less than an hour had passed since his departure. Her voice when he answered was tinged with regret—even though she was the one who had urged him off to Mujin by himself, leaving her and their daughter in Seoul.

"Are you driving?"

"No, I just pulled into a rest stop."

Kang wondered if she had called for a specific reason. Or was she only now aware of the emptiness he had left behind? For a brief moment he felt for her, but the next instant he felt sorry for himself, away from home and alone on the road.

"You're smoking, aren't you? Well, there won't be anyone to nag you now."

After a brief silence Kang responded: "It's all right, no worries. I'm hoping I can bring you and Saemi down next spring. She can go to kindergarten there."

He heard a brief giggle before she replied: "Yes—but first they have to take you on for good."

The teaching job that awaited him in Mujin was temporary. And it would never have come about if not for his wife. Quite by chance she had run into a high school classmate who had family ties with the Home of Benevolence, and as far as Kang could tell, his outgoing wife had asked this friend to see what she could do about finding him a position there. Kang had briefly taught school after graduating from college, then had started a garment business with a friend. If not for the global recession of the previous year, he would be on an airplane

instead of in his car, traveling to the factory in China. His
return to teaching had been his wife's idea. After six months
without a job, he needed a new livelihood. Fortunately, he and
his partner had had the good sense to close down the factory in
time to avoid bankruptcy. Fortuitously as well, he and his wife
had managed to hang on to their apartment in the outskirts
of Seoul. On the other hand, he had long ago had to cancel
his long-term savings plan, as well as forfeit his life insurance
policies.

At first he was puzzled by his wife's suggestion that he go
back to teaching: "Special education? With hearing-impaired
kids? My certification is for mainstream classes, and that was a
long time ago—I'm not even sure it's current."

"You're so stuck in your ways." His wife had smiled trium-
phantly; the teaching position she was presenting to him was a
plum opportunity. *No wonder your business went belly up,* he had
imagined her murmuring. But then she seemed to realize how
dispirited he had been of late, and she softened her tone: "You
know, it's a private school, and like my friend said, you'll be
fine now that we have a connection there. All you have to do is
take a few special ed grad courses at night. It sounds like they
pay well, and you won't be teaching all the time—what could be
better? So you work hard and get yourself a permanent position
and then who knows, maybe you can get something back here
in Seoul." She had sealed her pep talk with a bright grin.

〜

Kang resumed his southward journey. Born and raised in
Seoul, at the center of the Korean Peninsula, a man who had
rarely ventured far from home, he couldn't imagine life in
the southern region. The people there supposedly had thick
accents, and their food tasted strong. Apart from this, all he
knew of the south were the names of unfamiliar cities. Mujin
was an exception. It was the locale of Kim Sŭngok's signature
story "Record of a Journey to Mujin." A story that brought

back memories he didn't care to remember. Memories that, at
his wife's mention of Mujin, had loomed over him like a ship
emerging from a fog bank and preparing to dock.

"'Record of a Journey to Mujin' . . . when you taught us
that story—wasn't it right after you came to our school?—
somehow I knew this day would come." Myŏnghŭi had paid
him a surprise visit at the army base, insisting she would spend
the night. In bed at the nearby inn, he had been hesitant, and
finally she had drawn him close and spoken into his ear: "Do
you remember Ha Insuk from that story? Did you ever wonder
what happened to her after the guy left?"

Myŏnghŭi's body had smelled faintly of peaches. She had
been a student at the girls' high school where he had taught
while awaiting his induction notice for compulsory military
service. But the girl he had taught then now wore garish
makeup that couldn't conceal the fact that she was barely
twenty years of age.

"Don't be afraid," she had told him. "It's . . . not my first
time."

He had been the one trembling. He recalled how she had
giggled as she placed his hands on her naked bosom. That
giggle had chilled him; he had felt he was in the presence of a
girl who had given up on life. But at the time he hadn't dwelled
on this. After seeing her off he had gotten drunk near the bus
terminal, and back at the base he had been able to dispel any
nagging feelings of guilt. Myŏnghŭi had returned from time
to time, and if not for his affair with her, the sex so intense
that he had sometimes felt on the verge of strangling her, he
might very well have turned his army rifle against others—or
himself.

Around the time he was discharged, Myŏnghŭi's letters
stopped arriving. And when he returned to Seoul, he learned
she had taken her life a few months earlier. That was when he
recalled her question—"Do you remember Ha Insuk? Did you
ever wonder what happened to her after the guy left?"

⤳

The sign for Mujin appeared, and Kang exited the expressway. The city was over the next hill. But what Kang saw as he crested the hill was the stolid mass of clouds, the vast sea of fog banks composed of delicate tendrils of white that shrouded Mujin. The car tunneled its way into the clinging fog, the fine, damp mesh of the mist calling to Kang's mind a witch's gray hair. He couldn't have said why, but for some reason he recalled the time many summers ago that he had almost drowned. He had been fishing, and he could still remember the sticky, slimy feel of the vegetation on his bare legs when he had jumped into the reservoir to retrieve the fishing rod that had been pulled from his grasp. He had felt that the water weeds clinging to him would swallow up everything, and instead of swimming back to shore, he had called to his friend for help. The energy had drained out of him, and even though he knew how to swim, he had felt paralyzed. That this memory had surfaced just now gave him a bad feeling. He stiffened, overcome with a brief surge of terror: if he wasn't careful, this journey might be the end of him. After a nervous gulp he turned on his hazard lights and heard their rhythmic click. The GPS navigated him through the fog: "Now entering a fog zone. One kilometer ahead turn right."

And one kilometer farther along, he turned right.

⤳

The Home of Benevolence appeared through the fog. Kang drove past a vacant custodian's booth and into a parking lot and was about to pull up next to a blue luxury sedan when he heard the vehicle's engine come to life. Kang lowered the driver's-side window to speak to the other driver. But the car had already lurched into motion, and it sped off surprisingly fast and in no time had penetrated the white fog bank. All he had seen of the driver was a balding head and a nonchalant expression. Kang inched his car into a space in the obscured lot. Once or twice an offshore breeze lifted the curtain of mist just enough for him to see the huge stone structure, but before long the sheer veil had lowered again. He got out. The twenty-minute drive from the Mujin turnoff had left his shoulders more stiff and sore than the four hours of expressway driving from Seoul to the exit. He windmilled his right arm a few times, then lit a cigarette. He heard a soft crunching sound. Whatever was making the sound came near, and then a shape appeared, that of a small girl. The crunching sound was coming from her mouth—cookies? She was a scrawny little thing, and her hair was cropped so that it looked like the rim of a bowl. As she walked toward Kang, she kept reaching into a large bag for more to eat.

"Hey, there!" Kang called out. "Can you—" And then he realized the girl was fixated on what she was eating, and in the same instant he remembered that he had arrived at a facility for the hearing-impaired. While he was thinking how ridiculous his attempt at conversation had been, the girl seemed to have spotted him. The crunching sound came to a gradual stop. Clumsy though it was, he tried out the sign language he had studied before departing Seoul: *Hello. Nice to meet you.* But before his hands could complete the greeting, a look of unworldly terror came to the girl's eyes, and with an inarticulate shriek she turned and ran.

Kang watched her receding form, baffled, until the fog had absorbed her. There remained only her shrieking, an alien sound from a human mouth.

⁀

"It was probably the fog."

As Sergeant Chang listened to Kim's report, he felt the vibration that announced a text message. Listening with one ear to Kim, he glanced down at his cell phone.

i'm mad, oppa, *really mad—i told you i need it today!*

Chang smiled in spite of himself. He could still feel the pasty inside of Misuk's thigh on his fingertips.

"If the boy was hard of hearing, then he never heard it coming. Probably couldn't see it either."

"For sure . . . damn thick fog," Chang countered as he pecked out a reply to Misuk: *can't wait a few days? lack of patience is so charming in a girl. . . . how about chewing on some fresh octopus with me tonight?*

Chang sent the message and looked up just in time to see the last trace of a sneer pass from the patrolman's face. He carefully placed the cell phone on his desk and in response to Kim's gaze cradled his head in his hands in a gesture designed to convince Kim that the boy's death actually bothered him.

"Any other particulars?"

"About what you'd expect with someone hit by a train. But we did recover something unusual from his pocket." So saying, Kim produced a plastic evidence bag and deposited it on the sergeant's desk. Inside was a bloodstained scrap of paper that looked like it had been torn from an appointment book. "Two names written there—Yi Kangsŏk and Pak Pohyŏn—with a bunch of *X* marks above."

Chang's eyebrows rose to attention, and thoughts of Misuk at the Night Blossom Café were forgotten. By now Chang worked half on instinct, and he had caught a whiff of something in what Kim had just said. He considered the bloodstained scrap. Yi Kangsŏk was the principal of the Home of Benevolence. And Pak Pohyŏn, if he remembered correctly, was one of the dormitory guidance counselors. He recalled attending a dinner party hosted by Yi, who had arrived with Pak tagging along behind him—a man with thin eyelids and a dark, sickly complexion. *The principal treated him like shit the entire night, and all he did was hang his head—spineless bastard.* Yes, he remembered Pak Pohyŏn now.

"All right, you can go. I'll give the school a call."

As soon as Kim turned to leave, Chang returned to his cell phone and tapped out another message: oppa *gets it—3 million? no problem*

Chang felt more relaxed now. He was, as his wife had once said, a lucky fellow. Whenever he needed something, the situation always developed in his favor. His thoughts went back to the previous month, to another day of thick fog, when he had seen the body of the girl at the foot of the cliff at the far end of the school playfield. The train tracks and the cliff. Two months, two deaths, two kids from the home. The one at the cliff had been ruled an accident; probably ditto for the one at the train tracks. You could blame everything on the damn fog. Chang broke into a grin as he looked out the window. The fog was gradually lifting, and he could see the outlines of cars slowly appearing. Everyone was fed up with the fog, but sometimes it came in handy. *That's right. All you got to do is watch your step, and everything comes in handy sooner or later.*

᠊᠊᠊᠊᠊᠊᠊᠊᠊᠊᠊᠊᠊᠊᠊᠊᠊᠊᠊᠊

You may not have much in the way of belongings, but moving them can be a chore. You don't notice them in their usual places—it's only when you have to pack them that you see how pathetic they are. At least this was Kang's impression as he began to organize the kitchen in the 430-square-foot apartment he'd leased in Mujin. Cookpot, coffee cup, glass, a few small plates—these were the sum of his kitchen items, and it was not until he'd arranged them in a cupboard and placed his notebook computer on the kitchen table that he began to feel he had actually left home and started a new life here. But there was also a familiar feel to the place—it reminded him of the studio apartments of friends he'd hung out with at college when they'd all had to skimp—and truth to tell, it was kind of refreshing. Just then, *ding-dong.* He opened the door and there she was, Sŏ Yujin.

"It really is you! Who would have thought we'd meet in a place like this? It's good to see you."

Setting down a shopping bag containing the requisite housewarming gift of detergent, she extended her hand. Kang clasped it and they exchanged smiles. She had graduated the year before him, and a classmate had mentioned that she'd settled here in Mujin. And so they had reconnected. All it took was a further exchange of emails and text messages, and she had found this apartment for him. And now, for the first time in ten years, they were face to face. Kang searched the woman standing before him for the slender student with the cropped hair he had known back then. But the intervening years must have been steeped in hardship, for all delicacy had disappeared from her face, and she now resembled a woman on the verge of middle age.

"She got divorced and raised the two girls by herself," a buddy had told Kang during a drunken confab in which the buddy had revealed that he'd fallen for her at one point. "One of them was always getting sick. She's had a pretty rough time of it. . . . Strange how all the right women—the ones who are pretty and smart—end up with all the wrong guys and a shitload of problems."

"And your wife is a perfect example, sad sack," Kang had said in an attempt to mollify his maudlin friend. But it wasn't just his buddies who felt sorry for Sŏ; anyone who had known her would have felt the same way about the succession of political defeats that befell her husband, the congenital heart defect that afflicted one of the girls, and the want of money that inevitably followed. How she had ended up in Mujin, nobody knew. But now that Kang was finally reunited with her in a new setting in an unfamiliar city, he noticed in her once-gentle face and fine features the fresh girlish silhouette of the woman he used to know. Her presence here had instantly rendered Mujin less forbidding, and the fog-induced tension that had gripped him began to dissipate.

"I was worried about the fog, but here you are. It must have been quite an ordeal. Fog is the one thing you'll have to get used to here. But look, it's starting to lift."

So saying, she turned toward the window, arms across her chest. Seeing her from the rear, Kang realized how small she was.

"We live in the next building over, on the top floor, where the lights are on." The building she indicated was half misted over, its outlines blurred, but not before Kang instantly noticed two windows lit from within. He guessed from the splotches of bare cement that the building had once been shiny and immaculate.

"I've got two kids, you know, and my mother's living with us. My brother and his wife are in the area too. She's from here, and he managed to find a business opportunity locally. So we decided that one of us would take Mother in." And then she said, "I really had to get out of Seoul."

To Kang the cheerfulness of this last utterance sounded forced; what it sounded like to him was *I'm not all that unhappy.* But however she wanted to phrase it, he had to do the right thing and respect her feelings.

"You must be starving—can I offer you dinner? Or maybe we could go somewhere. . . ." The second suggestion came out sounding noncommittal because by rights she, the older of the two, should invite him to her place.

"Oh, let's just go out. That way I can have a look at the city."

Kang's response seemed to put her at ease, and she gave him a bright smile that revealed a dimple he had forgotten until now. Observing that dimple, Kang for a brief instant was taken back to the rented room he had occupied as a twenty-year-old, when Sŏ had visited him. And with this thought came a sense of anticipation: life in Mujin might not be so bad after all. He couldn't remember the last time he had experienced this buoyant sensation. It was a feeling to savor, and he didn't want to let go of it.

〜

Off they went, Sŏ leading the way, the fog filtering between them like smoke from a dying fire. They were in the busiest part of Mujin, the night still young and the city just coming alive. But the awakening lights failed to dispel the impression of drabness Kang got from the city. There was a smell of chronic decay in the air and a sense of urgency you might feel at the sight of makeshift beach structures confronting the massive waves of an ocean storm. A flock of chattering girls in their late teens were descending into a basement karaoke bar; the girls wore short skirts, tall boots that were out of season, and tops with scooped necklines. Kang and Sŏ entered an alley where a cat was clawing through litter looking for scraps of food. It perked up at their approach. Farther down the alley a young man was clutching a wall and vomiting.

Just then a hand grabbed Kang's arm and a woman with long permed hair and a revealing neckline came into sight. She was very short.

"Hey, *oppa,* let's go have some fun."

As Kang silently removed her hand, he realized she was not a woman but a girl, likely in her mid-teens. And then he became aware of Sŏ's gaze. He tried to turned away, but the girl blocked him. She had unusually dark eyes, which might have been crossed, and they shone with a strange gleam, giving her a peculiar sensual aura. She wore heavy makeup, though there was no ugliness to hide. Kang tried to sidestep her, but the girl stuck her nose into his chest and sniffed.

"Wow! You smell like Seoul, *oppa.* A fine and dandy smell." She cackled.

Finally, with a stony look Sŏ took Kang by the shirttail and tugged him off toward the main street.

"My fault—I'm sure you're hungry so I thought we'd take this short cut." Sŏ bit her lip as if an embarrassing family secret had been exposed. To Kang her reaction bespoke an artlessness that he associated with former honor students, many of whom seemed to think that they carried the world on their shoulders. That artlessness must have been a factor in her present misfortunes, he decided.

"Why feel sorry?" he said with a smile. "Is it your fault that there are pleasure quarters in this world of ours?"

She smiled with him, sweeping her hair back over her ear.

"Well, it's just that Mujin doesn't seem to have much to show for itself these days. Mujin, the Historic City—sure, it has a nice ring to it, but so what if it was once the fountain of democracy? All it is today is a poverty-stricken, rundown city. Its former glory doesn't mean much to the young people here. Once they graduate, where do they go?"

Sitting across from Sŏ over a meal of grilled pork belly, Kang sensed that she regretted having settled here. And now he had landed in the same dead-end place. His face clouded over. Just then she handed him her card. Above her name was the title "Director, Mujin Human Rights Advocacy Center."

"Why the smile?" she asked.

"Wow, advocacy, center . . . it's been a long time."

Kang suddenly felt tired. When had human rights advocacy become a profession? He wondered if she was paid for her work. He recalled the shabby little windows of Sŏ's apartment, and the next instant the buoyancy and anticipation he had felt upon first seeing her was replaced by a surge of fatigue. So when she asked, "What made you decide to teach at a school for the hearing-impaired?" he snapped, "To make the world a better place."

She responded with an indulgent grin, ignoring his sarcasm. "Good for you. You know, when that girl said you smelled like Seoul? Forgive me for saying this, but I felt something similar when I saw you earlier. I guess it's because I feel like a country mouse now that I've been here three years." And flashing a down-to-earth smile, she poured him a shot of soju.

Kang found himself wondering whether he had made the right decision in moving into an apartment a stone's throw from hers.

⌁

Day one at the Home of Benevolence. As Kang followed the school administrator down the hallway, the door to the principal's office opened and a man in a brown windbreaker emerged. His eyes met Kang's and then quickly took in Kang's appearance. *Very sharp eyes,* Kang told himself.

"Well, if it isn't the esteemed Sergeant Chang!" the administrator greeted him. "I just now submitted my report to the principal. These kids, I can't count the number of times I've told them *Do not leave the grounds on Sunday,* but they just won't listen. And look what happens. For heaven's sake, we do the best we can to supervise the children, but you know what we have to deal with. . . ."

Whatever the administrator was referring to, it was clear to Kang from his overblown delivery that he was talking out of both sides of his mouth, accepting and yet denying responsibility for something.

"Well, what can you do?" said Chang. "If they can't hear, then they won't listen." He and the administrator laughed long and hard, as if they had hit upon a brilliant joke. This too rang false. "These kids" and "won't listen" obviously referred to the hearing-impaired children. *Still,* Kang couldn't help but think. He wasn't expecting the administrator to say he managed a home for the disabled in order to make the world a better place, as Kang had said to Sŏ. *But still.* The exchange left Kang with a bad taste.

"It must have hit the principal hard. I want you to know, I was concerned enough about him that I dropped everything and hurried over here."

"How much of a nuisance is it going to be?" said the administrator, scratching his balding head.

Kang found the conversation tedious. He wondered if the administrator and the balding man in the blue car he had seen through the fog the previous day were one and the same. "Anyway," continued the administrator. "Do what you can—please. We've had a lot of headaches lately, what with audits and all." "What's there to do?" asked Chang. "It was an accident pure and simple. The fog was thick, and the engineer didn't see him. And if the engineer can't see the kid and the engineer's right there, then how could the teachers have prevented it? And that's what our finding will be. Please, no worries." And then, with a subtle grin, "Didn't I take care of that other business for you last month?"

Kang thought he saw the administrator's face briefly turn pale, but the next moment the man chuckled and gushed, "Indeed you did. It's good to know we can breathe easy. We're much obliged, Sergeant Chang."

Inside the principal's office, no sooner had Kang noticed the nameplate on the desk—"Yi Kangsŏk, Principal"—than the man himself returned from the bathroom, drying his hands. He too was balding. Kang shifted his gaze back to the administrator. Amazing—like the same actor playing different roles, so close was the resemblance between the two faces. Principal Yi Kangsŏk, Administrator Yi Kangbok—identical twins.

↝

Sitting opposite Yi Kangsŏk, Kang became aware of the man in the gilded portrait mounted on the wall behind the principal, as if lending moral support to the occupant of the office. The man stood at a slight angle, gazing out at the viewer. Below the portrait was the inscription "Paesan, Yi Chunbŏm, Founder of the Home of Benevolence." Yi Chunbŏm—the father of the twins, Kang decided.

The brothers were identical twins, but each projected a distinct aura. Was it their attire? The principal wore a dark brown three-piece suit, but the administrator preferred a more casual look—a dark-gray sweater and slacks. It was only natural, Kang told himself: the older you became, the more your job tended to infuse your person. He began to see the two men as individuals rather than twins.

"I understand your wife is a close friend of our niece in Seoul."

As Kang had expected of a man in his position, the principal spoke deliberately and with authority—plenty of authority. But instead of looking at Kang as he spoke, the principal was flipping idly through the newspaper on his desk. This neglect, combined with his failure to use the proper verb endings demanded by etiquette, left Kang wondering if the principal was trying to humiliate him, if what he really meant to say was *So you're the guy who hid under his wife's skirt while she got you this job.* Kang had to remind himself of the decision he had made that morning while shaving: he would earn his monthly wage and with it plan for the future and enjoy life like your average Kim. And then he remembered how he had agonized whenever payday drew near at his modest business enterprise in China, and he realized he should be thankful for his wife's assistance. Why, he'd be grateful for help from his little daughter if she could offer it. If humiliation was the price he had to pay in order to enjoy life, then so be it. With these thoughts he produced an awkward grin and bowed in deference to the principal.

"The new administration in Seoul keeps cutting the social welfare budget, the kids keep eating up our resources, it's a real bitch of a job . . ." The principal punctuated the statement by folding the newspaper and slapping it on his desk in frustration. At which point the administrator rose, signaling Kang with his eyes. Kang got up as well, and just as he was thinking that the principal ought to at least ask his name and shake hands, Yi Kangsŏk checked his watch and barked through the intercom to his secretary: "Call the computer room and tell

Ch'oe to get me those documents now! I have to leave before lunch. Make it quick!"

Something was going on. The principal was out of sorts, and there was a mood of urgency in the office. Kang followed the administrator out to the hall. At the window the man turned to Kang and displayed his thumb. Puzzled, Kang watched him spread wide the fingers of his hand. *Oh, he's testing me on my sign language.*

"Um, I was told I didn't need to be fluent in sign language," Kang faltered. "But I'll do my best to get up to speed. In the meantime I'll communicate with the children by writing."

The administrator made a face. "Do I have to explain every last detail? Here's the way it is: Normally, it's one large, but since your wife is friends with our niece, we'll settle for five small. Payable by month's end, in the office. And we don't take checks."

Thirty-four-year-old Kang Inho felt the blood rush to his face.

～

Kang was well aware of the adage that you haven't really lived until you've experienced some of life's indignities. Even so, his first encounter with the brothers Yi had left him embarrassed and ashamed, not unlike what he felt in nightmares where he found himself wandering crowded streets stark naked. With this thought, curiously enough, he thought he detected a faint stink emanating from the man before him, Yi Kangbok, that was partly the gamy smell of a sweaty beast and partly the rusty odor of a ship salvaged from the ocean depths. Such were the instincts that this first morning of Kang's new life had awakened in him, instincts that he associated with savagery, and this frightened him.

"It's time to meet your class—let's go." And off walked the administrator.

Kang thought back to his buddies who had found teaching jobs at private schools, about how they had mentioned, talking in hushed tones, a noble-sounding cause—the Development Fund, or some such title. And he recalled something his wife had told him not so long ago: "I'll take care of it. You just figure out a way to get yourself a full-time teaching assignment." Could she have known that paying a bribe would be part of "taking care of things"? As he walked down the long corridor, he asked himself if the Home of Benevolence was the right place for him. He heard several answers. "Haste makes waste," his younger self told him. His older self reminded him that he'd sunk a lot of money into his apartment here in Mujin and that going back to Seoul with his tail between his legs would be just as humiliating as paying the "five small." And in between his older and younger alter egos was another who told him the issue was not so much a hasty decision as a one-way street. It was the older Kang who rendered the final decision: unless you've inherited rank and realm, this is how you live, so just go along with it. At that moment Kang became aware of his footsteps, abnormally loud, in the hallway. The school was too quiet. Yes, that was it. There were no sounds here. Tension came over him until he imagined himself sinking deep underwater.

The administrator came to a stop in front of a classroom. "Second-year middle school," he said, "but they don't know squat. The main thing is to keep them out of trouble; then you can worry about trying to teach them something." He sounded aggravated at having to explain this. The way he went back and forth between blunt and polite speech left Kang speculating that his rudeness was less a matter of studied intent and more the result of ignorance of the proper way to communicate with others. Telling a new teacher to focus more on keeping the children out of trouble than with teaching them . . . for Kang it was one perplexity after another, starting with his encounter with the principal. He drew a deep breath.

The administrator opened the door to the classroom. The children were gathered in a circle, busily signing to one another, and none of them noticed Kang. He peered among them and saw within the circle a boy with his head down on his desk, crying. The administrator went to the far side of the chalkboard and pulled on a long string, whereupon a red light in the ceiling began spinning around and flashing like a strobe light. All the children turned toward him. Kang noticed first that their eyes were bloodshot, but his next impression was that their faces were swollen with rage. He had to resist the urge to retreat a step.

"Kang Inho," wrote the administrator on the chalkboard. And beside his name, "Homeroom teacher; language arts." The faces that regarded Kang had turned expressionless, like plaster masks.

⌁

Good morning. My name is Kang Inho. Nice to meet you.

The administrator had left, and Kang was greeting the class in clumsy sign language. Among the pupils was the one he had seen outside the previous day, the girl eating cookies who had fled upon encountering him. Kang saw that his struggle with sign language had brought a flicker of movement to the masklike faces. This was a good start. Kids are kids, he told himself, and his mood lightened. Next he wrote a poem on the chalkboard:

> **Paris at Night—Jacques Prévert**
> I strike three matches in the dark, one by one
> With the first I see your face, all of it
> With the second, your eyes
> With the last, your mouth
> And the night all around us reminds me of them all
> As I hold you in my bosom.

Now he produced a box of matches and lit three of them in turn, reciting the poem in sign language as he did so, indicating one student's face, then another student's eyes, then a third student's mouth. Like opaque glass wiped clean, the expressionless faces began to reveal clear outlines. Kang could see in those faces a tinge of red, as if the children were in a black-and-white film that had been colorized. Perhaps his modest performance would shrink the distance between them. With this boost to his confidence, Kang felt his apprehensions ease. He examined the boy who had been crying. The boy's eyes were dark pools. Kang gave him a smile. The boy continued to regard him with those dark eyes. And then, as if under a spell, the boy began to sign, at first slowly and then more rapidly, while out of his mouth came a shrill, inarticulate moan. His pale face reddened and took on a look of hopeful urgency. But so limited was Kang's knowledge of sign language that apart from that sense of urgency he understood nothing of what the boy was trying to communicate. He made a gesture of apology, and when the boy realized he wasn't being understood, his hands stopped in midair, and the glimmer of urgency dissolved into the dark pools of his eyes. Before he knew it Kang had approached the boy, who had lowered his drawn, tear-smudged face. Kang offered his handkerchief but the boy remained still. Kang dabbed at the boy's tears. The boy regarded Kang, but the look of hopeful urgency had disappeared from his teary eyes.

Kang turned back, stepped up onto the platform occupied by the teacher's podium, and approached the chalkboard. And then something peculiar happened. He sensed the children "whispering" in sign language behind his back but realized he actually was hearing something. Kang wrote on the chalkboard: *I'm sorry. I'm a beginner at sign language. But by winter vacation I'll be fluent. I promise.*

He turned back to the class to see a girl holding up a sheet of paper. Written on it in large letters was HIS BROTHER DIED YESTERDAY. The girl's face was fearful, as if she wasn't sure she was doing the right thing.

Before Kang could answer, a second student, this one a boy, also held up a sheet of paper: WE KNOW WHO KILLED HIM.

⤺

"Hit by a train. It can happen—the fog gets real thick here."

Kang was in the teachers' room, listening to a man named Pak Kyŏngch'ŏl.

"I wonder," said Kang. "I mean, one of the children has just died, and the school is so—" He was about to say "quiet" but checked himself. Was "quiet" the right word? He silently tried out a few other possibilities: unconcerned? peaceful? bizarre? Yes, "bizarre," that was the word. His impression so far of the Home of Benevolence was just that—it was bizarre. "The kids are saying things," he said. "The boy who died yesterday— they're saying it wasn't an accident—"

"You've never taught at a school like this, have you?" Pak interrupted. His tone sounded neutral, but in his gaze Kang read a combination of naked contempt and pity. Or was he overreacting? He was beginning to feel he'd become overly sensitive since arriving in Mujin. *Be positive—the power of positive thinking!* His wife's mantra. Instinctively, he forced a neutral but awkward smile—when in doubt, play it safe.

"You'll learn for yourself by and by," said Pak condescendingly. "You'll learn that deaf-mutes have the worst victimization complex of any disability group. They don't trust anyone but themselves. If we think of a *people* as those who speak a common language, then they're a foreign people. I think you can understand. They look like us, but they use a different language—sign language—and they have a different culture. For example, they lie."

Just a few minutes earlier, Kang had approached Pak with an outstretched hand, and here he was being treated with aversion and cold malice. He felt the same chill go up his spine that he had experienced the previous day while tunneling through the fog. In Pak's face he could almost see the dark pools of the crying boy's eyes, the fleeting sense of earnest entreaty with which the boy had regarded him.

"They tell me you're a gentleman from Seoul, a temporary hire," Pak said as he navigated a website on his computer. "Maybe when your time here is up, you'll find it in your best interests to move on. You don't exactly strike me as the kind of person who would fit in here." Only then did he make eye contact with Kang.

Embarrassing but true, Kang thought. "Well," he mumbled, "as long as I'm here—" But when he noticed the patronizing look on Pak's face, he fell silent.

Just then his phone beeped. His wife. He left the teachers' room to take the call. Classes were over for the day, and the children had gone to the dormitory and changed out of their uniforms; they were now gathered at a bench at the corner of the playfield. Emerging from the school building, Kang walked toward the far end of the field.

"How was your first day? Did you get through your classes all right? Did you get to use your sign language?" Her voice was cheerful.

He answered in monosyllables, thinking about how for the past six months, day in and day out, she had bought soybean sprouts, a cheap source of protein, about how she would make bean-sprout soup one day, bean sprouts and steamed rice the next, bean-sprout soup again the following day—how could he possibly broach the subject of the "five small" with her?

"Did they tell you about the Development Fund?" asked his wife, beating him to the punch. "Well, guess what—I got some help from my family, and I just deposited the money in our account for you."

Kang had arrived at the far end of the playfield. At the edge was a cliff that resembled a fortress, with vast mudflats spreading out far below. That had to be the ocean beyond. He couldn't see it, the tide was so far out, but that's what he'd been told. Looking out at the mudflats, he breathed deeply to compose himself before answering. The mudflats had the slimy appearance of reptiles, and the residual pools of tidewater gleamed like aluminum foil.

"Tell me, when did you find out?" He tried his best to keep his voice level but realized he was practically growling. His displeasure must have been obvious.

"Well, I was going to tell you before you left, but . . ."

He ignored the whimper in his wife's voice, overwhelmed with the humiliation he had felt that morning.

"Then why didn't you? If I had known, I never would have come here."

When his wife didn't immediately respond, he felt a burning sensation. Half of him awaited her reply, while the other half tried to focus on the mudflats stretching out beneath the heavens, the silver shafts of sunlight reflecting off the tidal pools, the fields of reeds along the shore. He swallowed heavily.

"And then what?"

He was surprised at how composed she sounded. If instead she had begun crying, if instead she had raised her voice and started screaming, he might have exploded from the pressure building inside him since his loss of face in the principal's office. But the only effect of her dispassionate tone was to make him feel drained.

"I don't mean to say I'm not happy with you. Even though you were out of work for six months, you're still a fine husband. And a good father. But sometimes you're too fussy, you don't like the way the world turns, you start sounding like a high school civics teacher, and that's hard for me. What's wrong with a school having a development fund? If we had money, who's to say we wouldn't have made a donation to a school for the disabled by now? Would that be wrong? Why not just blink and pay up, that way you get some good returns. Do you think it's easy getting a teaching job the way things are now? Do you?"

He felt a surge of emotion, and to contain it he screwed up his face, as if in facing out toward the mudflats he were being blinded by the sun. If either of them spoke out now, they would surely end up saying hurtful, disgraceful things. Standing at the very edge of the cliff, he spoke slowly and carefully: "I'm sorry. I was thinking only of myself."

There was a brief silence, and he realized she was surprised that he had given up so easily. When she did speak, it was with a sob: "I want you to understand—I've lowered myself enough already." She sniffled before continuing: "I've decided to put Saemi in preschool starting tomorrow. And I found a job. Don't ask what. If I told you, you'd just ask me why. Don't worry, it's not like I'm selling my body. It's nothing bad."

Kang gazed down at the bottom of the cliff. *Not a bad place to kill yourself,* he thought.

↜

Alone in the teachers' room at the end of the day, Kang studied the roster of the students in his charge. Two were day students, and the remaining ten lived in the dormitory.

There were two groups of deaf-mute children: those whose mother or father was a deaf-mute and those whose parents had normal speech and hearing. The former group could be considered congenitally deaf and mute, whereas the latter, through some affliction or other, had suffered damage to the auditory nerve or the inner ear. Kang found the listing for the student who had been crying in class:

> <u>Name</u>: Chŏn Minsu—moderate hearing impairment
> <u>Family</u>: father, mild intellectual impairment; mother, moderate hearing impairment and moderate intellectual impairment; younger brother Yŏngsu, moderate hearing impairment, severe intellectual impairment
> <u>Home</u>: Oeso Island; remote location makes school-vacation home visit difficult for pupil
> Requires special attention

Now he felt he was beginning to understand why the children were so quiet in the aftermath of their classmate's brother's death. He was reminded of the look of hopeful urgency, the earnest entreaty in Minsu's eyes. Kang had wanted to ask Pak Kyŏngch'ŏl to interpret for him what Minsu had been trying to communicate with his signing. Even if Minsu's brother's death were in fact accidental, something needed to be done for the children, who considered the death a homicide and were terrified. But Kang had been confounded in his attempt to find an interpreter: among the thirty-five teachers at the school, virtually no one professed to be conversant in sign language. How then was it possible for them to teach these children? Kang had come very close to asking this question, but in the end, whether it was the mood he sensed here, the peculiar odor, or the stillness, he had felt compelled to remain silent.

On the next page was the listing for Yuri, the girl who liked cookies:

> Name: Chin Yuri—moderate hearing impairment, severe intellectual impairment
> Family: father, moderate hearing impairment, severe intellectual impairment; mother's whereabouts unknown; grandmother is guardian
> Home: deep in the mountains; pupil occasionally goes there during school vacation, for two or three days only
> Exhibits food craving, may follow strangers
> Lives in dormitory; requires special attention

Kang visualized the girl who had appeared from out of the fog, munching on cookies. A small, emaciated girl who had shrieked and fled when he had tried to speak to her. The girl who had left him associating the fogbound Home of Benevolence with shrieking.

The next page contained the listing for Kim Yŏndu, the girl who had written HIS BROTHER DIED YESTERDAY.

Name: Kim Yŏndu—moderate hearing impairment
Family: both parents, normal speech and hearing;
relatively well off, but with business failure and father's
chronic illness, she became a boarder starting in middle
school year 1
Relatively intelligent; very compassionate, looks after
homeroom classmates, especially those such as Chin Yuri

So they have a disability. This had been the extent of Kang's
thinking about the children he would be teaching here. He
realized now that the lives of these children were more stark
than he had ever imagined. Lacking the most important
faculties for surviving in the world at large, they had been cast
out of that world, and the majority of them seemed burdened
in addition with family misfortune. What if a lion were born
without claws, a deer without legs, a rabbit without ears, a
monkey without arms . . .

In his thirty-four years, not once had Kang contemplated
the fact that his own birth had been accompanied by good
fortune, happiness, and an abundance of talent. Only here
and now, after delving into the lot in life dealt these children,
did he realize how fortunate he was. *Strange that I never felt
this before.* He wasn't one to trumpet feelings of gratitude and
happiness, but couldn't he at least refrain from making himself
any more miserable than he had been at the edge of the cliff,
brooding over the "five small" conversation with his wife? He
opened his phone and tapped out a text message: *treat yourself
to a nice dinner with saemi. forever sorry, forever loving.*

After a quick tidying of his desk, he rose. He felt good about
the message he had just sent. His wife must have been stewing
over their conversation, and he really did hope that she and their
daughter would have themselves a nice warm dinner. With his
end-of-the-month pay he would open a savings account and
then feed that account. He looked forward to the day when the
three of them would once again gather around the dinner table.

2

Dusk had begun to fill the hallway, reminding Kang that the days were growing shorter. And then he heard the scream. Was it the same as the faint sound he had heard back in the teachers' room while texting his wife? Here in the still of the hallway at the entrance to the building, there was no mistaking it. He looked back. The scream had come from the vicinity of the bathrooms. He felt a brief but intense jolt, as if he had collided with a massive object. His instincts told him that if that scream were to involve him, it would forever alter the course of his life. He felt like a swinging pendulum in a clock that was the universe. The next moment he was running toward the bathrooms. He arrived at the first door, saw it was the women's bathroom, and hesitated. From inside came a hoarse, squawking outcry. He pushed at the door— locked!—then pounded on it. "Who's in there? What's going on?" he shouted. And then he remembered where he was; unless whoever was in the bathroom had normal hearing, his shouting and banging were futile. His hand fell limp to his side. Just then a dormitory counselor appeared at the far end of the hallway. He didn't seem to have heard Kang pounding on the bathroom door. And then from the stairway came the sound of children's footsteps—boarders presumably, the day students having left. Kang had never realized how crucial it was to be able to hear. And because you might not immediately see obvious signs of disability in the hearing-impaired, you could momentarily forget they were disabled. Kang realized that at this instant, in this vast building, he was the only one able to hear the screaming. He felt he had entered a spirit world.

The screaming stopped. Next to the women's bathroom was the men's bathroom. Kang tried that door, wondering if it was school policy to keep the bathroom doors locked. But the door was open. That meant someone had locked the door to the girls' bathroom from the inside. Kang took a couple of deep breaths, and when no further sound came from the girls' bathroom, he went outside. Maybe it was a girl with a bad stomach ache, he told himself. But he couldn't rid himself of the feeling that something was wrong. He tried again to dismiss it: because the children couldn't hear their own voices, their utterances probably always sounded loud to those with normal hearing—they weren't necessarily screams.

The air felt damp on Kang's face. As the day retreated, the fog advanced from the chill, dark ocean—not as thick as the previous day, but there it was, nevertheless.

In the parking lot Kang lit a cigarette. His hand holding the lighter was shaking. Suspicion reared its head again. Who was the screaming girl? And *why* was she screaming? What was happening behind that locked door? He sent a lungful of smoke streaming into the mist, then pressed down on his chest to try to calm himself.

Only a few cars remained in the lot, among them the blue car from the previous day. He turned back toward the school and noticed the lights were on in the office—and in the principal's office and the computer room as well. He climbed into his car. As he turned the ignition, he noticed a man and a woman approaching the building. The man was short with

wavy hair, and the woman had long hair. Kang recognized
the man as one of the dormitory counselors he had met in
the teachers' room that morning—Pak Pohyŏn. Like the
majority of the counselors, he was himself hearing-impaired.
Kang remembered the name because he'd had a very negative
impression of the man—thick eyelids beneath the wavy hair
and beady eyes that reminded Kang of a rat. The woman must
also have been hearing-impaired, judging from the way she
was signing to the man.

Kang pulled out of the lot and came to a stop at the check-
point at the school gate and lowered the driver's-side window.
The custodian rose and emerged from the booth to greet him.

"Don't work too hard," said Kang, trying to sound as if
nothing was out of the ordinary.

"No sir, I won't." The custodian had a broad face with a
sprinkling of pockmarks.

"You know," said Kang, "I'm just wondering. I thought I
heard a scream coming from the women's bathroom on the
main floor. Might be worth having a look?"

A look of surprise came to the custodian's face, but a grin
quickly replaced it.

Is it just me, or is he sneering at me? In the light from the
booth, Kang could see mist settling over the man's dark
silhouette.

"Those kids—when they don't have anything better to do,
they like to scream. They think it's fun. What do they care—
they can't hear themselves. It's nothing to worry about, sir. But
you be careful driving—the fog's coming in, and if it's like this
now, it's bound to get real thick." Again he grinned.

The man's tone was polite enough, but the message Kang
heard was something like *Stop fussing and get your sorry ass out
of here.*

Ever since arriving in Mujin twenty-four hours earlier, Kang
had felt something distinctly unpleasant in the air. He couldn't
explain the feeling, but it had left him with a terrific headache.

⤙

Not until Kang had pulled out of the parking lot and was inching along outside the school grounds, examining the surroundings, did he realize how isolated the Home of Benevolence was—five minutes by car from the nearest habitations, and in between grew a wild expanse of reeds. In the driver's-side mirror he tried to make out the building through the fog and gloom, but its outlines had been erased, and all he could see was an occasional patch of milky light coming from a dormitory window. The Home of Benevolence was like a huge, lonely castle, the school shuttered from view by Mujin's notorious fog. And when that fog descended like it had now, those outside the school had no way of knowing what might be taking place inside.

Kang's headlights were a poor match for the fog but strong enough for him to notice a human form appearing ahead. He slowed and saw it was Yuri. As before, she was eating from a bag of cookies. She stopped when she saw the car, and when Kang pulled over and rolled down the window, she regarded him, munching on a cookie. Why would a child from the home be roaming outside the dormitory on a fogbound night— especially a severely impaired girl with the IQ of a kindergartner? She had a small build compared with that of the other girls, but her chest was fully developed, and that's what Kang noticed now.

Yuri smiled when she recognized Kang. The eyes of this girl, who had screamed in terror upon seeing him yesterday, were clear and artless. Kang smiled back, then pointed toward the home and made a shooing gesture. Yuri flashed a sheepish smile, meekly turned away, and ran off toward the building.

Kang remained at the side of the road as he waited for Yuri to return to the school. He saw no other vehicles—presumably this road had been put in specifically for the facility. Finally, the girl disappeared through the misted gate to the school grounds, and Kang started up again. In the meantime a text message had arrived: _lets do our best. cant wait till youre back home. im sorry too and i love you too._ Reading the message, he felt a sudden urge to offer up a prayer. _Watch over us,_ he wanted to say. _Watch over me—my wife—Saemi, our only child—Minsu, who lost his brother—Yuri, so frail and vulnerable._ And one thing more: _Deliver me safely from Mujin._

⌐

That night as the custodian nodded off in front of his television, the songs from the variety program working on him like lullabies, one of the children, her hair cropped in school-girl fashion, felt her way through the fog and out the school gate. She took nothing with her and wore no jacket to ward off the damp and the chill. Once outside the gate she began to run, and by the time she arrived at the bus terminal a little over a mile distant, she was bent over and gasping for breath. Waiting for her was a man in a dark, worn-out suit. Anxiously checking his watch, he ushered the girl into his car, and off they went toward downtown Mujin, a curtain of fog descending behind them.

⌐

When Kang knocked on the door to Administrator Yi Kangbok's office the following morning, gift bag in hand, he was still trying to convince himself of the necessity of this act of—what should he call it—betrayal? Complicity? Irresponsibility? He was by no means impervious to feelings of shame or guilt. Heaven knew, if no one else, about the bargirls he had slept with even after his marriage and the income he had underreported, heaven knew he had prayed for the downfall of a classmate who had made a success of himself and liked to tool around in his luxury foreign car, and heaven knew he had lusted after a friend's wife, tempted by her beauty. And he was sensitive to these transgressions. But never in his thirty-four years had he gone along with such out-and-out bribery. And never before had he gone to work in the morning having to make such an effort to mollify himself. Once again his wife's words came to mind: if he were wealthy, if he were fortunate enough to have inherited vast landholdings, then by now they might have donated to the Home of Benevolence ten times the amount of money in the gift bag.

But when the door opened, the first person Kang saw was the man who had been in the principal's office the previous day, Sergeant Chang. Chang was in conversation with the administrator, and they must have been discussing something serious, for Kang immediately saw through the two men's forced attempts at nonchalance—a hollow chuckle by one and a meaningless cough by the other. But whereas Chang's face was relaxed, Yi's was tense.

"Ah, Mr. Kang," said Yi as soon as he noticed the gift bag. "Just put it on the desk."

At the same moment, Kang and Chang made eye contact—or rather their gazes collided in midair. Kang felt he had taken the brunt of the impact. Chang, though, smiled with perfect composure.

"Well, we meet again. And it looks like the fog's almost gone. When it's like it was last night, even a grown man like me gets rattled, you know? And here you are, the gentleman just arrived from Seoul, if my information serves me correct. You must have wondered what you were getting yourself into. It's worse than usual lately—the fog, I mean. I guess we can blame it on global warming."

But Chang was clearly more interested in the bag Kang held, the bank logo clearly visible. *He must have caught a whiff of the dough.*

"Right," said Kang as he walked past the two men and deposited the bag of cash on the administrator's desk. He moved stiffly, feeling he was committing a crime in plain sight of the police.

"And another heads-up for the good man from Seoul," said Chang. "There's something about Mujin—how can I say it— well, we like people from Seoul but—how to put it—we have our own ideas about Seoul. You see, when folks from here move to Seoul and then after a long time come back home and pay us a visit, they always bring a sack of complaints—'What is it with this place, anyway?' or 'Doesn't anything work in this city?' These folks pay their taxes in Seoul, they live in Seoul, they come back here whenever they want, and all they do is flip real estate. Now don't get me wrong—none of this applies to you, Mr. Kang."

Kang had to stand there like an idiot and listen to this spiel, no one having offered him a seat. He smiled the requisite social smile and was about to leave when Chang let fly one final remark: "In fact, you and me ought to have ourselves a drink sometime. Mujin's a great place to eat, drink, and make merry, you know."

～

It was during roll call that Kang noticed Yŏndu was absent. He should have been told if one of his boarding students was ill, but he'd received no such notice during the morning meeting with the dormitory counselors. Kang approached Yŏndu's desk and asked her classmates if they knew her whereabouts. They gazed at Kang, blinking, and gestured that they had no idea. After outlining the day's schedule and writing reminders on the chalkboard, Kang returned to the teachers' room.

There he found Pak Kyŏngch'ŏl, who occupied the desk next to his, slapping a third-year middle school boy. He's overdoing it, thought Kang, but the other teachers seemed to consider it standard procedure. The boy must have absorbed a good deal of punishment—his face was burgundy red and swollen. Just as Kang was about to sit down, the boy staggered against him. Kang managed to catch the boy and at the same time remove him from harm's way.

Pak, registering Kang's presence, brushed his palms together in a that's-that gesture. "Stupid, fucked-up kids," he muttered. "If I catch you throwing a fit again, you're dead."

How in God's name was a deaf boy supposed to understand what the teacher was saying? Kang asked himself. The boy was small for a third year and displayed none of the defiance Kang had found in abundance among other children his age. He merely stood there, puffy face downcast, tears dripping from his cheeks.

"Get out of here!" Pak shouted, giving the boy a kick. The boy walked unsteadily out the door. An awkward silence descended between Pak and himself. Here he was, Kang thought, a fellow teacher who couldn't bring himself to ask why Pak had been slapping the boy so viciously.

Kang approached the head teacher and asked about Yŏndu.

"Yŏndu? Oh, yes. Last night she left the dormitory without permission. The proctor is meeting with her now. Afterwards I expect she'll go to class."

"Um, do you know where the meeting is? If there's anything I can do . . ."

"Probably in the computer room."

It seemed odd to Kang—he would have thought the conference room or the counseling office. He didn't have a first-period class, so why not go look for her? And upstairs he went. He had just reached the second floor when Sergeant Chang and Yi Kangbok emerged from the computer room. The two were whispering, heads lowered conspiratorially, and after Yi had seen the detective off, he disappeared back into the room. Kang went back down the stairs until he was out of sight, still concerned about how Chang had detained him in Yi's office a short time earlier. Continuing down to the landing midway between the two floors, he stopped, found his phone, and pretended to engage in a conversation while gazing out the window.

"Yeah, it's me . . . that's right, I'm in Mujin. . . . The school? . . . It's okay. . . ."

And then he heard Chang's footsteps. They stopped behind him and Kang felt a cold chill ride up his spine and a tingle at the back of his neck. And then the footsteps resumed, Chang walking rapidly the rest of the way down.

Kang stood frozen to the spot and considered: Yŏndu, who seemed wise beyond her years, leaving the dorm without permission; Sergeant Chang together with Administrator Yi. Why hadn't he, the girl's homeroom teacher, been at this meeting? Stranger still, why the computer room? Back upstairs he went. The hallway was still. He passed a classroom, and only when he drew near the computer room did he hear the shouts.

⮑

"Who was it—huh?"

Silence.

"Who put you up to it? Who took you in the car? Who?"

Silence.

"Tell her if she doesn't talk *right now,* we're taking her to the police station!"

And then Kang heard a girl screaming.

He reached for the doorknob. The cold metal chilled him to the bone. He half expected, half feared the door would be locked, like the women's bathroom the previous day. To his surprise the doorknob rotated effortlessly. A vague sense of terror drifted over him—he felt he was being forced to watch himself set foot in a marsh, then sink and disappear. As quietly as he could, he opened the door. Partitioned desks filled the room; no one could be seen. In spite of his efforts, in the characteristic silence of the school the creak of the turning doorknob sounded abnormally loud.

"Who's there!"

"Um, is one of my students . . . ?" Kang faltered as he followed the voice to its source. Sure enough, there was Yŏndu. But instead of the proctor, it was Yi Kangbok who was interrogating her. And next to him sat a woman Kang had never seen before, who must have been one of the dormitory counselors. The woman was interpreting for the administrator, using sign language.

"Uh, one of my students was absent from class, and I was told she was here. . . . Told by the head teacher, actually . . ." Feeling his way along, Kang emphasized "told by the head teacher" while adopting a subservient stammer in explaining his intrusion. He knew it was silly to feel guilty about following up in his capacity as Yŏndu's homeroom teacher, but he attempted to project abjection anyway. It was obvious by now that the locus of power in the Home of Benevolence was the man before him, brother of the principal and son of the founder, and no good would come from rubbing him the wrong way. As these thoughts flashed through his mind, it struck him that after scarcely more than a day in his new teaching position, he was already on hair-trigger alert.

"Your student? What the hell do you think you're doing? Get out of here now!"

At the same instant, Yŏndu looked up at Kang. Her drawn face was riddled with fear, and her disheveled hair told Kang she had been slapped. For the briefest instant as they made eye contact, a sparkle came to her fearful eyes—a distress call rising from the dark pools of her pupils. Just as quickly she noticed Kang's hesitation in response to Yi's barking, and the faint glimmer went out. But Kang had noticed her appeal, and he responded to it, speaking slowly and carefully.

"I'm not sure what she's done, but as her homeroom teacher—"

"What she did was leave the dorm without permission," the woman interrupted. "At night. Such behavior cannot be tolerated—especially in a student who's not a little girl anymore." The eyes that regarded Kang held a cold gleam. Though she was seated, Kang could see that the woman was tall and slender and wore her hair in a ponytail. Her voice was metal-cold. Kang wondered if it was her thick makeup that made her look so menacing.

"I see," said Kang, "but shouldn't she be in class now, and perhaps the reprimand could be given after school—"

"For Christ's sake, how the fuck did we end up with you?" The administrator cut him off, a disbelieving smile on his face. "Who do you think you're lecturing? Didn't you see the police? Are you aware of the mess we have on our hands here? And in case you don't realize it, there are plenty of teachers out there who wouldn't mind having your job!"

Kang could hardly believe the administrator had said this without the slightest hesitation. *This child can't hear what you say,* Kang silently retorted, *but even so, this is a school. And even though I'm only temporary, I am a teacher.* He recalled his initial impression of Yi Kangbok from the day before, the sense of savagery, and the next moment was struck by a suffocating, fishy stink, along with a piercing sensation that left him reeling.

⌒

Yŏndu had not yet returned to class when school ended that afternoon. Impenetrable masks had settled once again over the faces of the children. Yesterday—his first day in the classroom—had ended with Kang feeling he'd been showered with filth; today he felt immersed in it. His treatment at the Home of Benevolence, the way the staff spoke and behaved—how to explain it? He still felt uneasy, still felt that unless he was strong and determined, his very existence was at risk, that he was nothing more than a sodden scrap of toilet paper about to be flushed.

As soon as classes were over and he was back in the teachers' room, he went online and visited the Home of

Benevolence website to learn about Yŏndu's dormitory counselors. There were eight of them. He found the woman with the ponytail; she was twenty-five and her name was Yun Cha'ae. Intrigued that her given name, Cha'ae, meant "benevolence," he read her profile.

After one last trip to the classroom to see that the students had tidied it up before leaving, Kang went to the dormitory in search of Yŏndu, walking down the long corridor that connected it with the school building. The girls' rooms were on the third floor. Kang found the room Yŏndu shared with five other middle-schoolers. It contained three double-decker bunk beds and a large desk set against the wall. Through the window Kang could see in the distance the dark contours of the mudflats spreading out like the backs of a cluster of huge reptiles. The lace curtains framing the opened window fluttered gently in the breeze. The girls kept the room clean enough, and the furniture appeared to be of fairly recent vintage—consistent with the commendations the Home of Benevolence had supposedly received over the years from the province in recognition of its facilities. If Kang had simply been touring the home without his current sense of unease, he might very well have submitted a report endorsing the care given these children by the province and the provincial Bureau of Education.

Four of the girls, obviously surprised, rose to greet Kang. A fifth girl remained seated—Yuri, the severely intellectually impaired girl—clutching a small stuffed bear to her bosom, a look of stark terror on her face.

Where is Yŏndu? Kang asked the other four girls in sign language. There was no answer. Kang interpreted their expressions to mean not so much *We don't know* as *We're not allowed to say.*

Next he tried Yuri. *You're Yŏndu's friend, right?* he signed. *Do you know where she is?*

Yuri kept her eyes down and stroked the bear's head, refusing to meet Kang's gaze. The bear was so threadbare that Kang was afraid a few more strokes would cause it to burst at the seams, and the cotton stuffing would spill out.

Kang knew that only 10 percent of communication is conveyed through utterance itself—vowels and consonants. The remainder consists of nuance, context, and body language—specifically, the speaker's demeanor. Which was why in his initial attempts at instant messaging with his wife they had almost ended up arguing—it was impossible to convey body language and nuance in cyberspace. But face-to-face communication had its own challenges. He recalled the time that five-year-old Saemi had told him, "I hate you, Daddy!" after catching a scolding from him. But there was nothing in the situation or in Saemi's body language that seemed to be saying this. Instead, Kang interpreted her utterance as follows: _Daddy, I'm sad you're not happy with me. Daddy, I want you to be nice to me. Daddy, I want you to love me._ And this interpretation came easily because he loved his daughter and understood immediately what she was conveying nonverbally. He imagined Saemi's face and, superimposed on it, the image of Yŏndu regarding him that morning with the sparkle in her shining eyes.

He tried signing again, clumsily, in an attempt to express himself. _I am very worried about Yŏndu._

The children glanced at one another and made faint movements with their hands. It was the sign-language equivalent of whispering, and Kang understood none of it.

Tell me. I want very much to help Yŏndu. I want to do whatever I can for all of you.

Kang had never dreamed that as a teacher he would one day be trying to convey these words to his students. He thought of how his former business partner had tried to dissuade him from going to Mujin to teach at a special-education school. He probably would have said something like this to Kang now: "You knucklehead, what kind of show are you putting on? Did you go there as a rescue worker?" The next moment he recalled what he himself had said to the college friend who had wanted to help Sŏ Yujin in her time of need: "Can anyone really help anyone else in life? All you're doing when you volunteer help is trying to boost your own ego—forget it. Instead, just wait till they ask!" And then he could hear his wife's voice: "What are you doing? Stop trying to hurt my pride." When she talked like this, Kang would hang his head, and his older and better alter ego would advise him. And now, that alter ego said, *Be honest with yourself. Like you did when you told Sŏ that you didn't come down here to make the world a better place. You came here for one reason only, the paycheck. Of course you can get paid and also do good—but it ends there! Otherwise you've learned nothing from your thirty-four years and all your failures— and you're no different from these disabled kids—except you might get a government pension. Only joking! Seriously, it's time to put on your concerned expression, ask them no more than you have to, then get out while the getting is good—see no evil, speak no evil, hear no evil. That's all you can do. Now that you're here, don't get involved. It's not as if you didn't answer the kids' questions—*they *didn't answer* your *questions. So you ended up here yesterday, and you don't know a thing. You think you came here to film a mystery or something? Wake up, you idiot.*

Maybe he would ask Sŏ out for a drink after work someday and say, "You and me, we're both just tiny cogs in this huge machine of a society. The world would get along just fine without us. Let's go to a karaoke bar and sing 'Que Sera, Sera' or something." And they would make their tipsy way home. Or else he would part company with her and slink off to the red-light district in search of the cross-eyed teen streetwalker. And if he were lucky—or unlucky—the girl would spot him first and latch onto him, saying, "Uncle who smells like Seoul," at which point he would pretend he couldn't resist and allow her to lead him away with a giggle. And if Sŏ were to see this and say, "Kang Inho—is that really how you want to live?" he would reply, "No, but I can't help it—everybody else does it." Yuri broke Kang's reveries by grabbing his sleeve. The faces of the other girls turned fearful, the change in expression like a dark countenance suddenly illuminated by a match. Kang understood immediately—severely intellectually impaired Yuri would lead him to the source of their terror. Kang was half ready to follow her; the other half of him recoiled.

~

Kang followed Yuri down the darkening hallway. She kept a few steps ahead of him, the stuffed bear wedged beneath her arm. If Kang got too close, she would speed up, and if he lagged behind, she would turn and wait. A group of boys on their way to the computer room, seeing Kang, offered perfunctory nods. The school building was visible through the window, sitting perpendicular to the dormitory, the lights in the teachers' room blinking in the evening glow—was it the wind? Kang asked himself, noticing the rippling of the leaves on the trees.

Kang followed Yuri like a man in a trance. How could someone walk so quietly? She was like an angel gliding above the floor. Kang was all the more conscious of the sound of his own steps as he followed Yuri up the stairs to the fourth floor. There to his surprise he heard the rumble of a washing machine; his ears perked up. The source of the rumble lay at the end of the dark hallway behind a door from which light leaked out. No sooner had Kang realized this than Yuri turned around, her navy-blue-clad form disappearing back down the hall. The next moment a scream came from the room.

Kang opened the door to a large space containing a washing machine and three big girls—high school students by the looks of them—huddled together around Yŏndu. Kang couldn't believe what he saw: Two of the girls flanked Yŏndu, each with a hand on her shoulder, while the third girl forced Yŏndu's hand into the washing machine. The machine sounded as if its cycle was ending, but it was still spinning fast—the reason for Yŏndu's screams.

"What's going on!" Kang shouted before he realized it. But only one person heard him—Yun Cha'ae. Her sharp upturned eyes met his, eyes that at first were filled with rage but that Kang found pathetic. Kang reached out for Yŏndu, and as he did, she and the three girls turned toward him simultaneously. Before he knew it he had drawn Yŏndu close. To his surprise she pushed him away. But then, realizing it was her teacher who had come to her aid, she took refuge behind him. Meanwhile, the washing machine, whose opened lid was bringing its spin cycle to an end, rattled to a stop, the sound grating against Kang's ears.

"What in God's name are you doing to this girl?" said Kang to Yun, the only person who could hear him. He glared at her, wondering how angry he sounded to this twenty-five-year-old. The fluorescent lighting lent a bluish tinge to the faces of the three girls.

"We're teaching her a lesson," said Yun.

The woman's clipped tone had the effect of easing the pounding in Kang's chest. He turned to inspect Yŏndu's arm. The impact with the agitator had left it reddened, but otherwise no injuries were obvious.

Are you all right? Are you hurt? he signed to the girl, who was still gasping for breath.

Yŏndu regarded him with a searching gaze, her eyes boring into his.

Seeing no obvious signs of injury and trying to control his anger, Kang turned back to the woman.

"You and your lynch mob, how can you do this to a student! You call yourself a counselor? You say you're teaching her a lesson? In the Republic of Korea this doesn't qualify as teaching."

"Well," snorted Yun. "I was expecting a teacher and an attorney shows up instead." She produced a high-pitched laugh. Her three helpers followed her example but were capable only of half-hearted tittering.

"So I'm an attorney masquerading as a temporary teacher?" Kang barked. "Then how would you like to be on the receiving end of a lawsuit?" First the principal, then the administrator, then a fellow teacher, and now this twenty-five-year-old minnow was mocking him? His shoulders practically shook with rage.

But to his surprise, all traces of amusement had vanished from Yun's face.

"This is an internal matter, something that concerns us here in the dormitory. You needn't be involved." The clipped tone was still there, but her voice had softened, and she was speaking more respectfully. Not so much out of deference to authority, Kang felt, as from fear of Kang as a man and the possibility that he might resort to violence. Kang glared at her, tight-lipped. If it had been up to him, he would have slapped her; he would have beaten her until he felt compensated for the insults he had endured here at the Home of Benevolence. And he could see she sensed these feelings boiling up inside him. Best to use her fear to his advantage, and with this in mind he fixed her with a cold stare and hardened his voice.

"I'm taking her. You call yourself a dormitory counselor and yet you and these girls are acting like thugs. If this happens again to any of my students, I won't let it go, I promise you."

Kang took Yŏndu's hand. It was stiff as ice, making it seem she was resisting him. And she looked extremely uncomfortable. Once they were outside in the hallway, he let go of her. *Don't break the rules,* he said in clumsy sign language. *I want to help you.* But the next words he could only shout: "Take care of yourself! You have to take care of yourself!"

Yŏndu's dark eyes opened wide, and instantly Kang hated himself for shouting at this girl who had been interrogated the

entire day and then cruelly punished. If they had been able
to communicate through speech, he would have phrased his
words differently. He would have spoken at length, reasoned
with her, conveyed a teacher's affection for a student, and
made himself understood. But he couldn't do this using sign
language. Again he took Yŏndu's hand, and as they walked
down the hall, he could hear behind them the footsteps of Yun
and the other girls. Had there ever been a time when he was so
cognizant of, so sensitive to, every kind of sound? Barely two
days here and he was exhausted.

"Damn it—can't hear—can't understand what I'm saying—
damn it all!" he couldn't help muttering. Yŏndu's hand wiggled
inside his—another sign of her discomfort, he told himself.
A sigh escaped him. He gave up trying to sign to her and
resumed his muttering: "This hasn't been easy for me. I had to
swallow my pride. I'm in a sad situation. But I never expected
this. I want you to trust in me, please! I want you just to go
along with what I say, please!"

Upset at Yŏndu's attempts to free her hand, he gripped it
more tightly. And then he realized she was trying to communicate with him, using her hand as a writing instrument and the
palm of his hand as a surface. He could still hear the footsteps
behind them and felt the hair rising on the back of his neck. He
released Yŏndu's hand and watched as she wrote on his palm
what looked like the numbers 010—or was it the syllable 앙?
Tight-lipped, he focused on his palm. Sensing the tension in his
hand, Yŏndu wrote slowly and carefully. And just as carefully
Kang followed her finger until she had finished. What she
had written was indeed 010, followed by eight digits—a phone
number—and then *phone mom come see me.*

Still aware of the footsteps behind them, Kang looked at
Yŏndu importunately, but she failed to return his gaze and to
his surprise didn't seem concerned. Once again she inscribed
the telephone number on his palm. Kang brought the busy
finger to a stop and used his own finger to write on her palm

ㅇㅋ—"OK." Only then did the tears pooling in her eyes begin
to drift down her cheeks.

After seeing Yŏndu back to her room, Kang repeated the
phone number to himself, practically holding his breath in an
effort to banish all other thoughts. Yŏndu was wise beyond her
years. That this precocious girl had placed her trust in him,
the trust extended to a teacher by one of his charges, pleased
him immensely. But he realized that his memory, clouded by
years of alcohol, nicotine, and despair, all too often failed to
hold even the telephone numbers of his closest friends, the
birthdays of his wife and daughter, and the date of his wedding
anniversary, so he rushed to the teachers' room, scarcely
daring to breathe, grabbed the first pen he saw, and scrawled
the phone number on a piece of paper. If he were younger, if
his memory hadn't been compromised by impurities and life's
reversals, if he were still capable of what he had done that time
Myŏnghŭi had given him her phone number—committing it
to memory that very instant—then he wouldn't have sensed the
urgency he felt now. There was no time to waste. Ripping the
phone number from the sheet of paper, he ran outside and got
in his car. No cigarette now. Making sure the windows were
rolled up, he punched in the number on his phone. After what
seemed an eternity of ringing, he heard the voice of a middle-
aged woman.

"Am I speaking with Yŏndu's mother? This is Kang Inho,
Yŏndu's new homeroom teacher at the Home of Benevolence."

And now it had started.

↜

"Ah, yes. I've been meaning to visit and say hello, sir. I'm
so sorry. Right now I'm at a big old hospital somewhere in
Seoul—Yŏndu's father is having an operation the day after
tomorrow. . . . I'm so sorry, sir."

Like all the good-hearted people Kang knew, she sounded as
if she felt sorry toward everyone and everything.

"I see. You say the surgery is scheduled for the day after tomorrow?" Kang felt the energy drain from his other hand as he ran it along the steering wheel.

"That's right. The doctors think it's cancer, but they won't know for sure until they open him up. We had to close down our shop in Mujin for the time being. . . . I don't know whether I'm coming or going. Is Yŏndu doing all right?"

"Oh, sure. But I can see where you must be very concerned about your husband."

"I'm so sorry we unloaded the girl on you all and then did nothing to show our appreciation. She went deaf at age eight, we didn't have the money to get her hearing fixed—felt like the world was collapsing all around us—but we're so thankful to our country and the school for taking the children in for free and teaching them. The year before last, when Yŏndu's father was healthy, he slaughtered a couple of pigs for a feast for the teachers, but this year . . . I'm really sorry, sir."

Kang looked out at the darkening school grounds as he listened. The wind had picked up and was whipping the branches of the camellia tree at the main entry to the school into a frenzy. At least there was no fog when the wind blew like this; even better, the air was so clear that the dark sky was beginning to look like iridescent gooseflesh as it lit up with stars.

Kang was reminded of a time in college when a line from a Su Shi poem was popular: "Green hills are to be found everywhere." When the students cruised for drinking places off campus, *ch'ŏngsan,* "green hills," became *ch'ŏngju,* "clear rice brew," transforming the line to "*Ch'ŏngju* is to be found everywhere" or "Soju is to be found everywhere." What young Kang had found everywhere in his world, though, was unhappiness and unfairness—and much more of it than he saw now. But at least the unhappiness and unfairness back then had not left him feeling wretched. The world had been, on the one hand, like a framed picture—clear and yet abstract—and on the other hand subject to interpretation and debate, like a classical phrase. A world that had allowed him to make mistakes and get away with them—because he had no others depending on him yet for their daily bread. But after scarcely three days here in Mujin, he found himself thinking *Signs of a wretched fate are to be found everywhere.* Maybe before long it would be *Misery is to be found . . .* or maybe *Beasts. . . .*

"About Yŏndu, ma'am—she misses you, wants to see you, in fact she asked me to call you. Nothing out of the ordinary— it's just adolescence, and she's sensitive to things. We all went through a phase like that. . . ." He couldn't finish. He was haunted by the image of the thick tears spilling from Yŏndu's eyes as she had marched down the hallway with him a short time earlier. And by the knowledge that one of these sensitive children who couldn't hear, an adolescent girl, had been locked up and slapped and brutalized. And then very quickly he regained focus. He was beginning to feel like someone who has been going about his business, who out of the blue gets slapped back and forth, who hears a laundry list of reasons— his mistakes—for the slapping, who apologizes and goes home, who revisits every last detail of the incident and at last comes to the conclusion that none of it makes sense.

Just then he heard a car start up and set into motion behind him. In the rear-view mirror he saw it was a foreign-made car, the same color but not the same model as Yi Kangbok's. Inside he made out the principal—his driver must have had the day off. Sitting next to him, of all people, was Yun Cha'ae. She was leaning toward the principal and appeared to be going to great lengths to explain something. There was a flirtatiousness to her movements, something Kang had not seen during their encounter earlier. He sat silently in the dark, and only when the principal's car had disappeared from view did he himself leave.

↬

The following day, as Kang awaited the morning assembly and drummed his fingers on his desk, wondering how to break the news to Yŏndu that her mother wouldn't be able to visit, he was met with a surprise—a call from the custodian saying that Yŏndu's mother was here to see him. He shot to his feet and went outside, his intuition warning him not to receive his guest in the teachers' room. He spotted her immediately, walking toward him from a distance. Republic of Korea middle-age womanhood, he told himself as she came into view—she was short of stature, overweight, and dark complexioned, and her expression suggested that life had dealt her more than a few blows. But the determined set of her mouth and her clear eyes beneath their thick lids put Kang in mind of Yŏndu's sweet face.

"You must be Yŏndu's mother. I'm Kang Inho—I spoke with you yesterday."

Lost in thought, the woman came to an abrupt halt, visibly surprised. "Good heavens, sir, you came out here to meet *me?*"

"Yes. But what about the surgery?"

"Well, it's been rescheduled. Yesterday was his final checkup before the operation, and one of the blood tests showed something about his liver that was too high, and so at the last minute they postponed it, said to bring him back in a month. So I came down to see Yŏndu. Then I'll go back up, and tomorrow or the next day I'll have to fetch him out of the hospital. I tell you, these days I've had nothing but bad dreams. . . . Yŏndu, she has a disability, but she's always thinking of her mom, and she knows darn well about her dad's operation, so why would she be asking me to come see her now? There must be something on her mind, something out of the ordinary. . . . Tell me sir, is she ill? Do you suppose I could see her briefly?"

As she said this, Kang ushered her behind the leafy camellia tree where they wouldn't be seen from the teachers' room or the office. He took a look around anyway to make sure they hadn't been noticed.

"First of all, I'd like you to ask at the office to see Yŏndu, and if necessary arrange for her to leave for the night so she can be with you. If anybody asks, don't mention our phone conversation yesterday; just say that something has come up at home—you could even mention the operation. And while you're with Yŏndu, could you try to put her mind at ease and then ask what's bothering her? You could communicate—"

"I can use sign language," the woman broke in. "When I learned there wasn't anything we could do about her being deaf . . . I thought I might as well learn it."

Kang, noticing the hesitation that followed "wasn't anything we could do about her being deaf," realized that Yŏndu's mother must have been revisiting a trying experience. The first—and most difficult—trial for the parents of a disabled child is to accept the disability.

"I don't know what else I can tell you. I've only been here a few days, but I have a feeling that something happened to Yŏndu."

"But what . . ." A cloud of fear had shrouded her face, giving Kang the impression that the merest layer of concern added to her life of hardship would send her toppling over the edge. But shining through that careworn expression was a ray of maternal light. To think that a woman so worn down would learn sign language in order to share her daughter's world. . . . For such a woman it would be like learning a foreign language to talk with her daughter. Kang had heard of the terrible isolation suffered by hearing-impaired youth whose families never learned their language—sign language. Such thoughts made Kang want to believe in this woman whose motherly ardor shone so clearly.

↜

For the first time in a long while it felt like autumn. The skies were clear outside Sŏ Yujin's office window, as if in atonement for the days of dense fog that had preceded them. As she sat at her desk sending out the last emails before leaving for the day, a knock sounded on her door.

"Yes?"

When there was no immediate response, she rose to receive her visitor, but then the door opened, and a short, overweight woman entered.

"What can I do for you?" Sŏ noticed that the woman's eyelids were puffy and her eyes, bloodshot—the result of a long bout of tears, she decided.

"Is this the Mujin Human . . . ?" And then the woman fell silent.

Sŏ wondered if her visitor had ever used the expression "human rights" before.

"Human Rights Center? Yes. What can I do for you?"

The woman bit her lip, eyes downcast, trying to decide what to say. Sŏ sensed that the woman was trying to contain a tearful surge of emotion. She must have had an eventful life.

"If there's something we can do to help, we'll do it. Why don't we talk in here?" Sŏ said as she led the woman to one of the interview rooms. The woman seemed hesitant until she was seated, when she looked up at Sŏ.

"I'm so glad you're here. If it was only men, I don't know what I'd do—I've been worried sick all the way here."

It was something related to sex, Sŏ sensed. She waited patiently as the woman looked down, gnawing on her lip.

"Heaven help me," said the woman, looking up again at Sŏ. "Who can I tell this to?"

As a gesture of confidentiality, Sŏ closed the notebook that lay in front of her.

"If it's within our power, we will help you, so please—try to relax and talk to me."

The woman began to weep. Sŏ allowed her to cry, placing a box of tissue before her. Finally, the woman cast an anxious gaze about the room and spoke with difficulty: "Would you mind closing the door?"

ᔍ

Sŏ stood at the window watching the lights come on along the streets outside. A staff member returning from an assignment stuck his head inside her office.

"This weather is something to die for! Just right for some fresh shad and a shot of soju down by the ocean—yeah! Hey, what are you doing sitting in the dark?" He turned on the light for her. The face that turned to regard him was stiff and tense. "Your face—something going on at home? Your younger one sick again?"

Sŏ regarded the man with a blank look, her face pallid as if emptied of something vital. Finally, she broke her silence.

"Mr. Chŏng, first thing tomorrow morning gather all the staff and all our advisors, as many as you can. I want *you* to launch an investigation of the Home of Benevolence—and be as thorough as you can. I had a visitor today, and it seems that something very serious is happening there. The sons of the founder are involved. And the disabled children too."

3

It was late at night and Kang was having a pot of ramen as he surfed the television channels. In recent days he had rediscovered what a hassle the simple act of eating was. Along with thoughts of his mother, and thoughts about women, this had been a recurring subject ever since his army days, when he had been thankful—no, amazed—to be served three meals a day. How could a person, day in and day out, three times a day, prepare meals for all the family members and make sure they were well fed? Kang felt all the more thankful now that at least he didn't have to worry about lunch—it was provided at the Home of Benevolence.

Just then his phone beeped. He checked the display—Sŏ Yujin's number. Should he answer? Well, she was his closest acquaintance here in Mujin, regularly delivering kimchi and meal fixings for him, and he hadn't been here even a week yet. He was grateful, on the one hand, but couldn't deny that it was also a bit annoying. From a man's point of view, she tended to talk a little too much. He didn't remember her being like that back in school—so why now? He decided on a simple explanation: maybe it was their nature for women to grow more talkative the older they got. During their reunion the previous

Sunday he had chalked up her loquacity to loneliness, but at this point in their lives no good would come from proceeding on that assumption. In the end he liked the way she could be talkative and also cheerful, but that same quality could be irksome if Kang was feeling spent, as he had been lately. With these thoughts in mind he took the call.

"Is this a good time to talk?" Her voice was flat, without the usual sisterly bounce. No *Have you eaten?* No *Shall I bring you some more kimchi?* "I'm sorry it's late, but something's come up, something important. Would you mind if I dropped by? Or would you rather come over here?"

Out of habit Kang quickly scanned the interior—dress shirt and socks tossed there, dirty dishes piling up in the sink here.

"It's kind of a mess here," he replied, and the decision was made. Dropping the pot of noodles unfinished in the sink, he went out.

Sŏ was standing, arms crossed, in the open entrance to her apartment. "I haven't eaten yet—let's go out somewhere." And she marched off without waiting for a response.

A short time later they were sitting across from each other in an eatery that specialized in potato stew. Sŏ had ordered a bottle of soju, and when it arrived she had three shots straight off. And with a deep breath, she looked across at Kang.

"So, something came up?"

"Yŏndu. Kim Yŏndu."

Kang was about to pincer a potato chunk with his chopsticks when he heard the name. He looked up at Sŏ.

"Her mom came to see me at the center the other day. She could hardly bear to talk about it."

The events of his stay thus far in Mujin flashed through Kang's mind. *Finally. Something bad has happened.* He deposited the potato chunk in his mouth and chewed thoughtfully.

"Yŏndu was assaulted the other day—sexually assaulted—at the school—by the principal."

Kang considered Sŏ. He couldn't believe it.

"He took her into the women's bathroom . . . tried to rape her, apparently . . . but I can't help thinking . . ." She fell silent, wondering how to say this to a man. And then she made up her mind. "I can't help thinking he didn't succeed—she's so young, after all." She bit down on her lip.

⌒

There were moments etched with lightning clarity in Kang's memory—the moment he heard his father had been killed in a car accident, the first time he was beaten without reason in the army, the moment he heard about Myŏnghŭi killing herself. But these were events that anyone might experience, events you acknowledge with the clink of a shot glass of soju while telling a pal, "And that's what happened" and hearing the friend say, "I think I can understand." But what he had just heard from Sŏ was so unreal and not of the "so that's what happened" category. If the earlier events had hit him like lightning, then this news about Yŏndu brought thunder as well, hammering at him, leaving him shuddering as if a bolt of electricity had shot right through him. All he could do was gape at Sŏ and say, "Huh?"

Sŏ stirred her stew, lost in thought, but when she noticed how shaken Kang looked, she smirked.

"Hard to believe, isn't it? Same with me. But her statements are amazingly consistent in their details." Again her expression hardened.

Kang recalled his first encounter with the principal—the arrogant thrust of the man's shoulders, his disdainful gaze, the receding hairline, the thin lips in the small, colorless, oblong face, the sum of it giving an impression of cold cruelty. But why would any man, especially a school principal nearing age sixty, want to sexually assault a deaf-and-mute second-year middle school girl? As son of the founder of the Home of Benevolence, the principal presumably had the wherewithal to purchase the services of any woman he desired. The streets of

Mujin were lined with women of the night. Whether working in room salons, risqué cafés, karaoke bars, massage parlors, or phone-sex lounges, they were arrayed all along the garishly lit streets and alleys of the pleasure district, perky young women eager to sell their bodies but looking to Kang like so many sodden fish laid out for filleting. As Sergeant Chang the policeman had said, Mujin was the perfect place to eat, drink, and make merry. And the principal, simply put, had the financial resources to keep several young mistresses if he wanted. There was a correlation, Kang knew, between a man's possessions and his sex life, both its frequency and its quality.

"What sort of man could sink to the pits like that—a school principal who's almost sixty going after one of the students—and in the school bathroom!"

Kang finally made the connection—so that was the reason for the scream from behind the locked door of the women's bathroom. That scream was from Yŏndu, and the principal, hearing Kang knock on the door, must have put a hand over her mouth. If Yŏndu had only known that her new homeroom teacher was knocking on the door, she would certainly have put up a fight. As it was, the principal must have continued his indecencies after the knocking stopped, culminating in the assault. Kang wished he had been more persistent. Why couldn't he have broken into the bathroom or at least summoned someone to open the door?

His heart was pounding, and he had to look away from Sŏ. He recalled the look of shame that had come across her face when she saw him being accosted by the streetwalker that first night in Mujin. That's how he must have looked now. And he recalled asking Sŏ rhetorically if it was her fault that there were pleasure quarters in Mujin. And just as she wasn't responsible for that streetwalker, Kang bore no responsibility for the character of the principal, but this realization left him no less ashamed of himself. As a teacher and having heard the scream from the bathroom, he felt a sting in his heart. And were the

feelings of shame that had accompanied his arrival at the
Home of Benevolence what prevented him now from telling Sŏ
he had heard that scream?

Sŏ regarded Kang even as he avoided her gaze.

"That same night, this girl Yŏndu sneaked out of the
school and met one of the school counselors, a man named
Song Hasŏp, and he took her to the Rape Crisis Center, where
she filled out a report. She gave a statement and asked them to
notify the police, and then she went back to the school. You'd
think a rape center would send a victim, especially a child,
to the hospital right off, or at least shelter her for the night.
It mystifies me that they sent her back to the place where
this man had assaulted her. And I don't understand why her
mother didn't pull her out of there—of course she has other
things on her mind. Anyway, the police could have investi-
gated right off, but we found that the very next morning the
complaint was dropped. If the victim of a sexual assault is
under thirteen, then a complaint is automatically filed; if the
victim is thirteen or over, she can file the complaint herself
and can also have it dropped, and that's the end of it. So why
was Yŏndu's complaint dropped? Well, you would guess,
would you not, that it's because they beat Yŏndu and made
her recant? That they made her write a second statement
saying the first one was false? And then Yŏndu asked you to
call her mother."

So, she knew—presumably through Yŏndu's mother—of his
involvement. He had become, he realized, one of the princi-
pals in this case. Which meant he might be subpoenaed as a
witness. Which meant in turn that he might have to testify on
behalf of the prosecution against Yi Kangsŏk.

His thoughts turned to Saemi and his wife, who had
reassured him about her new job with these words: "Don't
worry, it's not like I'm selling my body. It's nothing bad." The
thing was, he hadn't heard from her in the past few days. In
their last conversation she had talked about Saemi: "She's such

a wonderful girl. Every morning she straps on her yellow book bag and goes off to preschool without a fuss. Her teacher told me that one time she watched Saemi say goodbye to me— said she had this big smile—but then after I left she went over by the window where the other kids wouldn't notice and she started crying. She knows that kids cry when they're separated from their mother, and I'm sure she told herself not to cry in front of me. What a wonderful girl—or maybe she's already mature enough to know sadness."

Kang's eyes revealed the worry this conversation with his wife had caused him.

"The question now," Sŏ continued, "is how the school found out so fast about the complaint. And that is where I'll need your input. We helped Yŏndu's mother file a new report, but it's been two days now, and the police haven't acted on it. We're told that it's Sergeant Chang's case—our center has had some friction with him before. But even if we get the investigation going, there's another problem. We can't go inside the dormitory, and the children can't leave the dormitory unless they're accompanied by a parent. The mother had to go back up to Seoul to take care of Yŏndu's father, and for all we know, the school could be taking matters into their own hands with Yŏndu, and there's nothing we could do about it. And there's more. Yun Cha'ae, the counselor who was administering the frontier justice to Yŏndu, turns out to be the foster child of the founder, which must be why her name means 'benevolence.' And everyone's heard the rumor that she's the lover of her own foster brother, the principal—is that sick or what? I have to wonder if her own messy background is a factor—why else would she be so cruel to one of the children? When she was interrogating Yŏndu, apparently she asked why the girl was flirting with the principal. I couldn't believe my ears. It's insane—the place is a crucible of insanity!"

As she finished her briefing, she noticed that Kang's face had turned ashen like the fog. The reason for this was that the players in this drama, starting with Yun Cha'ae, were crossing Kang's mind. When he considered the surreal sense of hostility the woman had projected and what he could only explain as bad karma, he thought he could begin to understand her behavior. And he thought he could understand the savagery of the principal and the administrator, though each seemed to have his own way of manifesting it. The question mark was Chang the policeman. He seemed to have sized up the situation immediately, and Kang could only guess that Chang happened to be at the school to cover things up on Kang's first day there. What Kang couldn't understand was why the policeman had taken such an interest in him, while at the same time displaying such obvious hostility. He felt that the two of them would someday be brought together in a duel and that Chang had already made the first thrust. Had the policeman's feral instincts told him that Kang, the newcomer from Seoul, was his most formidable obstacle, something to be removed? Chang had warned him not to form hasty judgments about Mujin like Seoul people were wont to do. Kang shivered. *No, Chang wasn't talking about me,* he wanted to say—*no way.* He wanted to deny as well what Sŏ had said—that for all they knew, Yŏndu might be on the receiving end of more frontier justice at that very moment. That he was able to suppress the urge was thanks to a sound and an image that overlaid themselves in his mind— the scream coming from the bathroom and the cruel welts on Yŏndu's arm from the washing machine.

Sŏ had more to say. "This is strictly a hunch on my part, but I think something very serious is going on. Kim Yŏndu is victimized by the principal, and we file a report. Now isn't there a child in your class, Yuri, Chin Yuri? Did you know she's been sexually assaulted by the principal, the administrator, and dormitory counselor Pak Pohyŏn—starting back in grade school?"

If the report of Yŏndu's assault had struck Kang like a bolt of lightning, then this news shook him like an earthquake. How to make sense of it? A faint realization came over him:

As for Yŏndu, perhaps her sweet loveliness was capable of sparking the interest of men with a sexual perversion—a Lolita complex. This in no way condoned a school principal's sexual assault of a fifteen-year-old student or denied that it was the most repulsive of crimes, and yet Kang wanted to leave open the possibility, however slight, that another factor might be at play—a basic human weakness. But if a principal or an administrator or a guidance counselor had sexually assaulted a girl as disabled as Yuri and had been doing so since she was in grade school—if there was any basis to what Sŏ was saying about Yuri, if there was any truth to it—then the scope of the act had expanded to a different dimension altogether. The enormity of it was too much for Kang to fathom, making it difficult for him to focus on Sŏ's words. Her voice sounded distant one moment and nearby the next.

"Can you believe it? I don't think we've managed to process it ourselves. But that's what Yŏndu told her mother, and she was all in tears. She said the children have known about it all along. They've told the teachers several times, but they're always shushed up—everything they try to say disappears into silence. Even Yŏndu's mother had a difficult time believing it—I can imagine the state she's in. So we're launching an investigation here at the center, and first off we'll have to file a report—say, are you all right?"

Only then did Kang realize he'd dropped one of his chopsticks. He retrieved it and, to hide his embarrassment, popped some spinach into his mouth and crunched into it. But he was still so flustered that he lit a cigarette before he had swallowed the spinach. As he was thinking how ridiculous he must look, he noticed with relief that Sŏ, instead of observing him, was lost in thought. The fat on the pork neckbone in his stew pot was congealing into a creamy white. Kang finally broke the leaden silence.

"Chin Yuri functions at the level of a six-year-old. If you give her cookies, she'll do anything for you. Isn't it a bit much to make an issue out of the entire school just based on what children like her say? You mention that you have a hunch. But what if these allegations get out and then go wild—are you willing to take responsibility? The bottom line is, in a rational world . . . things like this just don't happen, do they?"

In emphasizing *a rational world,* Kang was seeking the power of reason. Sŏ sighed, frowning, and then puffed up her cheeks in a pensive expression.

"If you were in my line of work—I'm not sure I can explain this—you'd find that rationality"—and here she paused, trying to lock in Kang's wavering gaze before saying in a pained voice—"doesn't exist."

༺

"This is the twenty-first century," said Kang. "Of course the police will investigate."

Sŏ's frown deepened. "Yes, it's the twenty-first century, all right, and I'm telling you the police are *not* investigating!"

"Let's just wait a little—it's only been a few days," Kang managed to say.

But Sŏ would not back down. "Listen to me, will you. Let me tell you something about the man who founded the school, Yi Chunbŏm. The school dates back to 1964—that's after Park Chung Hee took power and right after he made himself president. Yi Chunbŏm started out working for the Public Welfare Bureau at City Hall here in Mujin and then he set up the Mujin Home for Deaf-Mutes—which makes me wonder if he caught on early about the huge welfare budget for the disabled. I don't know this for a fact, but sources say he decided on deaf-mutes because they're more capable of physical labor than people with other disabilities. It's ridiculous, I know— when people can't speak up. . . . Anyway, he bought up land around and about Mujin, put up temporary housing, and then put his deaf-mutes to work building permanent housing. From that point on he received a great deal of funding. And then when Mujin started to expand and the outlying areas were incorporated into the city, land prices skyrocketed. So he got all this funding from the city, and then—and God knows how he did it—he put his land under corporate ownership. Eventually the city bought it all from him, and he moved his operations outside the city again, to the present seaside location. The capital gains were huge, and because they were _corporate_ capital gains, they were safe. But of course the corporation in question consists of the founder, Yi Chunbŏm, and his two sons—the principal and the man who holds the purse strings, the administrator. You don't need any video to see how it plays out. The twins' academic background isn't much to brag about, but the father made sure to send his daughters off to the US for high school and college and then got them high-powered husbands. We found out that one of them is a prosecutor.

"And there's another piece to this puzzle that sticks out— where the school used to be is where Mujin police headquarters is now. Meaning, the land was bought by the government. Nothing's come to light in the way of a relationship between the police and the home, _but,_ during the dictatorship, when there were demonstrations and the old police station got filled up with protestors who'd been arrested, the Home of Benevolence occasionally let the police use an entire floor of the dormitory to handle the overflow. The demonstrators were unlawfully detained and they were tortured but so what—nobody could hear them. Knowing this, don't you think there's something fishy about the police dragging their feet in this investigation?"

Hearing this, Kang imagined Sŏ confronting a massive iceberg with only a tiny hammer. He, on the other hand, had been trying to give the impression that he had risen above the inevitable fact that there were bad people everywhere. But his efforts were eroded by her words, which had dashed over him like a cold shower.

"You don't know, because you've only been here a few days, but don't you _feel_ there's something strange going on?

The principal assaults a student in a school bathroom, the girl screams—is there any teacher capable of hearing, who wouldn't know what was going on?"

Kang could only hang his head in response.

⤸

When Kang arrived at the school the next morning he found a commotion taking place outside the principal's office. A man he had never seen before, dressed neatly in a suit, was talking loudly in a peculiar voice while the custodian and Pak Pohyŏn attempted to detain him—each had taken hold of one of the man's arms. Standing nearby was the administrator, obviously displeased. Also present was Yun Cha'ae, arms folded across her chest. When she spotted Kang, her frown turned frosty and she looked away. Pak's eyes, small and shiny like a rat's, seemed to have been watching out for how Yun would respond to Kang, and when he noticed her chilly look, he adopted a menacing expression.

"You can't get away with this!" shouted the man in the suit. "You have to give me a reason! You can't get away with this! You can't just fire me!"

This was the first time Kang had heard a deaf-mute speak. The man's tone was unsteady, but his pronunciation was clear.

"Can't I?" barked the administrator. "We hired you, we'll fire you, and there's nothing you can do about it! So shut up— you're making a fool out of yourself!"

The administrator must have known the man was a deaf-mute, but he wasn't using sign language, wasn't even bothering with gestures to make himself understood. Kang knew by now that this was the worst insult a deaf-mute could suffer. Failing to show the least effort to communicate— no sign language, no gestures—was no different from an American, arms folded, carrying on endlessly in English to someone who didn't speak that language.

The man in the suit looked at Yun with an expression that showed he didn't understand what the administrator was saying. She responded with a look of contempt mixed with what Kang could only describe as sheer hostility. But the way the man regarded her indicated that he was asking her for help, and Kang realized that Yun was the only communication link between the two men, one with normal hearing and the other deaf. For a brief moment Kang sensed the grief that the hearing-impaired must feel in such situations, followed by a stab of pain in his heart.

"Doesn't he have to give me cause?" the man shouted. "A reason for firing me?"

With an expression of annoyance, the administrator gestured with his chin for Yun to interpret. She did so, signing to the man, her cold expression unchanging. The moment she finished, the man screamed once, broke free from the two men restraining him, and charged toward the principal's office. The door was locked. He rammed the door with his body, then kicked at it.

"Come out! You can't fire me like this! What did I do to deserve it!"

The teachers arriving for the day paused only long enough to see what was happening, then continued on their way. They reminded Kang of drivers who slow down to gawk at an accident and then speed up again, their faces uncaring. Several men rushed into the building, and the man in the suit was carried away, each limb in the grip of a separate man.

"You can't do this to me! You can't do this!" he screamed as he was taken outside.

In the teachers' room Kang approached Pak Kyŏngch'ŏl, who was changing into his school slippers. The man was struggling to get his shoes off.

"What was that all about?" asked Kang. "Who was that?"

"You're a determined fellow, aren't you?" asked Pak as if nothing had happened. He finally managed to remove his shoes and don his slippers. Then took his time turning on his computer. "Didn't I warn you? Why are you so nosy, anyway? You have something in mind?"

Kang cringed at these words.

⌒

The bell for first period rang, and the teachers began filing out, a succession of unsettled faces. Kang joined them, class list in hand. The long hallway to the classrooms was still, and Kang felt an overwhelming fear, as if he himself were deaf.

"Got to see Sŏ," he muttered to himself. "Got to find out who that man is and what's going on between him and the school—it's unbelievable." And then a strange thought hit him: What if the words he had just mumbled, words heard by his own ears, were not audible to others? He was suddenly revisited by the same vague unease he had felt since his arrival in Mujin. Could he ever have imagined, as he did now, that tranquility could be so oppressive?

In the classroom he found Minsu crying while the other children stood nearby communicating feverishly in sign language. Putting his class list on the teacher's desk, he went straight to Minsu.

What is it? He had barely signed the question when his hands dropped to his sides. Minsu had a black eye, his face was bruised, and his neck bore discolorations. Kang rolled up the boy's shirt sleeves—abrasions on his arms as well.

Were you fighting with someone? Kang signed.

Minsu, head lowered, didn't answer.

Kang recalled the listing for Minsu in his student roster:

Name: Chŏn Minsu—moderate hearing impairment
Family: father, mild intellectual impairment; mother, moderate hearing impairment and moderate intellectual impairment; younger brother Yŏngsu, moderate hearing impairment, severe intellectual impairment

<u>Home</u>: Oeso Island; remote location makes school-
vacation home visit difficult for pupil
Requires special attention

That listing would eventually be updated:

Younger brother struck and killed by train; remains
unclaimed by disabled parents; compensation provided
to parents by Railroad Administration.

What now? The prospects for this boy's very existence seemed
more remote than the island where his parents lived.

Who hit you?

It was all Kang could do to sign this question but Minsu
remained silent. With a sigh, Kang carefully lifted the boy's
shirt. More startling than the bruises on the boy's chest were
his bony ribs. Noting the bruises, he lowered Minsu's shirt.

No ointment?

_No._

Can you tell me who did this?

No answer.

All right. Let's go see the nurse.

But when he took Minsu's hand, the fear-ridden boy
resisted.

What's the matter? You need some ointment for those bruises.

The next moment Minsu shot to his feet with an inarticulate
scream, wrenched his hand free, and ran frantically from the
classroom. While Kang tried to decide whether to follow, the
other children regarded him. Their faces were cold and once
again guarded. Kang managed to compose himself.

Take your seats and open your books. I want you to read today's
lesson.

He sat down at his desk, beside the platform and podium,
and summoned Yŏndu. The girl's face looked calmer now that
she had seen her mother. He wanted to ask if she was all right

but couldn't bring himself to do it. First, he needed to regain his presence of mind.

Do you know what happened to Minsu?

Instead of answering, Yŏndu lowered her gaze.

Who did it?

Yŏndu looked up hesitantly toward Kang, bit her lip, then slowly began to sign.

Sometimes he comes to class looking like that. He told us it happens at night in the dorm. When Teacher Pak Pohyŏn has night duty, Minsu gets taken out, and we think that's when he gets hurt. Before his brother died, sometimes they were both taken out at night. Even if they get beaten, no one objects—you know.

Teacher Pak—Pak Pohyŏn?

Yŏndu looked intently at Kang.

Yes. And the day Minsu's brother, Yŏngsu, died? The night before that, they were both beaten.

⌒

The night was dark and the area was tawdry. The dim lights in the surrounding establishments were going off. A salty smell and a sticky feel rode the wind blowing in from the sea. Kang kept trying to focus his blurred vision; he had no idea where he was. From school he had driven home, parked, and started walking. He had walked until he was too tired to walk more, found a drinking place, and drank. He had repeated the process at least twice that he could remember.

Once more he narrowed his focus, and there in front of him, revolving like a barbershop pole, was a gaudy neon sign. Kang peered at it, trying to make out the words—The Extravaganza—Hot Beauties of Mujin—Seoul Style, Anything Goes! The sign was grimy and the borders, top and bottom, were chipped.

Kang gaped at the sign a while longer, then started moving again. Light, a shaft of light from behind him—and then something smashed into the back of his head. Down he went

like a sheaf of straw. Instinctively he reached out, but the
motorcycle was already speeding off, and he realized the
suit jacket he had slung over his shoulder was gone. Before
he knew it he was on his feet chasing the motorcycle, but it
disappeared around the corner and into an alley. He arrived,
panting, at the mouth of the alley, and suddenly everything
was bright—a profusion of signs in red and yellow and beneath
them a throng of women in short skirts. Kang was reminded
of a children's book he had read in which the characters fell
through a manhole and into a vastly different world. But the
children's book was fantasy and this was real. The women
wore garish makeup. Some sat in chairs, others stood; all
were angling for customers. Kang thought he saw two men
on a motorcycle—_bastards!_—but then they were gone. He kept
blinking, wanting his alcohol-blurred vision to clear, as he
tried to figure out where the motorcycle had gone. It was so
frustrating.

A woman approached. Her hair was a gray tangle, and she
was shaking her head back and forth. She put her face up to his
and examined it. Her own wrinkled face resembled a sponge,
her complexion the murky color of sewage, and she clutched
a bundle. To Kang she seemed half human, half ghost. The
woman shoved her face closer.

"Kim Inshik, right?"

Kang was hit with a blast of gamy, excremental breath.
"You've got the wrong guy," he said, backpedaling.

"No, you're Kim Inshik, all right."

She was like a pesky fly, and when she tried to press even
closer, he retreated to the now-darkened main street. The
woman hurried after him.

"You're Kim Inshik, all right. Kim Inshik, you lousy bastard!
Where's my money? You lousy bastard, give me my money
back!"

Kang quickened his pace and the woman did likewise. He
broke into a run, figuring the hag would do the same. When

next he looked back, she had stopped and was gesticulating
frantically in his direction. The pumping of her arm beneath
the solitary streetlight made this Mujin street scene look like
something out of a nightmare, only worse.

~

When Kang had caught his breath, he tottered off into the
night. The dense air promised rain. Holding his hand out, he
could almost feel the moisture condense on his palm. Taxis
whizzed through the thick air. He felt a tickle at the back of
his neck and reached there—sticky. He looked at his hand, saw
blood on his fingers. He tried to wave down a taxi, staggered,
and grabbed a utility pole to steady himself. Where was his
wallet? In his suit jacket, damn it! Wallet, credit cards, suit
jacket—bye-bye. He clenched his teeth, then felt in his pants
pocket—his phone was still there. Thank the Lord for little
favors. He felt sick to his stomach. Holding fast to the pole, he
retched and spat. He looked up and felt rain. The raindrops
thickened. The heavens were darker, the streets wet.

> I had a dream, I did, and though it was abandoned,
> ripped, and ragged
> I treasured that dream and kept it in my heart.
> If on occasion someone, for whatever reason, were to
> sneer behind my back
> I endured, I could endure, until the day that dream came
> true
> I always talked anxiously, said that a pipe dream is poison
> And the world is like a book: once you know the ending
> you can't go back and change it.
> That's right—I have a dream, I do, a dream I believe in
> Look at me—I stand tall before that cold wall of fate
> Someday I'll fly over it, fly high into the sky,
> The weight of this world cannot tie me down
> That day let's celebrate the end of my life's journey.

"Goose Dream" by Insuni—the answer tone that Sŏ had programmed into her phone. Kang had difficulty appreciating that dream, so immediate was the impression left by his spectral encounter with that dirty old woman. *Dream—ha, a dream.* Listening to the song, Kang forgot for the moment that he had called Sŏ, and when the song was cut off, replaced by her voice, he startled.

"Inho? Kang Inho?"

He must have awakened her.

"Are you all right? What time is it anyway?"

"I'm sorry . . ."

"What's the matter? What happened?"

The back of his hand holding the phone was getting wet. It was all he could do to speak, and he had to keep gritting his teeth before he could say anything.

"Yes, it's me. I'm somewhere downtown . . . wallet's gone—a couple of guys snatched it—everywhere it's dark, and now it's raining . . . can't find my way home." And with that he plopped down onto the sidewalk.

⌒

Sŏ exited her car and slammed the door shut. She could almost hear her colleague chiding her, the way he did when they had to drive to an appointment: "Please, easy on the door—we don't want the car to roll over."

The next moment she was talking silently to herself: *Sergeant Chang—Chang Hamun—face like a dried pollack . . . knew I'd have to deal with that creep someday.* And off she marched across the parking lot toward the Mujin Police Station, swinging her arms like a boxer. *Hold on*—she stopped. Where was her handbag? She remembered dropping her keys inside it after she'd parked, then making a grand display of locking the car and slamming the door shut, so zeroed in was she on Chang. Were the keys in her jacket pocket? She felt around—no. This wasn't the first time she'd zoned out. *Come on, you really need to focus!* She heaved a sigh. Maybe she needed more sleep. She recalled how wretched and ghostlike Kang had looked when she had found him near the bus terminal the previous night. *No taxis,* he had whimpered over the phone.

"No cab? Where are you anyway, in the middle of a rice paddy? In a mudflat? Do you see a shop anywhere? Just give me the name—or read me the phone number on the sign."

She had then called information for the address of the shop Kang had reported, climbed into her car, and found him waiting with sunken eyes, like a voyager just returned from the other world. He hadn't been here even a week and yet had taken on an aging, seedy look. She'd felt peeved pulling up at the utility pole where he was standing—why couldn't he have hailed a cab and then knocked on her door to borrow the fare? Instead she'd had to fetch him. It was only when they'd arrived at his apartment and she'd helped him out of the car and noticed his bloodstained shirt that she understood why he'd felt compelled to call her. With his bloodshot eyes and the fear and sorrow he had projected, he reminded her of an orphan— even more so when she recalled how he had whimpered over the phone: "It's Kang. I'm somewhere downtown . . . wallet's gone—a couple of guys snatched it—everywhere it's dark, and now it's raining . . . can't find my way home." She'd had to help him inside, where he insisted she join him for more soju at his messy kitchen table, so she hadn't gotten to sleep until the wee hours of the morning.

"I want to go home. . . . I want to go back to Seoul." Eyes half closed, still clutching his shot glass, he had laid his head down on the table.

"Of course you do, you've been here a whole week, you miss your family, you miss your mom, poor boy, what are we going to do with you?" she had *tsk-tsked* as she practically carried him into his bedroom and laid him down. She remembered Kang at college as being smart and mature enough that she couldn't really treat him as someone junior to her. He seemed much changed since then. But she herself, once settled in Mujin, had immediately begun to feel she was withering on the vine— especially when she realized that time here seemed to move at a different tempo. She recalled a nightmare in which she had visited Seoul to find that all her friends had retained a semblance of youth while she alone had aged, looking like all the life had been sucked out of her.

She set off again, slowly now, wondering about the keys. Well, they weren't about to materialize in her jacket pocket, nor was a savior about to appear to unlock her car. Best to focus on her business with the sergeant. She arrived at the glass door to the station and shoved it open. If Kang had seen her, he might have thought to himself that here she was again challenging that huge iceberg, but this time without the hammer.

⤳

Sergeant Chang was on the phone, snickering about something. His face tensed the moment he noticed Sŏ, but when he saw she had recognized him, he returned to his conversation. When Sŏ arrived at his desk, arms folded, he gave her a nod and with one last chuckle ended his conversation. Then he cleared his throat importantly and spat.

"I want to know _why_ you haven't started an investigation," said Sŏ.

This was the third time she had had to deal with Chang. Slowly and deliberately, the policeman looked her up and down. To her co-workers Sŏ had described this way of gazing at her as unsettling, disgusting, brazen.

"Won't you have a seat, Miss Sŏ?" Chang indicated a chair. "May I offer you a hot drink?"

"When a child is sexually assaulted, when the assault takes place at a school, and when a report is filed alleging that the school principal is the perpetrator, isn't it to be expected that the police will obtain a statement from the victim and launch an investigation of the principal?"

"Absolutely," he said with a smile, the picture of leisure as he rubbed his bearded chin.

Sŏ had made up her mind not to fly off the handle as she had during their previous encounter, and to this end she willed herself to keep her voice steady and calm. But at the nauseating sight of Chang, who always seemed to be one step ahead of her, she felt herself stiffen with tension and grow red in the face.

"Then why haven't the police done anything? The girl's been sexually assaulted and she's still at the school, she's still vulnerable."

"Well, we were about to investigate, but the school informs us that they won't release the child unless the parents are present. It's school policy—what can we do? I told you the last time—we can't remove the girl from the school. So as far as the investigation is concerned—"

"And *I* told *you* that the mother went to Seoul and couldn't come back down as planned, because the father's surgery has been rescheduled. But the point is, when a parent files a report with the police, there has to be an investigation. And the principal hasn't been questioned, and I want to know why."

Chang flashed another smile and struck an affable pose. "Miss Sŏ, you know this as well as anyone," he said in a hushed voice. "The principal is known to *everyone* in this area as a gentleman of refinement and excellence. Would you have us go up to this gentleman on the basis of what a deaf child says and tell him, 'Let's go down to the police station'? You know how things work these days—human rights or whatever. It's difficult for us too. We can't just bring someone in."

"And that's why you need Yŏndu here, along with us, so you can take a statement. And then you can bring in the suspect."

"Well, as much as we might like to do that, without the parents present, the school won't release her, as I said." Chang leaned back comfortably in his chair, fingers laced together behind his head.

"Then can't you just get the investigation going—focusing first on the child and the principal—the victim and the suspect?"

Sŏ's voice had risen in spite of herself, and now all the other policemen were looking her way. Again she felt her face turn red. And yet again Chang smiled, fingers still laced behind his head, enjoying the moment.

"Well, without clear evidence I can't very well go up to this distinguished gentleman and say, 'Sir, let's go down to the police station.' And on a charge of sexual assault? Just between you and me, Miss Sŏ, we're not talking about bribery or breach of public trust, we're talking about _sexual assault_. I just can't imagine myself saying those words to him—do you think you could? I mean, just the day before yesterday he was awarded a medal by the governor."

Sŏ swallowed heavily. She wasn't accustomed to dealing with this breed of man, who lures his opponent with obscure, multi-layered words, who seizes upon the other person's simplistic interpretation of those words and then drives her into a logical corner. She did, though, have good instincts, and those instincts were telling her not to continue this argument. And so, suppressing an urge to grab the man by the scruff of the neck, she lowered her voice and spoke.

"In that case, if we speak with the school and bring the student here, will you take her statement?"

"Please. You're talking as if we don't want to investigate, and _that_ is a big misunderstanding. The fact of the matter is, we haven't been directed by the prosecutor's office to investigate." By now Sŏ was trembling with anger. As if he found her reaction cute, Chang began to alternate between formal, honorific speech and familiar, plain speech. "You're aware of this, the authority of the prosecutor's office to order an investigation? We've been asking the government for independent investigative power—the technical term is 'the right to exclusive indictment'—but they won't do it. So until the prosecutor's office gives us their blessing, there's nothing we can do."

And with that, Chang unlocked his fingers, placed his hands on his desk, and looked Sŏ in the eye as if to say her audience was over. Sŏ had come up against Chang before, but not until now had he so obviously attempted to shirk his responsibilities—and the complaint was so straightforward. She had expected him to drag his feet and to be partial, and she realized that the previous issues bringing them into contact might have had political ramifications, but never had she dreamed that Chang would act as he did now when the complaint seemed crystal clear—a child, a school, a principal, and a sexual assault.

Sŏ met the policeman's gaze head on and sneered, "The prosecutor this, the police that—is that the best you can do? You'll pay for this, my good man, mark my word." There was a glint of righteous anger in her eyes. Truth had a way of strengthening one's words.

"Good man? Well, Auntie, so I'm a good man now. When did we become so close?" But Chang could no longer hold Sŏ's gaze.

"What—'Auntie'? So, Uncle, you don't like 'my good man'? Then how about 'Hey you!' Don't confuse me with one of the girls at your Night Flower Café hangout just because I call you 'my good man.'"

This drew stifled chuckles from the other policemen, who had buried their heads in their paperwork, pretending to be busy.

∻

"All right, then, since there's no other way, we'll proceed on our own." With this heroic parting shot, Sŏ took her leave. But outside the police station, she was overcome with feelings of helplessness. How to bring Yŏndu's sexual assault to the attention of the public? Maybe she had been naive to assume the police would launch an investigation as a matter of course. She had raised her voice to Chang, had been direct in her approach, wanting to show him what she thought was right, and now what?

As she hurried toward her car, she reached for her keys by habit. Of course they weren't there, and though she knew it was fruitless, she looked inside the car. But instead of the keys, there where she had left it on the passenger seat was her phone. A call had arrived, the name of one of her colleagues appearing on the display. Back at the office she had asked him to contact Yŏndu's mother. That must have been why he had tried to reach her. She needed to hurry. There was a spare key in her wallet—an acknowledgment of her frequent bouts of forgetfulness—but by now it was pretty much an empty gesture, the wallet more often than not ending up in the car when she locked it. And she had already exceeded the limit on free road-service calls through her insurance. Nothing to do now but swallow her pride and call her brother, who owned an auto repair shop. But how? Her phone was inside the locked car. With a sigh she turned back to the station. Chang was just outside the entrance, smoking.

"Was there something else?" he asked politely, on guard once he had noticed Sŏ making a beeline for him.

"I'm very sorry, but could I use your phone?" she asked, forcing herself to speak deferentially.

"My phone? . . . And what might you need it for, my good woman?"

Sŏ flared up. "It's just a local call—not international, not long distance. Do I need to tell you every detail? Don't tell me you need an okay from the prosecutor's office." She turned to leave.

"Wait, I'm not that bad—really. Here, help yourself—since it's not an international call."

She took the phone, called her brother, and asked him to send someone over. When her brother asked what the problem was, she glanced at Chang, hesitated, then mumbled, "It's that matter we talked about last time." And then, realizing her brother didn't understand, "I locked myself out of my car." Embarrassed that Chang might have overheard, she thrust the phone at him and said, "Thanks. And please get going on that investigation."

"That's exactly what I'd like to do—too bad you aren't the prosecutor."

While Sŏ waited for help to arrive, Chang watched her intently until he was joined by a policeman named Kim.

"What do you think of her?" he asked Kim.

Kim, based on his long experience with the sergeant, produced an ambiguous smile.

"She's single, lives by herself, right?" Chang continued. "Women like her, always carrying on about 'the people,' democracy, stuff like that, they're not much to look at, are they? Women with a mindset like that, they're more hysterical than usual, don't you think?"

So saying, Chang took a deep drag on his cigarette.

4

The video recorder was in place in the conference room of the Mujin Human Rights Advocacy Center, and the director of the Rape Crisis Center for People with Disabilities had arrived. A sign-language interpreter from the local district office was expected at any minute; he was a high school classmate of one of the Human Rights Advocacy Center staff members and had volunteered his services.

Sŏ had brought a small pot of begonias to soften the mood, and though it didn't have much effect in the conference room, at least it would help the children feel more comfortable as they gave their statements. Yŏndu would be arriving with her mother, and Kang would bring Yuri from the school, and the recording of the statements would begin.

Earlier that morning Sŏ, together with two other staff, had decided they could wait no longer for the police to act on the allegations regarding the Home of Benevolence. Their plan was to videotape the testimony of the children and then notify the newspapers, broadcasting companies, and other media, as well as the National Human Rights Commission in Seoul. Also that morning it had been reported to the Greater Mujin Workers Assembly that one of the counselors at the Home of

Benevolence dormitory, a hearing-impaired man named Song Hasŏp, had been fired without cause. The grounds for the firing given by the home were verbal abuse of the principal and conduct unbecoming a teacher, but the real reason seemed to have been that it was Song who had driven Yŏndu to the Rape Crisis Center after her assault. True to her foreboding, Sŏ now sensed something massive looming in the darkness—a threat that left her no time for further wrangling with Sergeant Chang.

Yŏndu and her mother arrived first. Her father's surgery had finally taken place a few days earlier, and her mother had come down to Mujin first thing this morning to be with her. The mother's face was more troubled than when Sŏ had first met with her—the father's prospects were not encouraging, she reported. Sŏ had decided some time ago that if there were a God, He would not allow life to bear down on a soul as mercilessly as this. She saw in Yŏndu's mother's face her own as she had hoisted her baby girl onto her back, the child fever-ridden and convulsing, then awakened her four-year-old and hauled her outside in the wee hours of a cold morning, trying frantically to find a taxi to the hospital. Also vivid in her memory was the illusion that the deep blue sky at first light would shatter and rain down on her.

There was tension in Yŏndu's face.

Here you are. Nice to see you. Using simple sign-language phrases she'd learned from Kang, Sŏ greeted the girl. Yŏndu brightened momentarily and signed something back, but Sŏ could only guess she was being asked if she, too, were deaf. With a smile she waved her hand in a "no" gesture. Disappointment passed across Yŏndu's face.

Sŏ next distributed pastries and milk to the children. Yŏndu hesitated before finding a place off by herself and then biting into the pastry with its red bean jam filling. The size of the mouthful made Sŏ wonder when the girl had last enjoyed a snack. She gazed at Yŏndu, the girl's plump cheeks bulging with every chew. Those cheeks were the color of peaches, and her thick black hair had a nice luster. Her eyes were clear, the lids fleshy, and she was a bit taller than other girls her age. The legs showing below the hem of her school-issue skirt were long and firm like a doll's. Sŏ's mind was awhirl with all that the age of fifteen suggested in a girl—the fuzz on an apricot, a light emerald color, rose petals on a spring day, morning dew, drizzle, the vulnerable wings of a butterfly in early spring, the delicate fragrance of tea. She tried to imagine for a moment what had befallen Yŏndu in the freshness of her girlhood; what came to mind made her dizzy. It was then that her eyes met the girl's. She saw in those eyes a flicker of bashfulness followed by a smile, brief and hesitant. Sŏ thought of her own daughters, of how she had named them Pada and Hanŭl in hopes that the entities signified by those names—sea and sky—would offer protection no matter what might befall the girls. And as she always did when faced with a challenge, she produced a brave smile for Yŏndu.

⁓

Yŏndu, clutching her mother's hand, had taken her place at the table in the conference room. Across from her sat the director of the Rape Crisis Center. Sŏ turned on the VCR, its whir sounding abnormally loud. Nobody dared make a sound. She nodded to the director, signaling the start of the proceedings.

"What is your name?" the director asked. The interpreter signed the question for Yŏndu.

Kim Yŏndu.

"And you are a second-year middle school student at the Home of Benevolence school?"

Yes.

"You are under no pressure or threat of penalty to testify in these proceedings. You may stop your testimony at any time. Do you wish to proceed?"

Yes.

"You have said that on Monday of last week you were sexually assaulted by the principal of the Home of Benevolence. Can you talk about what happened at that time?"

Yes.

"Then please tell us. How did this incident come about?"

After class that day I went to the dormitory to change out of my school uniform. Then I went out to the playfield. I was with Yuri, and she said she was going to the bathroom. When she didn't come back out, I went to look for her. I went in through the main entrance and I was walking toward the teachers' room when the principal came out of his office. When he saw me he asked me to "come here," going like this with his hand. I went up to him, wondering what he wanted; he doesn't use sign language, but I guessed he wanted to see me in his office. I went in his office and he took me to his desk. Something was showing on his computer monitor—something strange—a man and a woman, and they didn't have any clothes on—

Yŏndu's hands came to a stop in midair, and she turned to her mother, biting down on her lip. The young volunteer interpreter likewise fell silent. Unaware of the reason for the proceedings, he was clearly pained at what he had just heard. The gazes of Sŏ, Kang, the Human Rights Advocacy Center staff members, and the Crisis Center director were focused on Yŏndu. Silence blanketed the room. Yŏndu's mother regarded her daughter, the slow blinking of her eyes the only movement visible in her face, which had frozen more solidly than ice. She would stake her entire being on expressing herself to her daughter, her eyes communicating a mixture of sorrow, anger, and compassion with such intensity it seemed she was about to explode. Her plump hands were perspiring, dampening the handkerchief she clutched. Yŏndu's expression bespoke acknowledgment of her mother's conflicted feelings. It was suffused with gravity and with the dignity of one who is blessed with a love that is constant and true. Nothing girl-like remained in that expression.

Yŏndu resumed her testimony.

I guess it was a movie about naked people, and the man and woman actually had their private parts showing. . . . I was scared and I wanted to run away. But the principal grabbed me and stood me in front of the monitor, and he put his hands on my chest and . . . I got free and ran out into the hall. Nobody was there. I saw the women's bathroom and went inside. I thought I would be safe there. But the principal came right in behind me. And he locked the door.

Yŏndu's hands moved slowly, the movements transformed into vowels and consonants by the interpreter, and when Sŏ heard them embodied as speech, she put her hand to her mouth in shock. If not for Yŏndu's mother—who was doing everything in her power, power marshaled from a life of ill fortune, to maintain her composure—she would have screamed. As it was, her stifled outcries reverberated inside her, slowly to coalesce as tears.

And then he pushed me up against the wall and pulled my pants down . . .

By now the voice of the young interpreter was trembling, and he would break off in mid-word to sign a question to Yŏndu. Yŏndu's mother sat statue-still, aware that Yŏndu in the course of her testimony would suddenly search her mother's expression, gauging the effect of her words. Her mother's occasional nervous gulp was the only indication that she was focusing on her daughter. Yŏndu, as she observed her mother, seemed to be telling her with her eyes how sorry she was, her testimony so overwhelming that her mother couldn't even shed tears in response. A young woman staffer moaned, then turned toward the window and began silently to weep.

"If there's a part that's too difficult you can skip over it," the director said in a measured tone.

Yŏndu looked to her mother with fearful eyes. Her mother extended a trembling hand and caressed Yŏndu's head. For the first time Yŏndu was about to break down.

Child, do you want to stop there? signed her mother.

Nodding, Yŏndu nestled herself in her mother's bosom. The silence resumed, the VCR recording it. And finally her mother, still stroking Yŏndu's head, broke into tears. She said nothing, merely smoothed her daughter's hair. And then Yŏndu ceased weeping, grew thoughtful, and began signing violently:

And suddenly the principal put his hand over my mouth and dragged me into one of the toilet compartments. And we stayed like that for a while, with his hand over my mouth, and . . .

Kang clamped his lips together and felt beads of cold sweat in his armpits.

. . . when I tried to pull up my pants he slapped me. He took my pants off and stood me against the toilet. And then he made me bend over . . . and he . . . my behind—

Her mother grabbed hold of Yŏndu's signing hand. The interpreter's lips stopped moving. Kang's head sunk to his chest.

"Isn't this enough, ma'am?"

No one answered Yŏndu's mother. The silence was broken by Yuri, who had been looking on the whole time. With a weird outcry she rushed to Yŏndu and began a frenzy of signing. Instinctively, Yŏndu recoiled but kept watch as Yuri signed. The interpreter did his best to keep up with the two of them, but he seemed to be missing parts of the conversation—colloquialisms, slang, or idioms used by deaf-mute girls. Yuri's signing was punctuated by her weird outcries; she was agitated in the extreme. Yŏndu's expression was one of astonishment.

"What's happening?" asked Sŏ. "What's the matter with Yuri?"

Kang rose, approached Yuri from the rear, and took her in his arms. This brought a fierce screech from the girl, who tried to jerk away and, in doing so, lurched against the table, sending the pot of begonias crashing to the floor. The red petals lay strewn about its stark surface, their blackish roots exposed.

↩

Kang flashed back to his first encounter with Yuri. The girl had appeared out of the fog, munching on a cookie. The screech she had produced upon seeing him—it was identical to her scream just now. A scream of naked terror . . . but this same girl had warmed up to him, if only momentarily, leading him down the hall, clutching her teddy bear, toward the laundry room where Yŏndu was enduring vigilante justice. These images were followed the next instant by the memory of Yuri gliding swiftly along the hallway, moving so lightly she was practically floating above the floor. Yuri the angel, Kang had thought. He now took hold of her hands, noticing that the girl was screeching so fiercely the whites of her eyes were showing. She thrashed about like a raptor enmeshed in a net. Before he knew it, he had stilled her hands and was looking into her eyes and talking.

"Yuri, don't be scared. It's me, your teacher. I want to help you. It's all right, Yuri. No one here is going to hurt you. Now look at me. And follow me while I breathe—one . . . two . . . three. That's it—good! Good job, Yuri!"

It didn't matter to Kang if Yuri couldn't hear him. This was how he calmed Saemi when the girl's temper got the better of her and she started throwing her toys around. It had amazed him that it was possible to communicate in this way with a toddler who could not necessarily understand what he was saying, and he had realized then, if only imperfectly, that words were not the sole means of communication. And so it was that his tenacious gaze held that of Yuri, a girl who functioned only at the level of a six-year-old and whose actual age showed only in her physical development. The next thing he knew, the girl was breathing normally, and her eyes were calm. In those eyes he caught a fleeting glimpse of her soul— like a larva, its development arrested, inside a frozen cocoon. The next instant he seemed to hear a crack, as if that cocoon were beginning to open.

"Yuri, don't be afraid. We're all here to help you from now on, to . . . keep you safe."

In saying "keep you safe," Kang realized he had crossed a bridge. There she was, nestled limp against his chest, her outburst of signing having drained her. She felt much lighter than the fifteen-year-old girl she was. She felt as fragile as a butterfly just emerged from its cocoon, and, true to one of the meanings of the word for her name, *yuri,* fragile like glass.

Just then Yŏndu tapped the shoulder of the interpreter and signed to him: *Yuri has something to say—she wants to tell us everything.*

Yuri then signed to Yŏndu. The interpreter spoke.

"Yuri wants some cola—a cold bottle of cola. And a Choco Pie."

The male staffer, who until then had worn a blank expression, came to life: "Yuri, *oppa* will get them for you—a whole bunch. I'll be right back." And with that he rushed off to a nearby supermarket.

Silence filled the conference room. Yuri rested her head against Kang's shoulder, just like his five-year-old daughter would do.

Yŏndu, lost in thought, seemed to come to a decision and looked up at the others. She began signing: *The week before last, something happened to Yuri too—something with the principal. That's what Yuri wants to talk about. We saw it too.*

The interpreter, as he put this into spoken language, wore an uncomprehending expression. He began making grammatical mistakes.

"Something with the principal?" the director broke in. "And you saw it? You said 'we'—who is 'we'"?

Yŏndu bit down on her lip, then with a pout approached her mother. Rather than probe further at this point, the director and Sŏ decided a short break was in order. Presently, the staffer returned with a bag of sodas and Choco Pies. Yŏndu and Yuri beamed in delight. All drank, while Yuri alone munched on the small cakes.

"If we wait too much longer I'm afraid the girls will be too drained to continue. Should we resume?" said Sǒ, turning on the VCR again.

Kang gently removed the sweets from Yuri, who had eaten her fill and was now sucking the residue from her fingers. "After you've told us everything you can have the rest. But now you have to answer truthfully what you are asked."

When this was interpreted, Yuri took one last drink of soda and nodded.

Like Yǒndu, Yuri was first asked several basic questions for the record, starting with her name. And then the director got to the heart of the matter.

"Can you tell us what happened to you the week before last?"

Calmly, Yuri nodded like a good little girl who is quick to forget her tearful outbursts.

⌒

Yǒndu and I were going out to buy cup ramen. We get dinner around six o'clock but most of the kids don't eat it—actually they can't eat it, it's so bad. So instead we always go to that little store across from the school and buy pastries or ramen, and that's what we have for dinner. It was about eight o'clock and I was hungry. So Yǒndu and I were going to that store, but then I got a tummy ache, so I asked Yǒndu to get something for me while I waited at the door. And while I was waiting, the principal came out—I guess he was going home—and he saw me and he smiled and he took my hand. I didn't want to go with him, but he said he would give me cookies. He took me into the principal's office and gave me some cookies and while I was still eating them, he laid me down on the table in front of the couch and pulled my sweat pants down to my knees. And then he dropped his pants and his underpants down to his knees.

A short outcry escaped one of the staffers. Yuri of course didn't hear it, but Sǒ shot the woman a stern warning glance anyway. Perspiration streamed down the interpreter's forehead. Yuri was the only one present who was calm and collected. The heat rising inside the others was soon visible as sticky sweat seeping from their brows.

And then he took his pepper and . . . put it in me.

By now Sŏ's face was waxen and stiff, like paperboard.

And then the door opened and Yŏndu was there. The principal was moving his bottom back and forth and when he saw Yŏndu, he motioned with his hand for her to come in. But she ran away, and then the principal tore off a piece of tissue and wiped his pepper and pulled his pants back up. And then he shook his fist toward the window—maybe someone was outside—and pulled the curtain down over it. And then he went out into the hall and came back with Yŏndu.

Now it was Sŏ who cried out, the sound bursting through her clenched teeth. And with her outcry came a chorus of gasps. The interpreter rose and left the room, looking as if he had reached the limits of his endurance. Kang stepped out into the hallway for a cigarette, heard the sound of water from the men's room, and guessed that the interpreter was splashing cold water on his face. Puffing on his cigarette, Kang looked out onto the dark streets of Mujin and watched as a dog in a back alley pawed through a trash can before scampering off.

↬

The director's face was drained of color, but strengthened by years of experience, she managed a calm expression as she prepared to continue with the statements from the two girls.

"If you're ready to resume, sir," she said to the interpreter, "I would like to question Yŏndu to get her account of the incidents."

The interpreter, more composed now, nodded.

"All right, then—is it true what Yuri said just now?"

Yes, it's true, all of it.

"Then, could you give us your recollection of what happened that day?"

Yŏndu pondered, then regarded the interpreter with her clear, shining eyes and began to sign.

When I came back with the cup ramen, Yuri wasn't there. I thought maybe she had gone back to the dorm, so I went inside, then noticed light in the dark hallway. I went toward it, and it was coming from the principal's office. I could just barely hear some music from inside, and I thought someone was there. So I opened the door, and that's when . . .

Yŏndu hung her head. Her ears were flushed. When she looked up again, tears had pooled in her eyes.

"You don't have to say it if you don't want to," said the director.

Yŏndu nodded and gathered herself.

All right. It happened just like Yuri said. I was shocked—and scared—and I ran out. At the entrance I saw two of the boys from our class running toward me. They said they saw the principal with his pants down and his pepper hanging there and Yuri was lying on the table. They said if the teachers found out we had seen it, they would do terrible things to us and so I should hurry back to my room. The boys ran off, but I just stayed there. I was afraid and I wanted to run away too, but I couldn't—I was worried about Yuri. And then the principal grabbed me by the back of the neck and took me into his office. He sat me down and he told me in sign language that if I said anything, he'd make me pay for it. I was scared and so I told him I wouldn't say anything. And then Yuri and I went back to the dormitory and went to bed.

"The principal used sign language?" broke in Kang, who had been listening intently. "Didn't you say he doesn't know sign language?"

The interpreter signed Kang's question. Yŏndu looked doubtful, then replied.

That's right. Well, that day with Yuri, that was the first time I ever saw the principal up close. And he did use sign language.

But now that I think about it, last week when he took me into the bathroom—I think he said the same thing to me in sign language when he let me go.

"And did he say anything else in sign language?" asked Kang.

Yŏndu cocked her head thoughtfully before answering.

As far as I can remember, I don't think he said anything else in sign language. Just that if I told anyone, he would make me pay for it.

"But why didn't you go straight to the teachers and tell them?"

We've been telling them since we were third graders, broke in Yuri.

"What!" shouted Sŏ. She had forgotten for the moment that the questions implied in her exclamation—*Why didn't you say something? Why did you go along with it? Why didn't you resist?*—should never be asked of the victims of violence. Still, she simply couldn't believe it had gone on that long—since the third grade? Really? And thus her misdirected shouting to Yuri. Not only her raised voice but her flushed face testified that for Sŏ just then, emotion had eclipsed rationality. The staffer who had been cautioned by Sŏ now considered her with a look of surprise.

"Since you were third graders?" Sŏ followed up.

The two girls hung their heads and didn't reply.

"Ma'am," Sŏ said to the director, "how is it possible for such things to happen?"

The director adjusted her gold-rimmed glasses. A pained expression flashed across her face before she replied.

"I'm sorry you have to hear this. You wouldn't believe some of the cases I've dealt with. And with disabled women, there's really very little protection for them. . . . They get walked all over. I'm sorry—but we do need your help in continuing with these proceedings."

Sŏ had to remain tight-lipped as the director continued with her questions.

"Can you tell us what you remember about what happened when you were a third grader?"

Yuri searched her memory, then calmly began to sign.

It was right after winter vacation, after third grade, and I told our new homeroom teacher about it.

"And what did the homeroom teacher say?"

He told me he asked Teacher Pak Pohyŏn about it, and Teacher Pak said, "How could that be possible—it's ridiculous." And he told me not to go around saying things like that because it would hurt the teachers.

"And what was it that happened?"

I was living in the dormitory. During school vacation the children went home, but not me, unless my grandmother came for me. One day the kids no one came to get were playing in the dormitory, and Teacher Pak Pohyŏn came in. He was our guidance counselor. We were happy because we thought he wanted to play with us. During vacation the counselors would come once a day to see us. But it was night when Teacher Pak came. He gave me a hug. He smelled a little like alcohol, but I felt good— because I thought he liked me. And then, with all the boys there, he pulled down my pants and put his mouth on my privates, and then he pulled up my sweatshirt and sucked on my titties. I was so ashamed I wanted to die.

Again the director turned pale. Her voice trembled as she asked her next question.

"And . . . did anything else happen?"

And then one day when all the boys had gone home, I was in the dorm by myself. I missed my mom and I missed my dad, and I thought I was all by myself in that great big dorm, and I was so scared, and I wrapped myself up in my quilt and I was crying. And then someone came in my room and lay down beside me. It was Teacher Pak. He told me not to cry and said if I did what he told me he would buy me some cookies tomorrow. I said all right, and then Teacher took all my clothes off and then he took all his clothes off and then he tried to put his pepper in me.

By now tears were streaming down Sŏ's cheeks. With a faraway look Yŏndu's mother kept dabbing at her eyes with her handkerchief.

It really hurt, and I started crying. Teacher got really mad and told me he couldn't do it, and it was my fault because I was crying. I was scared and I begged him, I told him I was sorry. And then he told me to hold his thing and rub it. So I did. And then his eyes rolled up inside his head and some yucky white stuff came out of him, and he wiped it up with a tissue. The next day Teacher really did bring me some cookies. All day long the only person I saw was the auntie who worked in the cafeteria, and I didn't have anything to do, so I was happy when Teacher came, and I forgot all about how he hurt me. Teacher told me to get in bed even though it wasn't at night, and he said that if I listened to him he would bring me cookies every day, but if I didn't listen to him he would go away right then and never come back. There was a rumor that an older kid in our dorm had killed herself and turned into a ghost and the ghost sometimes came up from the ocean to the dorm, and I was so scared I begged Teacher not to go away, and I promised him I would do anything. And then Teacher took a tube of something clear, like an ointment, and smeared it on my privates, and then . . .

Kang shot to his feet and then sat himself back down. It wasn't an iceberg they were confronting as much as a tidal wave that would sweep away everything between heaven and earth. Yuri, hearing-impaired and intellectually disabled as well—ten years old at the time. Ten years old. *What the hell!?* At such times Kang reached for a cigarette by reflex—but not now. He felt utterly helpless. He thought of Pak Pohyŏn with the beady rat eyes—the one who had gotten Song Hasŏp fired. How could he do that to a poor little girl who couldn't go home during school vacation? And what about the principal? What about the school? What about the world? Could this really be the twenty-first century? Could this really be Korea? And he himself, Kang Inho—who exactly was he? He couldn't believe in anything anymore. But still he listened.

"And how much longer did this happen to you?"

Yuri thought for a time before answering.

A lot.

The director rephrased her question: "How many times?"

A lot. Can I have some more cola? I'm sleepy.

The staffer who had bought the soda and the Choco Pies obliged. While Yuri was devouring the cakes, Yŏndu began gingerly to sign.

The administrator and Teacher Pak and the principal took turns with Yuri. The administrator gave Yuri a thousand won every time he did it.

The adults, too disturbed to regard the girls further, could only listen listlessly to the interpreter.

↬

The drawn faces of those gathered in the Human Rights Advocacy Center conference room flickered beneath the old fluorescent lights. A ghostly gloom had enveloped the center, the Home of Benevolence, all of Mujin.

Yuri kept her eyes on Yŏndu's signing, all the while munching on her Choco Pies.

The image of the fog-shrouded school as he had first seen it flashed through Kang's mind—Yuri coming his way munching on cookies, the blue luxury car leaving . . . Kang's first encounter with cruelty worse than a massacre. He became aware of Yuri busy with her Choco Pies, then noticed the director's ashen face.

"A thousand won?" asked the director. "And what was that for?"

As he signed the questions, the interpreter wore a stricken look, as if he himself had been victimized. Yuri for her part was showing signs of fatigue.

When he took me into his office, he gave me a thousand won and then took off my pants. That's the money I used for cup ramen and pastries for dinner. If I told him I didn't want to do it, sometimes he gave me another thousand.

By now the questions were coming more slowly. Yuri, her concentration flagging, pawed with her feet at the petals of the begonias that had fallen to the floor.

"When was the first time the administrator took you into his office?"

I don't exactly remember. I think it was a little after Teacher Pak in the dorm. So it must have been the start of fourth year. It hurt so much with Teacher Pak that I started crying—I told the administrator I didn't want to, and I tried to run away. But he laid me down on the table and took my arms and legs and—

The interpreter's face clenched and he broke off. Yuri munched nonchalantly on a Choco Pie. With everyone waiting for the interpreter to continue, he looked to the staffer who had been his classmate. He was on the verge of tears, his expression a combination of outrage and astonishment that told his friend he could not possibly continue. His lips trembled.

"What is it?" asked the classmate. "What did she say next?"

The interpreter hung his head.

Kang, who had been watching Yuri all along, shifted his gaze to the others. "He tied her," he said in a low voice. "Tied her arms and legs to the table."

⌒

The interpreter nodded, confirming Kang's words. Another cry escaped the staffer who had cried out earlier, but this time Sŏ didn't respond with a disapproving look. The interpreter, gritting his teeth and trembling, had still not looked up. His expression had changed to shame, as if he himself had been the one victimizing Yuri. Or perhaps being a male, an adult, or a virginal man prevented him from holding his head high or even speaking in the presence of this disabled girl. He shook his head no—perhaps he found it horrifying that he inhabited the same world, breathed the same air as those who had abused this small, birdlike girl who looked light enough to lift with one hand.

Oblivious to the young man's predicament, Yuri began signing again. Instead of the played-out young man it was Yŏndu's mother who interpreted, her face moist with tears.

He told me that if I didn't listen to him, he would tie me up again, he would kick me out, and he wouldn't give me money to go home. I hate all of them—the principal, the administrator, Teacher Pak. I hope they get punished.

And then Yuri yawned.

⤶

Kang was reminded of the impassive eyes of Palestinian and African children he had seen in photos. Overwhelmingly painful circumstances had left no feeling in those eyes. He couldn't help thinking of his daughter, Saemi. If she had been born a boy, would he be feeling any less heartache now?

His musings were broken by the voice of the director: "Now that we've finished recording for the day, we need to remove Yuri to a shelter. We can't return her to where she's being abused. The same goes for Yŏndu." She then spoke to Yŏndu's mother: "Considering Yŏndu's father's situation, you'll allow us to place Yŏndu at the shelter as well? We'll be contacting Yuri's guardian tomorrow. And filing a report with the police about Yuri's abuse."

"Ma'am," said Yŏndu's mother, "even though this is a difficult time for our family, I would like to take Yŏndu home with me. I want to think everything over again and maybe withdraw her from the school. And . . . I'm sorry for asking this, but would it be possible for me to take Yuri home with me too, just for tonight, seeing as how she's Yŏndu's friend?"

Just as Sŏ was about to ask a question, the dam holding back Yŏndu's mother's feelings gave way and she began weeping again.

"I know Yuri's mother is poor and weak and ignorant, but it must break her heart to know that Yuri is deaf, and if she knew what has happened to her here. . . . Oh how Yuri must have cried for her mother! How she must have cried, left all alone in that dark dormitory in that big old place. You wouldn't mistreat a birdie that's fallen out of its nest—how could those people do those things to a little girl? Those heartless bastards. Even though I'm not Yuri's mother, if for just one day I could take her in my arms and put her to sleep, if I could just make a nice warm meal for her. . . . Because that's about all I'm good for. And please make sure those people are punished so that this never happens again. We're ignorant people, we have no power. Please, I beg of you, make sure they're punished so it never happens again."

So saying, Yŏndu's mother dried her tears.

"All right," said Sŏ, who had been listening tight-lipped. "Tomorrow morning the director will come for Yuri. You'll have to be ready. Since the police haven't moved forward with an investigation, we'll release this video nationwide—to all the broadcasting stations, the Human Rights Commission in Seoul, the Mujin Bureau of Education, and City Hall. Every place we can notify, we will. We'll be preparing a news release, and we'll accept requests for interviews, so we'll need your testimony. We need your help—we need the help of all who are present here today."

Sŏ's gaze passed among all the others before coming to rest on the interpreter. The young man regarded his classmate, looking like he was in a fix.

"To be honest, I didn't come here out of a sense of duty, but now I feel really shaken. I never thought I'd regret learning sign language . . . but in any case I will help too."

Yuri was off in the corner, half asleep. Kang went to her and swung her up onto his back. Yes, she was light as a bird. What manner of humanity would tie down this feather-light girl, strip her naked, beat her, penetrate that softest of flesh, assault her?

Down to the streets of Mujin went Kang, Yuri on his back. A faint mist was descending.

〜

By the wee hours of the following morning, the mist had
thickened to a dense, milky fog that bottled the city of Mujin.
The only access to the Home of Benevolence in its remote
seaside location was the road, and to get there Kang had to
drive. And so it was that later in the morning Kang had felt
his way along the road, visibility nonexistent, and had inched
up to the school grounds when he saw a shape rising from the
fluid white fog. He braked at the entrance, which was narrow
enough for a single person standing there to block traffic, then
resumed crawling forward until the shape revealed itself as a
man neatly clad in a dark suit. The man was displaying a sign
with large lettering. By instinct Kang gave a short beep on his
horn, but then he recognized the man: the guidance counselor
who had been dragged from the school several days earlier.
Song Hasŏp, was it? Kang pulled up short.

On the sign was written FIRED WITHOUT JUST CAUSE.
The message struck Kang as having come straight from the
man's heart. Against the misty backdrop it looked like a
subtitle in a movie and the man, a figure in a video game. He
looked so vulnerable standing there, as if on that white screen
a window might open with the question "Exit game?" and
he'd vanish with the click of a mouse. But the tight line of his
mouth seemed to say, "I know what I'm doing, and I won't back
down even if it kills me." At intervals his lips would relax as if
he were gasping for breath, and fear would cross his face like
wind sweeping across a barren field in autumn.

Close up Kang saw that the dark suit was the same one the
man had worn the previous time. He briefly imagined the man
fussing over his tie, taking pains not to wrinkle the suit as he
put it on, then making his way here through the fog. Tears
welled up in Kang's eyes, and just as he was lowering his gaze
to the dashboard display, a horn blared behind him. He turned
to see the headlights of a blue car. The horn continued to honk,

asking Kang what he was doing, stopped in the fog like that. It had to be either the principal or his twin brother; Kang wasn't sure which. The headlights were on bright, and when they didn't elicit a response from Kang, the horn grew more strident. And then from out of the background haze popped the custodian, dressed in black. He grabbed hold of Song while the din from the blue car reached full blast, then yanked him off while scowling at Kang. Nothing for Kang to do but pull forward and park. He thought he could hear Song shouting—a deaf man who could speak.

"I was fired without cause—I didn't do anything to deserve this!"

Never had Kang imagined—not when he had taken Yuri to the Human Rights Advocacy Center the previous day nor when he had returned home afterward—that this morning he would be feeling as he did now. The antique edifice of the Home of Benevolence appearing faintly through the fog, which had settled over it and the surroundings like a monstrous creature, gazed down at him. And then he heard the cursing.

"You fucking idiot—here we are first thing in the morning and you're wasting my time gawking at that deaf piece of shit!"

The outburst disoriented Kang, and for an instant he forgot where he was and had the sensation that he'd popped up on the computer screen from which Song had just been ejected. The next moment he turned back to see the hostile gaze of the administrator, whose head had appeared from the driver's-side window of his car.

"You again! I don't need another pain in the ass! What are you looking at? Fuck off!"

All Kang could do was blink. His first thought was that the administrator had mistaken him for a deaf teacher. And then he realized he was gasping for breath. His thoughts were jumbled with a nightmarish image: he was rushing down a flight of steps to catch a subway and came instead upon a herd of hyenas, but he felt no fear, no anger, no sensation at all. And then the image became clearer—here in concrete form were the lurid details of the girls' statements. Biting down on his lip, he emerged from his car and approached the administrator. He managed to compose himself before he spoke.

"How can you curse like that, sir? You saw there was someone in front of me. Even if I asked him to get out of the way, he couldn't have heard me."

"*You* get out of *my* way! You want to end up like that deaf asshole? Get out of my sight, dammit!"

The administrator got out of his car and walked past Kang, almost bumping into him.

Gave me a thousand won . . . laid me down on the table and took my arms and legs and . . . if I didn't listen to him . . . wouldn't give me money to go home.

Kang recalled Yuri's blank face. No—not exactly blank. He hadn't realized it until now, but the slack jaw and the dark eyes in that face concealed a kind of heat. It was like a wisp of steam from a dormant volcano, still faint but clearly present. And now, this morning, in the faint tingle in his nose, Kang felt that heat.

As soon as Kang entered the school building he recoiled, hit by an imaginary stench in the hallway, the stink of carnage. He swallowed heavily and tasted something sour and bitter and nauseating. Back outside he went for a cigarette. He thought about how he couldn't bring himself to hug Yuri after her statement the previous day. He regretted that. In his astonishment at what he had heard, he hadn't immediately thought of the children. And so he was thankful that Yŏndu's mother had taken the girls home for the night. Only now did he realize what it meant to be a parent.

Looking in from outside the entrance to the school grounds was Song Hasŏp. His sign was crumpled, and the dampness of the fog had made the ink run so the words were no longer legible. Aware of the custodian's gaze, Kang coughed a couple of times in Song's direction as if to say *I see you.* And then he approached the fired teacher. Song's face was ridden with fear. Kang produced Sŏ's business card and offered it to him. Song took it, looking back and forth between Kang and the card. Kang signed to him: *She can help you. Please go see her.*

The two men made eye contact. Song shook his head almost imperceptibly and took several steps back. Kang realized the man no longer trusted anyone at the school. He watched as the retreating man's outline grew blurry, as if Song were being sucked into the fog's huge maw.

Kang went back inside, and as he had expected, the head teacher summoned him, wanting to know why the girl Kang had left with the previous day, Chin Yuri, had spent the night away from the school.

"Her grandmother came to visit her—she's the girl's guardian. Oh, didn't I tell you? She said she'd take the girl home for a little while, and I was the one who delivered Yuri to her."

This was what Kang and Sŏ had agreed upon as an explanation.

Dubious, the head teacher cocked his head. "Well, then, you should have obtained a consent form first," and with that he ended the conversation.

That day, one and perhaps two things would happen with respect to Yuri: a Human Rights Advocacy Center staffer would attempt to bring Yuri's grandmother to Mujin, and if that didn't work out, the staff would fill out a form on their own enabling Yuri to transfer to another school. Yuri's case was different from Yŏndu's, but because it was obvious the police were not actively investigating what had happened to Yuri, this seemed the only expedient.

Just then Kang's phone buzzed—a text message from his wife: *when are you coming to seoul? payday? buy something for me and Saemi?^^ we're having fun cooking up something for when daddy comes home*

〜

"And where did you obtain this information?"

The question was posed to Sŏ by Ch'oe Suhŭi, chief inspector of the Mujin Bureau of Education. Ch'oe was a lean woman with a long neck who projected tenacity. After asking her question, she removed the bag of green tea from her cup, plucked a tissue and dabbed at a drop or two of liquid on the coffee table between them, then primly folded the tissue and deposited it in her wastebasket. And then, still not looking at Sŏ, she flicked her fingers against the hem of her tight-fitting skirt to smooth any wrinkles in the garment. These acts were designed to buy time. Ever since she, a woman, had risen to this position from a humble beginning at a countryside elementary school when she was fresh out of teachers' college, she had prided herself on her unbiased comportment, her uprightness and prudence. But here was this dwarfish woman with cropped hair presenting her with a request that threatened to turn her life upside down. Why, the very next month her daughter would be formally engaged, and the brothers Yi would be distinguished guests at the reception. She thought of all she had contributed to the Yi family whenever one of their children had married. She needed to keep calm. And with this thought, she recited to herself the litany she reserved for that purpose: *Ask, and it shall be given you; seek, and ye shall find; knock, and it shall be opened unto you.*

She straightened her back and then her legs, girding for whatever was in the envelope Sŏ had placed on the coffee table.

"Inside is a DVD of the children's statements and a transcript of the interpretation," Sŏ explained. "We are formally requesting that the director of the Home of Benevolence be dismissed, that the school's governing board be reconstituted with members appointed by the authorities, and that the perpetrators be brought to justice."

The request from the Human Rights Advocacy Center for a meeting had arrived three days earlier. Ch'oe had managed to put it off a day at a time before finally relenting. But the atmosphere thus far was not promising.

Sŏ for her part held out no great expectations but made a point of composing herself before continuing.

"What we originally reported to the police was a sexual assault by the principal on a second-year middle school student at the Home of Benevolence. It has since come to our attention that not only the principal but also his brother the administrator, as well as a guidance counselor, have been involved in repeated sexual assaults of a different student in addition, a girl with multiple disabilities. We believe that in the course of the investigation other victims will come forward. The incidents I mentioned have been reported to the police. It is so overwhelming you will find it difficult to believe, but if you will be kind enough to review the DVD and listen to the girls' statements, you will realize they are not lying."

The expression "sexual assault" brought a scowl to Ch'oe's face. But it was a confident scowl—perhaps she was indulging herself in the belief that it was somehow charming? For a woman in her early fifties, her face remained pretty and her body slender, and she relished in these attributes. She took a sip of tea in an effort to keep a lid on the conflicted feelings rising inside her. Both her husband and Principal Yi Kangsŏk were elders in the Mujin First Church of God's Glory, and once a month they met with other members of the We Love Mujin Society. What would her husband say if she reported these allegations to him in bed that evening? She herself wondered how they could possibly be true. Yi Kangsŏk was such a fine man. She recalled him on the golf course—his good-hearted smile, his quiet demeanor. As beautiful and willowy as she was, not once could she recall the principal ever leering at her. Something about this matter smelled of entrapment, her instincts told her, and Ch'oe Suhŭi, chief inspector of the

Mujin Bureau of Education, trusted absolutely in her woman's intuition.

"Just a minute—forgive me for interrupting but . . . this assault, did it occur during class? I mean, did it take place during class hours?"

Sŏ mulled over the question, trying to fathom Ch'oe's intent.

"Well, if you look at the DVD you will understand. Strictly speaking, it was after classes were over for the day— the children had eaten dinner and were coming back to the school—"

"Oh, so it was after school," Ch'oe interrupted; she had anticipated this. "In that case, we don't have jurisdiction."

Ch'oe grinned, and seeing Sŏ's head jerk up in bewilderment, she rose and pressed a button on her intercom. A man appeared in response.

"Section Chief Kim, do we have jurisdiction over the dormitory at the Home of Benevolence?"

"No, ma'am—that's under City Hall jurisdiction."

Ch'oe fixed Sŏ with a look that said, _So there. You people are a pain in the butt. Just thinking about this makes me sick to my stomach. Now leave._

Sŏ was momentarily speechless. Then, taking a deep breath, she continued. "Am I to understand that when the principal, the administrator, and a guidance counselor commit acts of sexual assault, sexual abuse, on school grounds, it is not the jurisdiction of the Bureau of Education? Then who in heaven's name does have jurisdiction?"

"What we mean," said Section Chief Kim, who after reading his superior's face had adopted a sure-footed tone, "is that our jurisdiction covers the _school_ at the Home of Benevolence. The _dormitory_ at the Home of Benevolence falls under the jurisdiction of the Department of Social Welfare at City Hall." He spoke as if he had hit upon a truth of incomparable brilliance.

"But Yi Kangsŏk is also the director of the dormitory, is he not? Yi Kangbok is his brother. And the children in question are students at that institution. Those students have been sexually assaulted by the principal, the administrator, and a guidance counselor, and the assaults took place in the school. How can you say that the Bureau of Education has no jurisdiction?"

Sŏ realized her voice had risen a notch and that Ch'oe was back at her desk leafing through some papers, and Kim had taken a seat as well.

"Well, I guess there's some logic to what you say, if you look at it like that." Section Chief Kim prefaced this remark with the chuckle of a good-hearted man indulging an ignorant, pestering auntie. "Administratively speaking, that is." Another chuckle. "Would you kindly take this matter to City Hall?" Kim chuckled one last time before rising to signal the end of the meeting.

Sŏ briefly regarded them both, then turned her gaze to the envelope containing the DVD and the photocopies of the interpretation of the girls' statements, which lay untouched on the coffee table. Then, head drooping and hands clasped together, she spoke in a soft tone.

"All right, ma'am, I understand. I will go to City Hall. But this matter concerns a crime—a crime involving the principal, the administrator, and a guidance counselor. The unfortunate victims of this crime are children who have no real power. Scars have been inflicted on these children by the very teachers whose duty it is to be teaching them; they will bear those scars for the rest of their lives. Doesn't it seem only natural that if there are allegations involving responsible parties at a school, the least the Bureau of Education could do is investigate?"

While Sŏ awaited their reaction, Kim attempted to read Ch'oe's face.

Ch'oe was scribbling on one of the papers she had been sifting through. She nodded as if to say *That much we can do, if that's what you want.* Finally, she spoke. "Yes, indeed. That has always been what we do. What we *must* do. Section Chief!" she barked. "Go to the Home of Benevolence and see what you can find out."

"Yes, ma'am."

With the order given and the factotum complying, Sŏ had no reason to stay longer. She opened the door and was about to leave when her eyes came to rest on a plaque on the wall. *Ch'oe Suhŭi, notable alumna of Mujin Girls' High School.* Sŏ looked back toward the chief inspector of the Mujin Bureau of Education. The woman's eyes remained fixed on her desk, but Sŏ read in her posture not disregard for her visitor but rather a heightened awareness of her presence.

Outside the building, Sŏ heard the faint sound of something dropping to the ground—the first fallen leaf of autumn.

5

The head of the Mujin Department of Social Welfare, a man named Chang, stared off into space as he slurped coffee from a paper cup. He was a middle-aged man of medium height and slim build, but the first thing Sŏ had noticed about him was his fine, wavy hair. As he listened to Sŏ, he scratched his head pensively, and by the time she finished explaining the purpose of her visit, he looked completely out of sorts.

"This is a school matter, and you should be seeing the Bureau of Education about it. We deal here with children's social welfare."

Sŏ wondered briefly if she should have come here first rather than to the Bureau of Education and decided if so, she would feel less angry. She moved very close to Chang and managed to keep her voice down to avoid giving the impression that she was about to fly into a rage.

"I *have* been to the Bureau of Education, and they told me that if the incidents took place after school or in the dormitory, I should go to the Department of Social Welfare. That's why I'm here."

Chang cocked his head dubiously and took another slurp of coffee. He still hadn't made eye contact with Sŏ.

How in God's name could a man in his position not even look at the person he's talking with? Sŏ asked herself. It was a nasty habit. She managed to remain respectful nevertheless.

"So this happened to the kids when they were in the dormitory?" For the first time Chang glanced at Sŏ out of the corner of his eye.

"That's why I brought this DVD and these transcripts. If you just look at them you'll understand—the children had finished school and . . ." She paused briefly and sighed. This was the third time she had had to explain it to him. "School was over for the day, and they were back in the dormitory and fixing to head out—"

"Now look, ma'am, that's all well and good but nothing I need to know because I'm not the one who will investigate. So what I'm asking is, did this business with the children happen in the dormitory?"

"It took place in the school—in a bathroom on the first floor, in the principal's office, in the administrator's office . . ."

Sŏ ended with a shudder as she recalled Yuri's statement.

Chang took another sip of coffee, the noisiest one yet, before answering. "Then you should be going to the Bureau of Education. Here we're responsible for the children's living conditions, budgeting, and such. So go see the Bureau of Education." So saying, he drank more coffee before swiveling around in his chair and turning his back on Sŏ.

If only I could take a whip to that back, thought Sŏ. *Maybe the use of force isn't always such a bad thing.*

"I told you, the Bureau of Education people say that since it happened after school, it isn't under their jurisdiction. Besides, at least one child *was* sexually assaulted in the dormitory. With all due respect, how can you say that *that* is not under your jurisdiction?"

In an audible show of displeasure, the middle-aged man at the desk next to Chang's rose deliberately to his slipper-clad feet and scuffed his way over to the window. His behavior made Sŏ feel like a door-to-door peddler.

"Please consider this, sir," she said. "The Home of Benevolence—the school and the dormitory—receives four billion won per year from the government. All of that money comes from our taxes. And so it's only right, is it not, that the good people here see to it that disabled children are taken care of and nurtured? I am telling you that a child was sexually assaulted in the dormitory—and by a counselor, the very person who should be guiding her!"

By now Sŏ was practically shouting. Chang frowned as if his ears hurt.

"And I'm saying that anything involving abuse by a teacher is under the jurisdiction of the Bureau of Education. Are you asking the Department of Social Welfare to watch over teachers? And as far as good use of the budget is concerned, that's for the City Council to judge, so maybe you should see them as well."

As the middle-aged man returned to his desk, he added, just loud enough for Sŏ to hear, "Really, do we have to hear about sexual assaults first thing in the morning—and from a young lady? It's kind of, well . . ." And then he chuckled.

"You gentlemen must have children yourselves—how can you talk that way?" Sŏ asked in exasperation. "The bottom line is, don't you get paid to oversee places like the dormitory at the Home of Benevolence?"

"How many times do I need to tell you—go see the Bureau of Education. Just because you come here first thing in the morning and raise your voice doesn't mean it suddenly becomes our jurisdiction. . . . It's a sad situation, but there's simply nothing we can do."

And with that, Chang drained his cup of coffee, his slurping sounding like a roar in Sŏ's ears, and his colleague joined him in turning his back to Sŏ.

Sŏ left the Department of Social Welfare on shaky legs and tottered to the parking lot. Her phone sounded—one of the Human Rights Advocacy Center staffers. He was petitioning the City Council, and it appeared his efforts had been in vain as well. Sŏ sank listlessly into her car and just sat there. She closed her phone, buried her face in her hands, and rested her head against the steering wheel. The phone sounded again. This time it was Kang.

"Remember Song Hasŏp, the deaf teacher? It turns out he can speak. I think I mentioned him to you—the guidance counselor who was fired for helping Yŏndu file her report? He was at the school this morning, protesting, and I gave him your card. . . . Are you there?"

"Mmm."

"If he stops by, try to help him. I talked with the head teacher and took care of Yŏndu and Yuri's absence last night, but the school is going to raise hell—it's only a matter of time. Are you all right? You're not crying, are you?"

"Oh, Inho," she said, her voice barely audible. And then she lapsed into a brief silence that Kang could almost feel at his end. "I always knew our country wasn't perfect, but I never knew it could sink so low. It looks like we have a big fight ahead of us. The Bureau of Education, City Hall, they're mixed up together in this—and for all I know, probably the Mujin Girls' High School, Mujin High School, maybe even the grade school, extended family, the We Love Mujin Society, the First Church of God's Glory. . . . Inho, there's four billion won involved here—four billion! These people get four billion of our tax money every year and look what they do with it. I sent one of the staff to the City Council— they oversee the budget—and he came away with nothing. And guess what? Several members of the City Council have themselves been arrested for sexual assault. One guy was charged with assaulting an elevator girl—in the elevator. I don't know whether to laugh or cry. Here we are trying to

raise our daughters in a country where everyone's in heat—
what are we going to do?"

⌇

The fog had lifted except for a milky haze over the roadway.
Sŏ kept blinking, as if an extra eyelid was preventing her from
seeing clearly. Such was the fog of Mujin, like a hag's hair,
making the local people want to plead with the sun and the
wind to disperse it.

Sŏ had never felt lonely raising two daughters by herself.
Each day she prayed that her girls wouldn't come down sick
that night, each night she hoped she could pay her apartment
maintenance fee on time, and she was grateful if once a month
the family could eat at a pork-rib restaurant. When the day
came that she no longer dreaded the prospect of the girls
asking for a second helping of meat, on that day she would
feel rich. She had long since decided not to feel sorry for her
lonely self until the girls were grown, until her number two—
the one with the congenital heart defect—was finally healthy.
But as she drove along now with her window down, the
cold, moisture-laden wind stung her cheeks like a pinwheel
of thorns. She recalled what the director of the Rape Crisis
Center, sniffling as she spoke, had reported to her over the
phone the previous night.

"I took Yuri to a gynecologist who examined and treated
her. It turns out her hymen is ruptured, and her vulva shows
severe abrasions and lacerations. And she's developed an
infection that prevents her from sleeping at night. I wonder
how she could have endured the times she was assaulted if
she hadn't been mentally deficient. Maybe it was better that
way . . . wouldn't you agree?"

Sŏ realized she was tromping down on the gas pedal.
The bayside reeds looked like they had turned blue, their
circulation cut off in the clamped maw of the retreating fog. She couldn't remember the last time she had seen

the clear, rippling surface of the ocean beneath a crystalline blue sky.

Her older daughter, Pada, was just a baby when she and her husband had separated and she'd realized she was pregnant with Hanŭl. Her stomach had looked abnormally large because of her small frame, and her face had turned a sickly mottled yellow. She had been hypersensitive, had felt she was always gazing into the depths—not a day passed when she hadn't thought of doing away with herself. And then came the little tap inside her stomach as she had traversed through a mega-bookstore. She had wondered if she'd bumped into one of the bookshelves—no, that wasn't it. It had been too early for fetal movement, so she hadn't dwelt on the sensation and had continued to browse. But then she had felt another tap and realized her baby was kicking. She had stopped and rubbed her belly. Through this faint impact had Hanŭl made her existence known, like a sprouting seed penetrating the frozen earth and biting wind of an early-spring day. Off in a corner of the bookstore, Sŏ had shed a few tears. Not out of sorrow or despair. Rather, they had been tears of awe that anyone might experience when in the presence of the majestic and sublime she realizes how insignificant arrogant humanity actually is.

Unable to afford a maternity ward stay, she had given birth in her small apartment, unattended except for a midwife. More frightening than her misfortune had been the prospect that others might learn of it. She couldn't deny that this had been one of the main reasons she had moved down to Mujin with Pada and her newborn. And the baby had been so small, its lips so blue—it must have been her fault for not communicating with Hanŭl in the womb, she had decided the night of the birth as she had laid Pada and the infant down to sleep beside her.

"Maybe Mommy won't be able to dress you up like a princess, maybe she won't be able to buy you a lace bedspread, maybe we'll never go to an amusement park with Daddy and take photos of all of us. I'm sorry . . . I'm so sorry. But there's one thing I can promise you—when the two of you are grown, Pada and Hanŭl, I'll have made our country a better place, a place where women like you can walk tall. It will happen a little at a time, you might not even feel it, but Mommy will make this world a better place, a place where people can live the way people should. Mommy will do this if she has to run herself ragged in the process."

Another phone call—this time from the office. Moisture from the fog was still condensing on the windshield, and she turned on the wipers before slowly checking her phone. It was one of the male staffers.

"Finally—you're going to like this. We heard from Seoul, and it's going to be all over the news. The network producers want to come down now and I said okay. Can you make it here as soon as possible? We need to get the materials ready for them, and we're kind of short-handed. And there's something else—the National Human Rights Commission contacted us. They're launching an investigation and they want us to send them more information. . . ."

Sŏ made a U-turn back toward the center. She knew she was flouting the law by crossing the yellow line, but there was no time to waste.

⌒

From her office Sŏ called Kang at the Home of Benevolence. Kang had just gone out to the playfield for a cigarette to compose himself after hearing her tearful voice on the phone a short time earlier. The voice he heard now spoke rapidly and with a tone of urgency.

"The TV producers from Seoul are on their way down. We're finally getting the spotlight. I think we should use this opportunity to highlight not just the sexual assaults but also the physical abuse of the boys and the terrible living conditions for all the children. So I'm wondering if you could bring that boy in your class, the one you said was beaten. Can you get him a day pass?"

If in her earlier call she had sounded like wind and clouds, her voice now was bright like the sun. Then again, anything was preferable to the fog and the damp and the gloom of Mujin.

"As for the sexual assaults and the indecent behavior, we have the DVD. But we need to know more about the abuse of the boys before we can brief the producers. Anyway, the sooner the broadcast is aired, the sooner we can get these problems addressed, don't you think?"

"All right. But are you okay now?" Kang ventured. "You were crying earlier."

He heard a sheepish laugh. "Oh, that. Well, you know how it is. Sometimes grandiose intentions end with a whimper!"

Her answer brought a chuckle from Kang. He felt a spurt of protectiveness toward her, an impulse so unexpected it almost brought tears to his eyes. But perhaps he should do a better job of looking after his wife and daughter first? This thought staved off his mixed feelings about Sŏ, at least for the time being.

That afternoon Kang left the school with Minsu. The boy went along without a fuss after Kang promised him a meal of noodles with black-bean sauce. Kang noticed that the bruises on Minsu's face were fading. After the boy had finished his noodles, they continued on to the Human Rights Advocacy Center. Once inside Kang sensed an unusual energy: television cameras had been set up in the conference room, and people were scurrying about tending to them. When Minsu saw the throng, he retreated a step and went back outside, his face fearful. He signed to Kang that he wanted to go back to the school. If Song Hasŏp had not appeared just then—he had left for the center after being contacted by Sŏ—the boy might very well have disappeared. Minsu's face brightened the moment he saw Teacher Song. If not for Minsu, this encounter with a man Kang didn't really know might have been awkward. Song summoned the trembling boy and signed to him, at the same time speaking so that Kang could understand.

"Minsu, it's all right. These people are here to help us."

Minsu stared intently at Song, who nodded slowly and encouragingly to the boy before signing again.

I came here for you—I want you to tell them about the people who were bad to you. If you can talk about the bad things they did, then those things won't happen anymore.

Minsu turned his gaze to Kang, who nodded calmly in confirmation. Kang then fished out his handkerchief and wiped away the sauce smearing the boy's mouth. He was reminded of his first day at the Home of Benevolence, when he had produced this same handkerchief to dry the tears of this boy whose brother had been killed on the railroad tracks the day before. He was reminded of how violently Minsu had signed to him then, not knowing Kang couldn't understand. That same boy was now gentle as a baby as Kang cleaned his mouth, gripping the boy's shoulder. It was so bony. The sensation of that shoulder penetrated him. *For God's sake, did anybody ever feed these kids? Did anyone try to make sure they slept well at night?* They were all so small and gaunt, every last one of them. He released the boy's shoulder and signed to him.

You're safe here. We are here to punish those who beat and bully the weak. So don't be afraid, and tell us everything that happened. And when you're telling us, you might be on TV all over the country. Minsu, think of it this way—you're going to represent your country, the country of the deaf, so do your best. All right?

When Kang signed *TV* the boy's face lit up, but the next moment it turned gloomy.

At this point Song stepped in and guided the boy to the conference room. Kang followed.

The recording began. The interpreter seemed more at ease, having weathered his experience with the two girls.

"Can you tell us why you don't eat at the dormitory?" Sŏ asked Minsu.

Lunch is all right. Because we eat with all the teachers. But for dinner they take the leftovers from lunch and they either stir-fry it or add water and heat it up. Sometimes we find a wooden chopstick in it. Those of us who live in the dorm call it slop. Hardly anyone eats it.

"Can you buy snacks?"

Yes, when our parents visit or if we get spending money. But if our parents bring sweets or cookies, the dorm counselors take them away.

"And do you ever get beaten?"

When this was signed to Minsu, his face dropped to his chest.

"I heard that your little brother died in an accident. Can you tell us why he went out on the train tracks? It was on a Sunday, and it probably wasn't safe to be outside the school all alone. Can you tell us why your brother went there?"

Minsu, his face pasty, chewed on his lip. Kang reached for the boy's hand, but Song discreetly deflected it, then began signing to Minsu. This time Song was not speaking as he signed, and Kang realized that he and the boy were having their own conversation. The boy's long, lean face twitched, and in the glare of the spotlights, sweat was visible on his forehead.

"Did something happen to your brother before he died? Was he beaten badly?"

Instead of signing, Minsu nodded. Kang saw tense faces all around. The conference room was dead quiet.

"Who beat him?"

Down went Minsu's head, then back up it came, to be met with gazes of entreaty from Song and Kang. The boy held their gazes, then slowly lifted his hands to sign. The outline of Minsu's bony back and chest became visible as cold sweat darkened his T-shirt.

Guidance counselor Pak Pohyŏn and some of the older kids.

"And when did these beatings happen, usually? Did you break the rules a lot?"

Minsu was about to sign when he suddenly looked skyward and cried out. Kang, as shocked as anybody, took hold of the boy's shoulders in an effort to calm him. But then Minsu began signing violently, not to the interpreter but to Song. When Song realized what the boy was communicating to him, he grimaced in disbelief. In the same instant the interpreter's face lost all color.

"What happened?" said Sŏ. "What's he saying?"

"Please, let him be," one of the producers said to Sŏ in a subdued voice. "Let's not push the boy or irritate him. We need to focus on the taping—we can get the interpretation back in Seoul."

Minsu kept signing, but Song's arms dropped limply to his sides, and a vacant look came to his tired, unfocused eyes. The interpreter swallowed heavily, as if he didn't know what to make of the boy's signing. Song covered his face. All eyes came to rest on the interpreter. He hesitated briefly, then signed to Minsu.

Could you please repeat that? Why did your brother go into the city that day?

By now Minsu appeared to be free of whatever had seized him. He met the interpreter's gaze and responded.

That morning Teacher Pak left the dorm to go home—when the dorm counselors have night duty they go home the next morning—and he told us we could play more computer games if we went home with him, so we did.

"And then?"

We got to his house, and he showed us the room where the computer was, and he told me I could play a game on it, and he took my brother.

"Where did he take him?"

To the next room.

A sharp look came to Sŏ's eyes. No one broke the silence. Sŏ felt as if she and everyone else in the room were being fed into a giant rotary press.

"And what happened then?"

I played a game for a while. Usually, Teacher would tell me to stop after an hour or two, but when I checked the time, three hours had already gone by. I went out to the living room, and Teacher Pak was there watching television by himself. I asked him where my brother was. He said he'd gone back to the dorm.

By now Minsu was sniffling.

But my brother didn't know how to get back to the dorm, and he didn't have any money—there was no way he could have done that. I went outside, and the fog was so thick I couldn't see anything. I didn't find out till later that the train tracks run by near Teacher Pak's house. I never saw my little brother again.

"Did he say why your brother left?"

I asked him, but he wouldn't answer. Instead he told me that if I tried to find my way back to the dorm in the fog like Yŏngsu and I got lost, some bad guys would get me. He told me that in a little while he'd make some ramen and then take me back to the school. But I was worrying so much about my brother I thought I'd go crazy. He didn't know how to write, and he couldn't memorize a telephone number. And then Teacher Pak pushed me down on his couch. And he took off my pants.

The woman staffer cried out.

⌒

A bug of some sort was wiggling on the child's slender forearm. It was early summer, so maybe an inchworm from an overhead branch? Thinking he would get rid of it like removing a grain of cooked rice, Kang gently pinched and pulled. Out it came from the child's tiny pores. His heart dropped. He managed to calm himself, blinked twice, steadied his breathing, and took another look. From where the worm had emerged was the head of another worm and it was wiggling. Again?! He'd have to get rid of this one too. He pincered it and what came out was long and pale and thinner than a Vietnamese rice noodle. In no time another worm was wiggling in the very same place. What was happening? Now the bugs were coming from the child's every pore. Kang couldn't bear to look. The pity he felt for the child was overpowered by his disgust at the sight. Disgust: the first sensation with which the gods endowed fragile humanity, to protect them against that which is monstrous and wicked.

Kang turned away. He wanted to run, but couldn't bring himself to abandon the child. Worms continued to emerge from the child's pores. They were longer and longer and now they were jittering. The child's face was expressionless. The child was eating a cookie. Oblivious to the worms dancing on its arm, the child took another cookie. The child was Minsu, and then it was Yuri, and then it was Yŏndu, and then it was his daughter, Saemi. He reached out and took Saemi's arm. *Don't,* he was about to say, and then he noticed worms dancing on his own arm.

〜

No . . . !

The scream shattered Kang's early-morning slumber, bringing him awake and sweating. He felt as if a net were settling over him—a creepy sensation. He drank some cold water but the feeling persisted.

There was a bluish tinge to the window. Was it dawn already? The buzz from his phone, next to his bed, announced a text message. He looked and saw it was Sŏ—she must have had trouble sleeping too.

just can't sleep so I came out to the water. dawn is approaching, I can see it over the mudflats. is the world telling the truth today? or is it telling lies? truth is so cruel and persistent. want to come out here if you're awake?

Kang rose and looked out the window. Everything was asleep except for a street-sweeper truck somewhere off in the distance, its brushes making a drawn-out scuffing sound.

Outside the air was refreshing but the cold breeze told Kang that autumn was here for good.

Sŏ was sitting on an embankment that looked out to sea. As Kang approached from his car, he noticed a bluish tinge to her face—the wind at dawn was colder out here.

"Well, that didn't take long. I always thought you were a sleepyhead. When we went on retreats back in college, weren't you always the last one up?"

Kang smelled liquor on her breath. In her hand was a small paper cup and beside her in a plastic bag a bottle of soju and some dried snacks.

"Well, if I said I was coming I always did."

Sŏ searched her memory, seemed to find confirmation of this, and grinned.

"Right. You weren't always on time, but you _did_ come. Yes, that's the Kang Inho we all remember." She took a sip of soju.

"Don't tell me you've been out here all night drinking," said Kang.

"Yes, with the interpreter and his friend—the guy on our staff. They left about an hour ago. I thought about going home too, but . . ." She drew her thin jacket about her and shuddered. And then instead of changing the subject, as Kang had antici- pated, she finished the sentence she had started. " . . . I decided to stick around and drink some more."

And then, in a self-conscious tone, "Remember the night you got lost and called me? And made me keep you company? Well, now it's my turn." She flashed a grin. The wind came up and with it, gooseflesh on one of the cheeks of her haggard face.

Kang took the paper cup from her, poured soju, and gave her the drink.

"I'd like to give you some payback for dragging me out here, but since I have to teach, I'll just keep you company. You can drink for me, and then you ought to go home and get some sleep."

Taking the cup gingerly in both hands, she slowly raised it to her lips. Kang was afraid she was about to cry. He removed his jacket and draped it about her shoulders. She flinched, then became still. Kang looked out at the sea under a faint layer of first light.

"Mmm, nice and warm," Sŏ said. "You know, I really liked you back then—didn't you know?"

Kang smoothed his hair back, then raised the jacket collar to protect the back of her neck before answering. "Yeah, I knew."

She looked at him in surprise. "I don't mean I just *liked* you—I wanted to get to *know* you. As a man, I mean. Among the younger guys at school you were okay, but that's not what I mean. . . . You get what I'm trying to say, yes?" She grinned proudly to herself, as if she had just completed a successful paper presentation.

"Yes . . . I knew that too."

She looked at him quizzically, then burst into laughter. "You're lying!"

"No, really." But it didn't sound very convincing. "Why do you think I didn't know? I did—I just did."

Sŏ hiccupped and cocked her head skeptically. "Hey, you're doing some serious damage to my self-esteem. Didn't I appeal to you at all? You always treated me so respectfully—because I was older, right?"

Grinning, Kang shook his head, then drew his face closer to hers. "You *did* appeal to me. But you were always right . . . and I lacked confidence."

Sŏ tried to make sure she understood this correctly, and then a look of dejection came to her eyes.

They became aware of the waves in the distance slap-slapping like a fish flip-flopping in water. They could see the waves struggling to advance toward them—slap, retreat, slap, retreat.

"What do you think's going to happen after they broadcast the children's testimony today?" Sŏ's voice was half slurred, half muffled. "We just played our last card, our trump card. Crimes have been committed, that's obvious, but the Mujin upper crust is coming together to cover it up. Even little kids know it's criminal, but that bunch denies it. I'm . . . to be honest, I'm scared, I've got a really bad feeling about all this."

Kang took her hand in his. It was so small. She couldn't meet his gaze. They sat together in silence. The sun rose almost imperceptibly, infusing the sea with the purple hue of an old bruise.

⌐

After school that day Kang went home, then set out on foot for the Human Rights Advocacy Center. The streets and alleys were bustling like the day he had arrived in Mujin and walked through this area with Sŏ. The young streetwalker who had accosted him then was still hovering about. Their eyes met, but she seemed not to remember him. Good thing, thought Kang. And understandable, too, because by now he had been steeped long enough in the murk of Mujin to smell of decadence and would no longer be a novelty but merely a source of cash flowing past on the human tide. The doors to restaurants opened, and people joined the flow. Cars went by, headlights glaring and horns blaring. Kang may not have wanted it, but here he was among the masses walking the streets.

⌐

Tension permeated the conference room of the Mujin Human Rights Advocacy Center. In addition to Sŏ and the staffers, Song Hasŏp and the interpreter were gathered around a television monitor. Yuri and Minsu had been delivered to a shelter by the director of the Rape Crisis Center. Just as the nine o'clock news ended, the telephone rang. The young male staffer—the friend of the interpreter—took the call, then turned on the speakerphone. The voice of the producer of that night's broadcast filled the room.

"We're on the air as scheduled. We've done what we can at this end; now let's see what happens. One thing I should tell you—the Home of Benevolence is protesting big time. Just now one of our Executive Board members got a call from someone there. They seem to have an army of supporters. We get this from time to time, but I thought I should tell you it looks like they're fixing to make trouble. If something comes up, be sure to let us know—since the police aren't moving forward—and if there's anything we can do to help, we'll do it. Are the children all right?"

His last question made it sound like the producer was trying to be cheerful. Even though he had "gotten this from time to time," he, too, appeared to be captive to the tension.

"They're safe," said the staffer, and the phone call ended.

The start of the broadcast drew near. Sŏ was calm and self-possessed as usual. If anyone had asked what she was doing drinking soju on the beach at daybreak that morning, she might have replied, "Who, me? That sounds like a dream." No one was talking. The ticking of the clock on the wall felt like raindrops on their shoulders. Kang steadied his breathing, went out in the hall, and lit a cigarette. His phone vibrated.

what's happening, dear? is something going on at the school?

He hesitated—it had been a day or two since he had contacted his wife—then carefully tapped out a response.

everything ok there? don't worry, i'm fine. since you've always had my back, i'm all right.

He heard a collective gasp from the conference room— they were on. He put out his cigarette, but before he got to the conference room another text arrived.

sure, if i don't believe in you, who will? give em hell. remember, we're strong. go, tiger.

He stared at the message, wondering whether to answer, then turned the phone off.

⤸

Teacher Pak Pohyŏn pushed me down on the couch. Then he took off my pants. And then . . . he took off his pants and then he put his penis into my anus.

"Couldn't you resist him? And run away, maybe?"

If I had resisted, he would have beaten me all night long.

"That same day, did this happen to your brother, Yŏngsu, too?"

I don't know. I'm not sure what happened to him that day.

"Did these things happen to you before?"

Yes.

"And where did they happen?"

At Teacher Pak's house, or else in the showers at the dorm.

"What were your thoughts after you learned about your brother's death? Do you think he killed himself?"

No, I don't. He wasn't like that. I don't think he was capable of something like suicide. But when those things happened to him it hurt. . . . It hurt him so much that for days afterward he couldn't walk right. . . . When I think about how my brother must have been hurting that day . . .

There on the television monitor was Minsu, crying. Watching him, Sŏ and the woman staffer held hands and cried as well. Without the children there, they were free to vent their tears. And then the male staffer, sitting in front of a computer, shouted.

"We're getting comments! Not just on the TV program website, but on our homepage too. It's working!"

More painful than violence is the feeling of being abandoned and isolated, the despair of knowing there is no one to help you. Those gathered in the conference room now knew they weren't alone, and they exulted in this realization, which moved them to the very depths of their existence.

◠

They weren't the only ones—the entire city of Mujin was shaken that night. The following day, the veterans of the pro-democracy movement, who had consigned their medals to drawers, got their suits out of mothballs, knotted their neckties, and took to the streets. The pro-democracy organizations, about to elect new presidents, put their campaigns on hold and focused instead on this small human rights center. Journalists flocked in from as far away as Seoul, and every news broadcast seemed to bring yet another dirty secret out of the Home of Benevolence closets. In the marketplace, the schools, the government agencies, the Internet, everywhere you looked you heard the name Benevolence—Mujin had become a crucible of Benevolence. Justice reared its head as if freed by a plow from deep in the earth, affirming the old saying "The world is worth living in after all." The Human Rights Advocacy Center had to be staffed through the night. There simply weren't enough hands to receive all the visits from supporters, to respond to the phone calls, letters, emails, and text messages of encouragement, and to process the gifts and donations.

The morning after the broadcast, Sergeant Chang went to the Home of Benevolence and personally took Principal Yi Kangsŏk, Administrator Yi Kangbok, and Guidance Counselor Pak Pohyŏn into custody. The principal and administrator were just then discussing a dismissal notice for Kang. Kang had appeared on the broadcast the previous night— although his face and those of the others were intentionally blurred during the broadcast, those who knew Kang had recognized him—and he had made statements defaming the Home of Benevolence: children were being beaten and sexually assaulted, virtually none of the faculty knew sign language, children were subject to summary punishment. Their next step would have been to summon Kang—but Chang stepped into the ring first.

Chang, for his part, didn't like the way the three men were responding—or failing to respond—to the situation. After the reports of abuse had been filed, the police had taken

no initial measures, precisely to buy the three of them time
to wash their dirty laundry. But they had made no attempt
to pacify their accusers or find a way to buy them out—
why, they hadn't even mobilized the thugs to intimidate
the complainants and drive them out of town. There was a
saying for such men—"Old power grows lame." Maybe they'd
grown complacent. Nothing had happened to them in the
past, so why worry today? In any event, there was no indication they'd prepared themselves for this eventuality—in spite
of Chang's hints. As far as Chang was concerned, he'd done
what he could. Long years of experience had taught him that
it's always the stupid bastards who get handcuffed and not
the bad guys. Beasts of prey never let their guard down, not
even with an injured fawn.

When the handcuffs snapped shut about his wrists, Yi
Kangsŏk gaped at Chang, incredulous. Chang could see the
principal searching for any signs of weakness in him. He
half expected to hear something like _This is the thanks we get
after all you've gotten from us?_ The principal just didn't seem
to get it. You had to be hard-core with people of his ilk. With
these thoughts in mind, Chang read the man his rights in a
monotone: "You have the right to remain silent. Anything you
say can and will be used against you in a court of law. You have
the right to an attorney." And then he added, "I'm going to go
easy on you. Classes just started, so there won't be anyone in
the hall to see you. But remember, there's no one to hear you if
you call for help either. So let's get going." The subtext, hinted
at in his tone, went something like this: _Yes, I did get something
from you, and the thanks you get is what I'm telling you now—I'm
going easy on you for old times' sake._

Yi Kangbok, the administrator, was trembling from head to
toe. Sergeant Chang's animal instincts had finally convinced
him—these three men most likely _had_ been sexually assaulting
the kids. But even though he had a long history of dealing with
such specimens, at this instant these three disgusted him.

"Sergeant Chang, it's not us. We never did anything like that, I swear. You know that, don't you? Sergeant Chang!" the administrator shouted, his face crinkling.

Chang gestured with his chin to Kim the patrolman before ushering the brothers into his cruiser. Kim and a third policeman took Pak Pohyŏn away in a separate cruiser.

"This is a conspiracy. You're doing this because of a broadcast on that Commie channel? How could you?"

Chang slammed the door shut. His concern now wasn't so much these clueless idiots but the fact that they were time bombs waiting to explode, and he, Chang, was in the blast area. He tried to keep his eyes on the road as he drove. But he couldn't help glancing at their weepy faces in the rear-view mirror—they must have thought he was betraying them. One moment their expressions looked so innocent, the next moment those same faces looked impossibly old and cunning.

Now it was the principal whining: "Sergeant Chang, call Pak, our attorney, will you? Tell him we need him *now,* all right? Come on, call him. Can't you do that?"

Finally, Chang turned back and gave them a disdainful look.

The principal pretended to ignore it, but his red face belied his agitation. "Sergeant Chang," he muttered. "We have a relationship, you and us. So give him a call. Pak can take care of this—he's the best lawyer in Mujin. Plus, he's on the board of the home. Do that and everything works out. That's right. And Sergeant Chang, you should know better. No matter what, you don't come into my school and put me in handcuffs. . . . You better believe me, I'm never going to forget this."

Chang stared at the two men in the mirror a moment longer, then turned back to his driving. He lit a cigarette, but as soon as the smoke began streaming out of his mouth, the two men started coughing. Nonsmokers, they probably found the smoke acrid in the first place, but as elders in the First Church of God's Glory, they couldn't let someone smoke under their noses without protesting.

"I'll make this short," said Chang in a voice that conveyed quiet authority. "And I'm not going to repeat myself. So listen carefully."

The exaggerated coughing immediately stopped, and the brothers strained to listen.

"It's a war zone at police headquarters. Now remember, I haven't turned you two gentlemen in yet, but if something goes wrong, I could lose my badge, and the damage could reach the prosecutor as well. I'm really going out on a limb for you. And the city is a war zone too. So once again, listen carefully. Pak, your attorney, he's a good man. And it's good you two have him in your back pocket—a man of his caliber is hard to find in Mujin. _But,_ he's running for mayor. What does that mean? It means he can't ignore public opinion. Why not? Because he's facing an election. So what do we do? I want you two gentlemen to call Pak but don't tell him anything except to find you a judge who's taken off his robe. And if that man hasn't hung out a shingle yet, all the better—he'll appreciate your business. Next, save all your bitching and moaning for church. Maybe God will be interested—I'm not. I want you to zip your mouth shut and keep it shut, no matter what anyone says, no matter if I come up to you with a threatening look and tell you I know all about what the two of you did; you zip your mouth shut and act like you're deaf and dumb, just like those kids you took advantage of. And if you have to open your mouth, you do it only with a guy who took off his robe. You need to find that guy! There must be someone with ties in Mujin, whether it's college, high school—hell, it could be grade school for all I care, could even be someone whose _wife_ has ties or, if all else fails, anyone who lives, breathes, and farts— as long as he's taken off his judge's robe. Once you find him, _then_ you can talk. All right, we're here—see all the hornets? So please, mouths shut. And if a miracle happens and everything turns out well, then after you give your tithe to God, please think about 1 percent for little old Chang here."

⤳

The reporters were waiting in full force. Sergeant Chang caught a glimpse of Sŏ among them. Short of stature, she would have been difficult to pick out from among the tangle of craned necks, but somehow Chang recognized her right off. The next moment he was recalling what he had learned from a detailed background check.

Her former husband was a politician who served a powerful man who, though not a national assemblyman, was a household name. Which was all the more surprising when you considered her pathetic plight at present. Her younger child had heart problems, for which the ex-husband didn't seem to have contributed much support. Well, she must have had a fling, Chang had thought initially, but he'd found no proof of this. And in her defense, there were quite a few of these deadbeat dads, Chang's own father among them. She wasn't all that bad looking, and she had a degree from a university in Seoul, so why was she living a life that appeared so wretched?

Chang let the brothers out of the patrol car and for appearance' sake—Sergeant Chang, at your service—he whispered a few words of caution. There was an arrogance to his manner that would have been unthinkable a few days earlier.

"No hangdog expressions, no pulling your jacket over your head—none of that stuff. Hold your head up, walk tall, throw a quick smile, and repeat to yourself, 'This is an outrage, a conspiracy, we're being sacrificed, but the police and the prosecutor are men of justice, they'll bring everything to light.' It won't be easy, but you've got to make an effort. Understood?"

The brothers nodded, their faces fearful. But Chang was already calculating: Before long the tables would turn. In the real world things weren't as simple as they were in fairy tales. The brothers were holding onto his pant legs like little kids now, but once this interval was over, life would return to normal, and once again they'd be flashing their money in his face like the pompous asses they were. Which made it even more critical for Chang to implant in their brains that he was their savior. The chances of getting a leg up on people who had so much were few and far between—closer to nonexistent, actually, since there were no opportunities to climb to their level. This was the reality.

⌒

The reporters swarmed close and attacked with questions. The brothers' faces were stiff, though the redness of agitation was gone. But even with the mantra Chang had supplied them, they weren't ready to talk. Down deep inside, Chang was contemptuous of their sort, people who inherited everything from their parents and lived like princes. All Chang had gotten from his drunk of a father were constant beatings that wore down his desire to study. Growing up in a hamlet an hour and a half by bus from Mujin, with a long walk from the stop, he had been in awe and fear of life. In contrast, the life bestowed upon this bunch was like a fully ripe watermelon—cracking open at the tap of a finger, the flesh dripping with sweet juice, something to gorge oneself upon. And so the advice Chang might have given himself, based on his experience—_be patient, people soon forget, time cures all_—he withheld from the little princes. Such an approach would only make things worse for them. But if Chang played his cards right, it would never be too late.

Cameras were flashing all around. As Chang had instructed, the brothers remained silent and made no attempt to cover their faces. But unlike the principal, the pale-faced administrator was trembling noticeably—he looked ready to collapse.

"Please come to our center an hour from now."

Chang turned and saw Sŏ. What did she mean, ambushing him like this?

"We're holding a press conference. Since the police haven't shown much interest or put any effort into the investigation, we thought you might like to know what we've come up with."

Chang saw a nastiness in the face framed by the blue sky in the background, and that face was quivering with rage. Chang was perplexed—never had he dealt with a woman like her.

"You police are crap—worse than those creatures you brought in!"

6

Ten years ago I graduated from the Home of Benevolence.
All this time I've kept something buried in my heart, but
after last night's broadcast I want to talk about it. I lived in
the dormitory, and the first time I was called from class to
the administrator's office, Yi Kangbok sexually assaulted
me. And he kept it up—even after I graduated, even when I
was engaged. He forced me to continue a sexual relationship
with him, threatening to reveal everything to my fiancé if
I didn't oblige. When I saw last night's broadcast, I realized
there were other victims like me, and I told my husband
everything. Even if my husband never forgives me, even if
he abandons me, I want that beast brought to justice before
the world. I want him punished.

Five years ago I had a temporary teaching job at the Home
of Benevolence. It was my first teaching position. I was told
to be patient and I would eventually be taken on perma-
nently. The satisfaction I gained from teaching the disabled
made it possible for me to deal with the uncertainty of my
temporary status. Then one day the principal, Yi Kangsŏk,
called me to his office and gave me a DVD and asked me

to make a copy of it. I was disgusted by what I saw—it was pornography. I had to continue that chore—copying pornographic DVDs, sometimes skipping a class to do so, and then delivering him the copies. So many times I felt ashamed of myself—how could I do such a godawful thing just to make a living? I feel relieved that all these incidents have come to light. For the sake of the children and me, I hope you punish them for what they did and help make our school into a genuine seat of learning for these poor children. Thank you.

I had a friend who was often called out of class. And sometimes I woke up at night in the dorm and she wasn't there. My friend was always crying, and if I asked her what was wrong she would lament, "I'm so ashamed I can't say anything. I hate the world—I'm so afraid. Why was I born deaf? Why did my parents leave me here? Why haven't they come to get me? In the next world I want to be born a healthy girl with good parents." Finally she stopped eating. She couldn't sleep at night, and all she did was look out the window. This went on for several days. And then she was called to the administrator's office. It was in the evening and I had a bad feeling. I told her not to go, but she went anyway. Before she left she told me that if anything happened to her I should keep her hairpin—it was a hairpin I'd always envied. She never came back. The fog was real bad that night, and my friend was found dead at the bottom of the cliff at the far end of the playfield. I asked myself why she had fallen to her death after the administrator called her. I wondered why the police never asked me about it. I hope you investigate, for the sake of the soul of my poor friend. I've always kept that hairpin.

The ripples from the broadcast were larger than anyone had anticipated. Testimony came from all quarters, petitions were filed. Details were reported by the press from one day to the next, and it seemed that in due course the alleged perpetrators—the two brothers and the teacher named Pak—would be punished. The directors and management of the facilities at this home, which had enjoyed full-scale welfare and educational funding from the government, would be dismissed. And after the government had dispatched a new Board of Directors, the home would return to normal.

⌒

Among those present at the First Church of God's Glory for the 10 a.m. worship were Ch'oe Suhŭi, chief inspector of the Mujin Bureau of Education, and her husband. The minister was in the Yanbian area of China supporting evangelical work in North Korea, and his son was conducting the service. The son was a good-looking young man, but today his expression was mournful. He was only lately returned from studying in the US, and apart from a tendency to sprinkle his sermons with English, he was judged quite decent as a minister. That morning his sermon began as follows:

"Among our congregation of Christ's disciples are two who are undergoing great suffering. Let us keep them in our thoughts."

A buzz of tension shot through the congregation.

"And not just these two, but their families and indeed all our flock are suffering as well. I have experienced deep anguish ever since that broadcast, though my anguish pales in comparison to that of the family members who are here today attending our Sabbath worship in spite of their great sorrow."

The young minister's voice was resolute. Silence enveloped the great sanctuary, which could accommodate some three thousand worshippers. The members of this congregation had suffered hurts to their souls that could not be healed. No matter which side was right, the worshippers were understandably confused. For their minister, God's shepherd, to go straight to the heart of an unresolved issue in the course of the worship was clearly a drastic measure. To bring out in the open during the Sabbath worship a matter that could determine the life or death of this church amounted to a declaration of war—regardless of the nature of the conflict. It was a valiant act.

"In the first place, according to the broadcast, these two have surely committed sins that are unspeakable not just to Christ's disciples but to educators or indeed any human being. But if they have not committed these sins, then we must assume that the hearing-impaired children are telling out-and-out lies. But it is said that those children are also slightly disabled intellectually, so we must also assume that the fabrication of such outlandish lies is—forgive me for saying this, but to be completely candid—beyond their brain capacity. And if that is the case, then are we to say that these two elders of our church who have offered up their lives, who have devoted themselves in service to the disabled, Yi Kangsŏk and Yi Kangbok, disciples of Christ, are they guilty of these sins? Are we to ask of them, did they really do that? This is the question I ask of you."

The sanctuary grew even quieter. A cell phone beeped. Normally, the sound would have been muffled by hallelujahs and amens, but this time it was loud and clear, and the owner hastened to turn it off.

Ch'oe Suhŭi cocked her head attentively. She seemed very interested in what the young minister had to say.

"I know these two gentlemen quite well. And if I were ever called to the witness stand, I would swear to the heavens above that these gentlemen would never commit *lesser* wrongs, much less those of which they are accused. I would swear it as I stand before you now, and if I am a hypocrite for saying so, then so be it! They would never do such things! I would swear it . . . but the police and the prosecutor will bring everything to light, so all we can do now is wait."

The quick-witted among the congregation could now see the direction the young minister's sermon was taking, and they were quick to shout "Amen!" For the first time breathing could be heard—the congregation was no longer holding its collective breath. With a broad smile the minister looked about the sanctuary.

"And so, what in heaven's name is happening? Last night I was unable to sleep, and I sat in the presence of the Lord and I asked of Him: 'Lord—please answer me!'"

This brought more shouts of "Amen!" from the assembly.

"'Dear God! What in heaven's name is happening? How is it possible for lightning to strike in broad daylight? I do not doubt these men. And so I ask of you, why have you presented them with this ordeal? Nor do I have the least doubt about those poor little students. And so, Lord, I ask of you, what in heaven's name is happening?'"

"Amen!"

"But the Lord did not answer. I asked and I asked and I asked and I asked. Sweat poured from me like rain the whole night through, soaking my clothes. And still I asked of the Lord. No rest did I take until the break of day. And just as I was despairing in the Lord's neglect of me, I received an answer. The moment I read the morning newspaper I knew that God had answered me."

Members of the congregation threw their arms high and cried out, "Hallelujah!" Chief Inspector Ch'oe Suhŭi kept her arms folded, focusing on the minister.

"This very newspaper," said the minister as he displayed it for the congregation. He began to read: "'After last night's broadcast, a Home of Benevolence Action Committee was formed. The Committee is centered in the Mujin Human Rights Advocacy Center, which is involved in an ongoing investigation of the situation at the home. The head of the Committee is Pastor Ch'oe Yohan, symbol of Mujin's venerable pro-democracy movement and former pastor at the First

Church of God's Glory, and currently pastor of the Church Without a Congregation.'"

The minister's gaze swept over the faithful. Again silence descended over them, broken by a few half-stifled exclamations. Pastor Ch'oe Yohan and the father of the young minister had been pillars of the First Church of God's Glory since its founding. But the father's attempt to bequeath the church to the son had drawn opposition from Pastor Ch'oe, and the resulting discord had prompted him to leave the church five years earlier. Many of the congregation had followed him, and to this day the wounds suffered by the First Church of God's Glory had never fully healed.

"Of course I have absolutely no intention of slandering the estimable Pastor Ch'oe by saying this. He is in my estimation a most excellent gentleman. He and my father founded this church, and ever since I was a sniffling child he prayed for me. But because of that, it is even more likely that he will be misunderstood if he now heads a committee that can accuse these two brothers, elders in our church. Did Pastor Ch'oe not know this? And so I thought again. If it were me, what would I have done? What if I had been in his shoes and accused *him*? I can tell you that I know this gentleman well. I would not occupy that position. And yet that gentleman does."

There were more calls of "Amen!" from the congregation, weaker than before.

"And what is more, my brothers and sisters, there are many peculiar individuals on this Action Committee. Consider this temporary teacher who was once a member of the National Teachers Union. About a month before these incidents, he suddenly shows up from Seoul. He was active for a time in the NTU, but strangely enough he has done no teaching since then, and now he suddenly shows up here, takes charge of the Action Committee, and from what I hear is the most fiery activist at the school. A very strange story—anyone would think as much. And the Mujin Human Rights Advocacy

Center—what about them? Well, I have heard that we have here our very own elder, the chief inspector of the Bureau of Education, Ch'oe Suhŭi, and that the Human Rights Center people demanded of her the dismissal of the Home of Benevolence director and his board and the dispatch of a government-appointed director. All right, let's suppose that the Bureau of Education and the mayor's office go along with their demand—then who will this new director be? You can count on the fingers of both hands the most qualified people in the city of Mujin, and every member of the present Board of Directors is among this choice group. I am of course one of them, and you may ask, 'Do you receive money from the school?' And the answer is, yes, we do. Every time we visit we receive a hundred thousand won in travel expenses. We have limited time at our disposal, yet in the spirit of service, we go there to work on behalf of those unfortunate children. And now it is demanded that the directors be dismissed and that the school be given up, the school that started fifty years ago as a wooden shack and for which these gentlemen sacrificed their family life so they could devote themselves in service to disabled children. Well, fine. If they are guilty as charged, they should give up the school. They should do so even if the law did not demand it of them. If an elder of the First Church of God's Glory did those things to those poor children, even I would call out to them, 'Give it all up!'"

"Hallelujah! Amen!"

The minister lowered his voice practically to a whisper and spoke gently.

"But, my brothers and sisters, the crimes of which these gentlemen are accused are so disgusting, so ugly. Isn't that the truth, my brothers and sisters? Yes it is. But after all we are human beings. After all, they are men. When we see adolescent girls with swelling chests, we are tempted like David was by the married woman Bathsheba. We don't realize that Satan is tempting us! These things happen! And so we would say,

'Our esteemed elder, step forward and accept your punishment!' . . . But what we have before us now, this is taking
things too far. It is so cheap, it is so obscene, to the level of
pornography. When you sink to that level, it is like the tempta-
tion of Eve in the Garden of Eden—everything is exaggerated, lies engender lies and more lies, and what we have now
is a comedy. At the very least we need to view this matter with
common sense. At the very least."

The eloquence of the minister washed over the congregation like a waterfall. He spoke with the energy of a storm and
with perfect logic. The sanctuary was turning into a crucible
of emotion. All were ready to be moved, ready to open their
hearts, ready to be intoxicated by his words. It was as if he were
infused with the Holy Spirit. Ch'oe Suhŭi was moved as well;
she dabbed at her eyes with a tissue.

～

"My loving and esteemed brothers and sisters, disciples in
Christ, my nephew is passionately involved with something
called the New Light. I asked him what it was. And he said
to me, 'Uncle, it's a group that wants a more healthy society.'
'Really?' I said. 'So what does the "new" mean?' 'Well,' he said
with a smile, 'we added it because we were ashamed of having
praised Kim Il Sung and his son back when we didn't know
any better.' And now, with the prayers of myself and my father,
through the tearful prayers of our entire family, the boy has
been reborn. He said that when he was an activist he studied
Hitler's theory of agitation. It's amazing how Hitler was able
to deceive his people, but that's how he did it—agitation.
For example, if he wanted to move the people to the right,
he would tell someone, 'If you go a hundred meters to the
right I'll give you ten tons of gold'—that's how he got them
agitated. The people who heard about this got to thinking. Any
of them would have wondered, *Even if all the gold in the world
were gathered together, how could one person get ten tons of it?* The

person next to him would have responded, *Well, he wouldn't be saying that unless he had* something *to give. I'll bet what he means is a hundred grams. Well, let's do what he says and find out.* . . . So, the lesson here is, the bigger the lie, the more convincing it is. That way, people may not believe they'll get everything, but they *will* believe they'll get something. This is Hitler's theory of agitation, the communist theory of agitation, Satan's theory of agitation, the false fathers' theory of agitation. My brothers and sisters, let us reconsider what I have just said. Two gentlemen, elders of our church, are at this moment locked up in jail for acts that are unspeakable to we who are joined here this morning in service to God our Father. Those who accuse them were either activists or are on the fringes of the activist movement. My brothers and sisters, we are standing at a crossroads. At the conclusion of this worship, my brothers and sisters, you must answer the questions of the citizens of Mujin. And when you do so, you must not speak with a false tongue, you must not speak as craven Peter did on the night of the Lord's suffering and say 'I know him not.' How, then, will you answer?"

The congregation answered as one: "He is not a person to do such things!"

"That's right. 'It is for God to know. To the best of our knowledge, they are surely not people to do such things.' That is how we must answer. Even if the accusers curse us, cast stones at us, we cannot become like Peter on the night of the Lord's suffering. As is written in the Epistle of Paul, we live only through our hopes in Jesus." And here he lapsed into English: "Jesus of living hope!" Then he said the same thing in Korean: "There is no despair in the presence of Jesus. Goodwives of these two, be strong. The special donation you have offered represents in the eyes of the Lord the tears of you good women and the tears of the two gentlemen languishing in a cold cell. My brothers and sisters! I ask you to join me in a round of applause for these two dispirited gentlewomen."

‿

"That woman came again."

Ch'oe Suhŭi, accoutered with earphones, was halfway through her online English conversation class when Section Chief Kim delivered this news. She knew that "that woman" meant Sŏ Yujin. Frowning, she made a "not-now" gesture to Kim. And then she muttered to herself: "I'll never figure out why women like her live the way they do. Always taking things to extremes, always so negative. She ought to do herself a favor and believe in God, accept Him as her savior . . ." She shook her head in disapproval.

‿

Not surprisingly, as the shock waves from the press reports subsided, the perfect logic with which the young minister had spoken at the First Church of God's Glory broadened its appeal. That logic manifested itself most persuasively in terms of common sense and at a level of rationality appropriate to the thought patterns of the average person. To those citizens who were ashamed that unspeakable incidents supposedly took place in their own city, pigeonholing them with the minister's perfect logic was above all else comforting.

‿

The only problem with truth is that it takes its sweet time coming out. Because of the arrogant propensity to equate *truth* with *my truth,* truth prefers to be naked and unvarnished; it does not try to persuade. And so it is occasionally awkward, usually illogical, and frequently uncomfortable. You might say that while untruth is bustling around working nonstop to plaster itself with makeup and cover up its contradictions, truth is biding its time, waiting for a ripe persimmon to fall within reach. All of which may help explain why everywhere in this world are situations in which people are reluctant to face the truth.

"Think about it—there are teachers all around, and the kids at least have eyes to *see,* so how is it possible that those things could have happened—regardless? And these are *educators* we're talking about. Well, maybe they were teasing the kids. And adolescents are so sensitive, maybe they took it the wrong way. But heck—how could a human being . . . ?"

Anyone who talked this way was likely to be met with nods of assent, and the listeners would be quick to conclude that the brothers Yi were merely the latest examples of all the stupid, incapable men in the world. Perhaps it was this version of "my truth" that accounted for what happened next: People felt that the ugly aftershocks that had rocked the city of Mujin were disappearing like mist giving way to sunshine, to be replaced by gentle breezes wafting in from the sea. People's expressions softened and the sunshine felt warmer again. People could once more drone on about the approaching university entrance exam, kimchi-making season, consumer prices—or anything else for that matter.

⌒

It was during this interval that Kang was paged to the administrator's office, where he found a middle-aged man he had never seen before. The man was counting a large sum of money, and surprise—next to him, arms folded, sat Yun Cha'ae. The moment Kang entered, Yun glared at him, making no attempt to hide her feelings.

"If you could please count this for yourself and then sign."

Perplexed, Kang accepted the money and a form from the man. On the form was written, "Yi Kangbok hereby repays Kang Inho borrowed money in the amount of fifty million won." When Kang looked up from the paper with a dubious expression, the man peered over his spectacles at him.

"The first thing our esteemed principal wishes to do," the man said nonchalantly, "is to clear all personal debts, and to this end I am acting on his behalf."

Out of the blue, the payment to the "School Development Fund" that had been extorted from Kang at the time of his hiring had become a personal loan and found its way back into his hands. Kang could only guess that there would soon be an audit—though there had been no sign of one from either the mayor's office or the Bureau of Education—and that school officials were taking all the necessary precautions. Kang let slip a grin, and with no questions asked he signed the document, conscious of Yun's brazen gaze. Yŏndu, Yuri, and Minsu were back in school, and Kang knew that Yun had summoned them numerous times from the dorm to threaten them: should they be subpoenaed, they were not to say anything that might prove injurious to the twins.

Kang was about to leave when he heard Yun's voice.

"You have quite the work history, don't you, sir."

He turned and for the first time met her gaze.

"A champion of the National Teachers Union back when it was illegal. And here you are teaching at a school for deaf kids out in the middle of nowhere." She snorted.

"National Teachers Union?"

Instead of explaining, Yun glared at him another moment before screeching: "Who are you, anyway? Who sent you here? What are you doing here?"

Speechless, Kang was searching his mind for an appropriate retort when he felt his phone vibrate.

It was his wife. Turning his back on Yun, he left the office and walked down the hall to take the call. But when he said hello, she didn't speak immediately. He had expected a call from her after the broadcast and had prepared himself for what he would say. But she hadn't called then and she hadn't called since. Finally, he heard her voice.

"Dear, I've never told you no about anything, have I. And I've believed in you, right?"

She must have put a lot of thought into this, Kang told himself. He had a hunch that she had something important to say and that he wouldn't want to hear it, so for the moment he merely answered, "Right." They had been apart only a short time, but so much had happened—how could he convince her that he was doing the right thing? He could imagine the fix she was in, having gone to the trouble of asking her friend for a favor in order to get him this teaching position. Which was why he hadn't called her or sounded her out. As a result he now felt as if she had emigrated to a distant land with a different system, language, and currency. But it was true—enough had happened to fill a lifetime. When you thought about it, time really was subjective.

"I've been thinking—you should come back to Seoul as soon as you can get away. I'm not saying they're right and you're wrong. It's just that this friend of mine who got you that job, she called me and went ballistic bitching at me. . . ."

She trailed off and he heard her swallow heavily. That swallow told Kang that the insults she had endured were much more painful than he could ever have imagined. Through the misfortune of marrying him, she had had to eat up this humiliation, and do so all by herself. If she were next to him now, he would gather her in his arms and hold her fast. He felt both thankful and apologetic that she hadn't called until after she had endured, digested, and come to terms with this experience, and to that extent he acknowledged the distance between them now. He gazed out to the far end of the playfield, where seagulls were skimming low in the sky. Lower, ever lower they swooped in search of prey.

"I know, those men are vile. And I know what you're doing is right. I feel so sorry for those kids. But enough is enough, don't do any more. Please, let it go and come back home. Just come back."

He lit a cigarette. It was a clear autumn evening. He sent a stream of smoke out above the display of milk-colored reeds bordering the bay. The sun was slanting toward the horizon, tinting the clouds in pastel pinks and purples. If only this scenery could be left as is and just the people in it erased, it would be heaven. Simple, uncomplicated, beautiful heaven.

"Just this once, close your eyes and walk away. For my sake and Saemi's. If you really feel sorry for the kids, there are plenty of other ways you can help them. Tell the school you're ill; I can come down and pack for you."

"But tomorrow . . . the trial starts."

As he said this Kang thought of the girl who had fallen to her death from the cliff at the far end of the playfield. That was more than a month ago. But now it was a peaceful autumn evening, the reeds gently filling out as they took the last of the sun's rays into their bosom. Their tassels had the fluffiness of a girl's freshly washed hair.

"I'm asking you, dear. Just this once, close your eyes. . . ."

There was nothing Kang could say.

"Dear, you love Saemi and me, don't you? And I'm sure you love those kids. But don't you love Saemi and me more? So . . ."

Kang bit down on his lip, then answered slowly.

"Honey, please listen. I don't love those kids as much as you might think. But that's not the issue. What happened here is just too much. It never should have happened, and I can't just say 'All right' and leave. And even if I left, I'd be telling myself it's not right, it really isn't right."

🍅

Back in the school, Kang encountered Yŏndu in the hall. She was holding hands with Yuri and seemed to be waiting for him. With a shy smile she deposited a small ribbon-wrapped envelope in his palm. Suspended from the pink ribbon were a pair of tiny bean-shaped golden bells. With adolescent giggles the two girls skittered off to the far end of the hall.

Inside the teachers' room Kang opened the letter. It started, *Mmm,* as if the writer were wondering how to begin. And then, "To our teacher Kang Inho,"

This is the first time I've written to a teacher since I came here from the regular school. After Teacher Pak Pohyŏn was taken to the police station we've had nice times here in the evening. Except when Teacher Yun Cha'ae is in charge of the dorm. To be honest, I haven't liked the teachers here. They always seem to have one eye on us and one eye looking somewhere else. Maybe it's because I can't hear, but I think that the look in people's eyes is extremely important. I still remember the way you looked at us that first day. And that you lit the matches. At that moment I felt as if a bright light had turned on inside me. Until then, I never thought of myself as being in the dark, but when you lit those matches, I realized I had been standing in the dark—do you know what I mean? That day, for some reason, I felt your eyes on all of us. Maybe that's why I had that impulse to tell you about Minsu's brother.

The principal, the administrator, and Teacher Pak will soon be appearing in court. And I've heard that you will testify. And Ms. Sŏ called my mom and said we might have to go up to the witness stand too. I believe you will do everything in your power for us. And we will do our best. I used to think that maybe all grown-ups were bad people, but meeting you and Ms. Sŏ, and the head of the Action Committee, Pastor Ch'oe, I've had many second thoughts. I think I've had too many bad thoughts about the world, and I regret thinking the world was bad.

Teacher, Yuri is asleep in the bed next to mine, but for some strange reason I can't sleep. I went to close the window because it was letting in cold air, and off in the distance I saw all the reeds glittering faintly in the moonlight. And they were swaying, I guess because of the wind. I remember when I was really little how the wind whispered past my ear. I remember the sound. But the memory is so faint now, I don't know if it's accurate. Anyway, that's why I wanted to tell you a story.

It's the story of how I lost my hearing. One day when I was in first grade I came down sick. I was very sick, all night long. That night Mom and Dad had to go to Big Uncle's house for the ancestral ceremonies, and a neighborhood granny was watching over me. Well, she was by herself and got drunk on *makkŏlli,* and no matter how I cried, she wouldn't wake up. Mom came home around dawn and noticed I had a fever and put a wet towel on my forehead, and after a while I finally went to sleep. When I woke up, it was strange—everything was quiet. So quiet. It was very peculiar. I felt like I was deep underwater. . . . I still had a fever, and it was hard to open my eyes, and I thought I had overslept and maybe everyone had left, and I called out to Mom while I was still half asleep. I kept calling her but she didn't answer. And then I got mad. "Mom!" I screamed. And I got up. And the moment I got up, I understood. They were right there beside me, sitting around the meal table, but instead of eating they were watching me with bug eyes because I'd screamed.

So I realized that while I was lying there sick at the warm end of the floor, they were right beside me eating. They said something—at least I think they did. I saw their mouths open and close. Even though I was too little to know better, my heart dropped. I had a feeling that something very bad had happened, something that shouldn't have happened, that couldn't have happened.

I wanted to believe it was just a dream. So I went back to bed. My family were all right there within reach, but when I turned away from them, it was like they had disappeared and I was all by myself in an empty house. I got scared, opened my eyes, looked around, and there they were, right beside me. Gone when I closed my eyes, there when I opened them. Mom shook me and said something. I guess she was saying I should eat. But I couldn't look at her face because I was watching her mouth open and close. I was afraid that if she learned the truth, then I would never again be able to hear. And so I buried myself in my quilt and acted fussy.

I went several times to the hospital and tried all the medications that were supposed to be good for me, but it was too late. Before I started grade school I could already read and write and people praised me for my singing. . . . And then I couldn't do anything. Teacher, that's when I entered an underwater world, a world in which all the people were like goldfish and I would watch their mouths open and close. I was forced to live in utter desolation. When classmates who couldn't sing as well as I would go up in front of the class and sing, it really pained me.

The day came when I stopped eating, wouldn't go to school, and all I did was cry. Young though I was, I wanted to die. Mom took my hand and wrote to me, "Just wait a little, and when you're grown up maybe you'll be able to hear. You have to eat and grow up to be an adult." I believed her. Oh how I ate—I wanted to grow up so fast. A day passed, and then two days, a year passed, and then two years—and I still couldn't hear. But I waited. Three years passed and then four. And still I couldn't hear. One day I started throwing my stuff at her and screaming—"What's wrong! I'm getting big, I've grown this much, didn't you say I'd be able to hear? Well, why can't I hear?" My mom was so sorry, she just held me and cried—even after I hit her with my notebooks, my books, and everything else. . . . Wasn't I a bad girl, Teacher? Don't you think I hurt her badly?

Teacher, in spite of it all, I am very happy now. It would be nice if dinner at the dorm tasted a little better, but that's all right. The school is better now. The children seem a lot more cheerful—I can see it. Yuri sleeps well these days. There used to be a lot of days when I couldn't sleep well because I was afraid Teacher Pak would wake her up and take her away. Once she and I even tied our wrists together before we went to sleep. Because if Teacher Pak came at night when I was asleep and took Yuri away, I wouldn't have heard her even if she had screamed. But when I woke up the next morning the string had been cut through. And so we didn't talk about those matters anymore. We did speak up to a few of the teachers, but they either ignored us or lectured us. But that was before you arrived and Minsu's brother died.

We can't wait for the trial. We want to go to the court to see those bad people who tormented us get a scolding from the honorable prosecutor and judge. We want to see them punished, and we want to see them promise never to do those things again.

Now Teacher, this is a secret. Yuri told me. She said she really likes you. Do you remember when you took her up on your back that day at the Human Rights Center when she finished her statement and kind of collapsed and was out cold? She told me she woke up on your back. She was so embarrassed she wanted to get down, but your back was so warm she pretended she was still asleep. She told me she was so sorry to put you to the trouble, she was so fat—and you know, she's actually just skin and bones—and then out of the blue she said she wished you were her dad. Teacher, Yuri said I should absolutely not tell anyone. So please keep it a secret.

Teacher, thank you for coming to us. And thank you for saving me that day that Teacher Yun Cha'ae and those scary big kids put my hands into that washing machine to threaten me. Thank you for trusting in me when I wrote on your palm, and for calling my mom. Teacher, we may not grow up to be the best people, but one thing is for sure—on Teachers Day we will come visit you. And pin a carnation on your chest. Now that I've given you this letter, I'm so embarrassed I'm not sure I can see you tomorrow. Tonight I will pray to God before I go to bed. I will pray for Him to help my dad get well soon, to punish those bad people, and to help Ms. Sŏ and you and Pastor Ch'oe live happily ever after. Good-night, Teacher.

↬

The first hearing took place on a day of clear skies and pleasant temperatures. Vehicles lined the curb outside the Mujin District Court, each sporting a car flag with the name of a newspaper or broadcasting station. At the main intersection nearby, the Home of Benevolence Alumni Association had held a press conference and issued the following statement: "We deplore the Home of Benevolence cover-up of ongoing sexual assaults, and we support the struggle of the victims—our fellow students—and the conscientious teachers." A group of parishioners—Sŏ guessed they were from the Mujin First Church of God's Glory—were singing a resounding hymn near the entrance to the courthouse.

Early that morning Sŏ had left for the courthouse with Pastor Ch'oe. The pastor, now in his mid-sixties, was a native of Mujin. Until he agreed to head up the Action Committee, he had received at best a lukewarm welcome within the progressive camp. Back in the 1970s and 1980s, when Mujin had stood up to dictatorship and emerged as a mecca for the pro-democracy movement, he had been much publicized for his consistently moderate views. A warm smile always adorned the face behind the glasses with their round lenses.

"Any lucky dreams last night, Pastor?"

All along the way Pastor Ch'oe had been lost in thought.

"Ms. Sŏ, the prosecution are confident there will be a conviction, are they not?"

Sŏ wondered if a deeper meaning underlay this question—conviction, after all, was a foregone conclusion. She had met the prosecutor only once or twice. He was an expressionless man, a bit peevish, perhaps, but he seemed to have an objective grasp of the case, and she had no concerns about him.

"Yes, I would think so—the facts are clear, the victims' statements are consistent, and when you add the witnesses'—"

She broke off and looked to the pastor for his reaction. He nodded briefly but said nothing, and in that instant Sŏ felt a gust of fear. Before she could get a handle on that feeling, the pastor spoke.

"Yes, I thought so too, but then I learned who the attorney for the defendants is. I know him pretty well. He was a couple of years behind me at the high school here, and he was always number one in his class. I think he ranked number two among the students accepted in the law department at Seoul National University. To everyone here he's been a prodigy since primary school. I thought he was still a high court judge, but it turns out he just entered private practice. And I think this is his first case."

"So you think everyone will defer to him because he was a high court judge? But he wouldn't go so far as to say that guilty people aren't guilty—would he?"

Seeing how serious Sŏ looked, Pastor Ch'oe responded with an indulgent smile. "No, I don't think there's any chance of that. But his background can't hurt him—judicial etiquette, you know. But let's give him the benefit of the doubt. We have to remember, though—these are highly educated, cultivated people, the cream of the crop in our country. Anyway, we should probably keep all of this in mind."

Any further thoughts were cut short when they arrived at the courthouse. As soon as their car came to a stop, the reporters were upon them. While Pastor Ch'oe answered

questions, Sŏ managed to distance herself from the throng.
And then she felt warm breath against her ear—an ominous,
sickening heat that left her feeling feverish. She whipped
around to see a heavily made-up woman in her mid-fifties
glaring at her. *What?*

"You dirty cunt, so *you're* the one. Let's have a look at that
mug of yours, you witch! So you're the one who's after my
husband, you're the one who slandered him. No husband, no
fucking, no wonder you're flipping out! You think everybody's
into screwing except you, is that it? You witch, our Lord Jesus
will drive you to hell, and I'll grind up your pussy once and for
all. You Satan bitch!"

Imagine you're going for a drive on a scintillating spring
day, whistling to yourself, and the road breaks up before your
eyes. This assault was incomparably worse—no notice, no
warning, no precedent. If morning had abruptly turned to
night and excrement had rained down from the heavens, it
would still have been less loathsome and chilling than those
words. Never in Sŏ's life had she heard a voice of such stark
barbarity. She was frozen in place, too terrified even to cry
out in response. The singing of the hymn, the chanting of
slogans, the honking of cars, the *whump* of camera flashes—all
became distant, and it was just the two of them, she and the
plastered woman, in a still, bleached-out space. Not until later
did Sŏ learn the reason for this encounter; for the moment she
understood only the icy fear experienced by the small, birdlike
children of the Home of Benevolence in the presence of unmit-
igated brutality.

꩜

After the foul-mouthed woman had unloaded her curses
and walked off, Sŏ stood where she was, heart pounding and
fingertips trembling, until Pastor Ch'oe finished with the
reporters. She set out after him and then took a look back,
and there was the woman, a woman she never wanted to

think about again, crimson lips mouthing "God our Father" along with others in the crowd. Later Sŏ would learn that the woman was the wife of Yi Kangbok. If the woman had grabbed Sŏ's hair during the tirade, she probably wouldn't have resisted, would have remained rooted to the spot. Not so much from the strength of the woman but from the suddenness of the attack. She observed the woman, her eyes still ridden with fear. The woman was in a circle of linked hands, praying. The subtle green of her suit, the pearl necklace, the thick waves of her hair bespoke refinement. If not for the outburst just now, Sŏ would have taken her for a typical cultured, middle-aged gentlewoman; she might even have felt womanly compassion knowing her counterpart was present because her husband was on trial. Sŏ watched as the prayer ended, and a man in a dark suit patted the woman on the shoulder and offered what appeared to be encouraging words, whereupon the woman managed to place a hand over her mouth, avert her face, and contrive a coy titter. How in God's name could people be so stupid, so low? Did that woman really believe her husband was innocent? Was that why she hated Sŏ—for lodging the accusation? Possibly. And what about the shower of curses? Sŏ felt she could have yielded a hundred times to the woman's grievances and still not have been spared. But then she realized that the old-fashioned rhetoric of the woman's obscenities, the subjugation of their gender it implied, made the wife an accomplice to the husband's crimes. The strange thing was, even after she had analyzed it this way, her fear remained—the instinctual terror induced by a predator with a blood-smeared maw.

$\backsim$

Sŏ sat blankly in the packed courtroom. The judge had yet to appear from his chambers. Photography was not allowed, but enough reporters and spectators were present that their collective body heat could be felt.

"We should be thankful that the judge is a reasonably decent man. And in my opinion he's not a dyed-in-the-wool conservative."

Pastor Ch'oe may have thought that the reason for Sŏ's vacant gaze was her concern about the defense attorney's background, as he had described it on their way here, and it was this concern he now tried to ease by commenting on the judge. In truth, the focus of Sŏ's gaze was the judicial bench. What was it like to be up there, looking down on everybody? What did it feel like to be a good three feet above those seated or standing below who looked up at you, awaiting your disposition? Didn't that lofty position make you different from those below; didn't it make you a kind of half god, half man?

〜

There was a stir as the three defendants in their turquoise-colored prison garb entered the courtroom. Some of the spectators wept, others called out, "You deserve to die!" Because of the uniforms, the brothers Yi were impossible to distinguish. Twins, Sŏ reminded herself. Even without the prison garb, the identical balding heads, bony appearance, and angular build would have made the two men difficult to tell apart. Standing before the bench, the brothers glanced behind them, acknowledging various individuals with a glance and occasionally a smile. Next to them stood Pak Pohyŏn with a wooden expression, his wavy hair and small stature rendering him all the more shabby in comparison.

"Why all the attorneys?" asked Sŏ.

"Well, well, well," said Pastor Ch'oe. "There we have the famous attorney Hwang, and that would appear to be his assistant next to him. And the next man is Pak Pohyŏn's attorney. I'm guessing he couldn't afford to hire one, so his is government-appointed."

"Same charges, different attorneys?"

Pastor Ch'oe considered the question, indulging Sŏ in her naivete, then nodded. "I guess so. The brothers get a good attorney and let Pak make do with a public defender. No loyalty among thieves, eh?" He produced a wan smile.

༄

"I have trembled with shame these past few days as I ask myself why I have been visited with such hardships. In the presence of God and my ancestors, I have had the opportunity to look back on my life. It has been fifty years since our deceased father, Paesan Yi Chunbŏm, out of compassion for the hearing-impaired, emptied his coffers and established the Home of Benevolence. From the time we were sniveling children, my brother and I grew up in that home, and I have never forgotten the words of our deceased father, who had such compassion for the hearing-impaired—and that is true of my brother, Yi Kangbok, the school administrator, as well. In the words of our deceased father, how could we take better care of these children, how could we feed them better, how could we teach them better—and if that is a crime . . ."

The trial was under way, the identities of the defendants duly established and the indictment read by the prosecutor. From the moment Principal Yi Kangsŏk had been sworn in, his voice had trembled.

There was a commotion in the gallery, and a voice called out—that of a deaf person, judging from the inflection: "Please interpret for us. In sign language!"

"What?" barked the judge. He gave the man a sharp look.

A pair of court clerks rushed to the man and hustled him away.

"Order in the court! Offenders shall be removed or arrested for disrupting a court of law."

Other deaf people took up the call: "We want interpretation!"

And then a single voice was heard: "Your honor, could we please have your words interpreted? Those of us here can't hear what you're saying."

Laughter burst out from the spectators. The judge grit his teeth and shot the gallery a look. His discomfiture was obvious. Another shouting deaf person was led out. The prosecutor and attorneys regarded the scene with disinterested expressions, then reflex took over and they turned to their case files and busied themselves making notes. By now the courtroom was a beehive of buzzing voices. And then Pastor Ch'oe rose.

"With my apologies, your honor. My name is Ch'oe Yohan, and I am the chair of the Home of Benevolence Action Committee. Inasmuch as this trial involves the hearing-impaired, I would like to request interpretation. It's our understanding that an interpreter has been provided for the defendant Pak Pohyŏn, and I would like to ask if that person would be so good as to interpret for the spectators as well. It shouldn't be too much of a burden, and it would be good for all concerned. If your honor—"

"Pastor Ch'oe, I order you to remove yourself. No one shall speak outside of the lawful proceedings of this court."

The judge seemed irritated not only by Pastor Ch'oe's request but also by the attention he was drawing from the spectators, who had suddenly fallen silent.

The pastor regarded the judge dispassionately.

"Your honor, isn't it only reasonable that interpretation be made available in a trial involving the hearing-impaired? Those in the gallery are present because they share the sorrow and anger of the defendants. Out of consideration for the disabled—"

"Order in the court!" shouted the judge. And the next moment, Pastor Ch'oe was escorted from the courtroom by the two clerks.

Again Sŏ considered the judge and his lofty position at the bench. He was slight of stature, and as he clutched his microphone, he looked about the courtroom with a hard expression on his colorless face.

"Interpretation for defendant Pak Pohyŏn has been provided for the benefit of this bench and not for the spectators. The defendant shall continue his statement without interpretation, and from this point forth, anyone who makes a commotion shall be prosecuted to the fullest extent of the law." Again the judge regarded the spectators.

Another man rose, and while the clerks rushed toward him, he spoke. "We are citizens of the Republic of Korea. We have the right to attend and listen to a public trial. I am told that you are ordering us to be quiet, but because we do not understand you—because we cannot *hear* you—you cannot lock us up. Is that not the case?"

The spectators responded with laughter and a smattering of applause. And so the trial had scarcely begun when the judge called a recess. Cell phones and notebooks in hand, the reporters began to file stories about the commotion. These reports would spell trouble for the judicial bench.

Outside, Pastor Ch'oe had found a bench at the corner of the lawn in front of the courthouse. He sat there at his ease, appearing to stare off into space, but when he noticed Sŏ approaching, he straightened to greet her, clearing his throat by habit.

"Not a dyed-in-the-wool conservative?" said Sŏ playfully.

"Well, if he were, he would have locked me up for disrupting a court of law," said Pastor Ch'oe with a chuckle. "I never imagined there would be no interpretation. I was just trying to inject some common sense into the proceedings. I feel bad that this happened right at the beginning."

Sŏ swept her hair back before murmuring to the pastor, "You know, the thing about common sense . . ."

7

"In order that we may proceed with the hearing, this court has temporarily engaged an interpreter." With this pronouncement from the judge, the trial resumed.

"The defendant shall continue."

Yi Kangsŏk rose.

"I have trembled with shame these past few days as I ask myself why I have been visited with such hardships. In the presence of God and my ancestors, I have had the opportunity to look back on my life—"

"Yes, and it has been fifty years since your deceased father established the school," the judge interrupted. "Please continue from where you left off."

The principal responded with a twitch of the shoulders that could be seen by the spectators.

It was very warm in the courtroom, and the judge sounded tired and irritated. But apart from spectator snickering in response to his directive, all was quiet.

"Yes, your honor. It has been fifty years since our deceased father, Paesan Yi Chunbŏm, feeling compassion for the hearing-disabled, emptied his coffers and established the

Home of Benevolence. From the time we were sniveling children, my brother and I grew up in that home."

In helpless exasperation the judge looked down and ran his fingers through his hair. Just as it's difficult for a child to recite a multiplication table starting from the halfway point, Yi Kangsŏk had to go back practically to the beginning of his statement.

"Ever since I was a boy, I have never forgotten the words of our deceased father, who had such compassion for the hearing-impaired—and that is true of my brother, Yi Kangbok, the school administrator, as well. In the words of our deceased father, how could we take better care of these children, how could we feed them better, how could we teach them better— and if that is a crime, so be it, and I will accept my punishment. If an extra pat on the back for these love-starved children constitutes sexual assault, if an extra caress of a student's hair constitutes sexual abuse, then please punish my brother and me. Here we have a group of young leftist teachers who are dissatisfied with our foundation, together with a left-wing movement that wants to swallow the foundation even as they brainwash these poor children to advance their shameless demands. It's a travesty. I in my turn would *accuse* those people. But, your honor, as the spiritual father of these poor children and as a Christian who believes in Jesus, I shall refrain from smiting them. During my confinement these past few days, I have been thinking of a poem—a poem that our deceased father often recited: 'Oh affection, you are a disease, and I sleep not at night; only heaven knows I am innocent!'"

A round of muted applause was heard from the members of the First Church of God's Glory in attendance. A glare from the judge quickly silenced them. Yi Kangsŏk, seemingly enchanted by his own words, wore an expression of utter satisfaction. It was fortunate, Sŏ felt, that Yŏndu, Yuri, and Minsu were not here. Though she had never encountered the brothers Yi or Pak Pohyŏn in person, she had to admit she felt helpless to contend with this level of humanity. The prosecutor, attorneys, and judge would know the three of them were lying.

The hearing ended with the three defendants having consistently denied all charges. Before adjourning, the judge examined some documents.

"I would remind the defendants that if these charges are factual, the crimes are indeed serious. It will be difficult to prove they are not factual. I have just one question to ask at this point: How far apart are the principal's office and the administrator's office from the teachers' room and the school office? Defendant Yi Kangbok?"

The heads of both brothers turned toward their attorneys. Hwang remained expressionless, but his young assistant couldn't conceal his glee.

"The principal's office is somewhat removed, with his secretary's office directly adjacent to it. My office is directly adjacent to the school office."

"Is the distance between the offices such that if someone were to scream, it could be heard?"

"Yes, that is correct."

The judge briefly considered this before adjourning the session. "This court will reconvene on Friday afternoon of this week. Prosecutors and counsel for the defense, please subpoena your witnesses."

⤸

That afternoon Sŏ and Pastor Ch'oe visited Chief Inspector Ch'oe Suhŭi at her office in the Mujin Bureau of Education building. The inspector was not completely at ease in the presence of the pastor. If Pastor Ch'oe had not been so contrary to the ways of the world, if he had not stopped going to church, then perhaps she would have asked him to officiate at her daughter's upcoming church wedding. Although she had refused Sŏ's requests for a meeting, she could not very well turn down Pastor Ch'oe. His influence had weakened

considerably, but he was still a stalwart figure in Mujin and not
to be ignored, and no good would come of leaving him with
a bad impression by refusing to see him. Cup of green tea in
hand, she spoke.

"We have looked into the Home of Benevolence and discovered no obvious irregularities. We did find that their job
listings aren't posted on the Internet and have instructed them
to remedy the situation."

She made a point of ignoring Sŏ as she said this. But Sŏ was
not about to take the hint.

"That's all?"

The inspector stole a glance at Sŏ and frowned in spite of
herself, as if to say she couldn't understand why the woman
was so combative, always charging blindly ahead—definitely
not to her taste. She knew Sŏ lived without a man—would any
man want to live with such a truculent woman? She responded
instead to Pastor Ch'oe.

"And that's the only issue we felt it necessary to point out."

But it was Sŏ who answered her. "Inspector Ch'oe, what
are you saying? The principal and the administrator are in
jail on charges of sexually assaulting children, and you're
talking about an Internet homepage? You told them to fix the
homepage and that's all?"

The vainglorious inspector could no longer hide her
contempt for Sŏ and turned away. The woman's voice sounded
to her like fingernails scratching on a blackboard.

Pastor Ch'oe broke in. "Inspector Ch'oe, I should remind
you that we have so far gathered the signatures of 5,292
citizens of Mujin on a petition, and we will file that petition.
And there will likely be more signatures."

The inspector glanced at the documents the pastor
presented to her.

"We are making a formal request to the Bureau of Education
to decertify the teaching program of the Benevolence Foundation and reconstitute that program in a public school. No

matter how the trial turns out, there is at present absolutely no oversight by public organs of facilities for the disabled. A structure in which there is no oversight of the expenditure of a forty-billion-won budget is problematic. Even if the present problems are smoothed over, there is reason to believe they will resurface. It would appear that the only alternative is the establishment of a public school. In addition, we would like to ask that you reinstate the teacher Song Hasŏp, who was the first to file a complaint about the sexual assaults that took place."

The inspector worked her mouth as though she were chewing bubble gum. She took her time examining the petition, then briefly closed her eyes, as if in prayer, before responding.

"Pastor Ch'oe, I too have a daughter, and if in the judgment of the court these men are guilty, then I can't help but be angry. But I sit before you now not as a mother but as a public servant. Simply put, everything about this situation is difficult. First of all, if we were to decertify, then where would the seventy pupils be schooled in the meantime? And as I have said previously, the social welfare component of the Home of Benevolence lies not under our jurisdiction but rather the jurisdiction of the Department of Social Welfare. Finally, we have no budget for establishing a public special education school."

Noticing that Sŏ was about to say something, Pastor Ch'oe spoke first. "Yes, I can see this must be difficult for a public servant. But if we on the Action Committee can put our heads together with those in the mayor's office and the Bureau of Education, can't we find a way? And isn't that why we have visited you today?"

The inspector managed a faint smile. "Yes, that's very well put. Lately, on account of the Home of Benevolence those of us here have been putting our heads together and agonizing every day. And I've had trouble sleeping at night. As you know, Pastor, I'm a sensitive person. . . ."

And then she covered her smiling mouth as a gentlewoman would. Pastor Ch'oe indulged her by chuckling.

"Please trust in us," said the inspector. "Since the city oversees the Benevolence Foundation, you can seek a solution in the mayor's office. And for my part, I'll be praying for you, Pastor."

So saying, she clasped her hands together, signaling to her visitors that it was time for them to leave.

⌒

"Doesn't it make you angry, Pastor?"

Outside, Sŏ was having difficulty understanding why the pastor hadn't pressed the inspector harder. Ch'oe offered a smile, but with his crow's-feet lit up by the autumn sun, he came off looking sad and forlorn, a man showing his age.

"I always assumed that after we achieved democratization we'd be done with this kind of business. So instead of feeling angry I'm, how to put it, wondering if maybe the biggest challenges don't necessarily go away just because the regime changes—maybe they wouldn't go away even with the second coming of Jesus if He died on the cross for us again. Those people, in the name of Jesus, would kill him all over again."

Sŏ clamped her mouth shut. She hadn't expected this.

"The situation may change once we get the verdict. If they're found guilty, then Chief Inspector Ch'oe and her cronies will be a little easier to pin down."

From nearby they heard voices from what must have been the press conference called by the Home of Benevolence teachers in front of the Bureau of Education building. Among the mass of reporters and television cameras was a banner reading "We Are the Ones Who Are Disabled—We Did Not Hear Their Pain." Thirteen teachers were present, including Song Hasŏp. All wore dark suits. Kang came forward to read a statement. Beside him was a sign-language interpreter.

"Look, Pastor, common sense at work."

This brought a rare chuckle from both of them.

"We the teachers at the Home of Benevolence are gathered here today to apologize to our beloved students, their esteemed parents, and all citizens of Mujin. At a time when most children are blossoming, our students were violated over a long period by individuals who are worse than animals, and we teachers lacked the ears to hear them. Even though they demanded bribes when they hired us, even though they humiliated us with demands that we make copies of pornography during class hours, we lacked the mouths to protest. The disabled in this case were not the children but ourselves. While we teachers blocked our ears and closed our mouths, our students, who genuinely are deaf and mute, were being despoiled and trampled; worst of all, during this semester two of the children lost their lives. As these facts have come to light, we teachers have agonized to the point that we cannot sleep at night. As teachers, and more importantly as adults, we have decided to speak from the heart so we will no longer have to live in shame. From the bottom of our hearts, we apologize to our students and to their parents."

From the platform prepared for the occasion, the thirteen teachers bowed deeply to their audience. A round of applause rose from the parents and the people of Mujin. Some of the spectators were in tears. But Kang's presentation was not over.

"From this point on, it will be our policy to hear that to which we should listen and to say that which should be spoken. We can no longer abide the silence of the Bureau of Education and the Mujin city government, which should be overseeing and directing the course of our school; we can no longer abide the silence of the directors of the Home of Benevolence. From this point forth, we will work in good faith toward the day when the truth comes to light, the day we teachers become mentors and our students become our charges, until the day when those who commit crimes are punished, the day when we have brought about a stable institution in which students can study fervently during the morning and afternoon and sleep soundly at night. We promise that with apologetic hearts we will fight, we will teach, we will love, until the day our institution, operating on funding provided by the taxes of the good citizens of Mujin, has become a genuine seat of learning. And we pledge to fight to the end on behalf of all disabled people, those who at this very moment lack money, lack support, who are tossed around like dishrags, who are the victims of all manner of violence, including sexual assault, who have no freedom of movement outside their institution, who are forced to perform manual labor without a copper of compensation, whose treatment is less than human, who live like slaves—this we pledge."

For the first time since Kang's arrival in Mujin, his face had a glow to it. Was it because of the cascade of camera flashes? The delicate lucidity of the autumn sun? At first glance, clad in his dark suit, he might be mistaken for a young priest, or a monk who has managed to grasp a shred of truth.

At the very back of the assembly of spectators, watching over all, stood Sergeant Chang.

⤴

One exceptionally clear day followed another. People's expressions were as open as the skies, and pleasant breezes blew in from the sea. As Kang pulled up in front of the Mujin District Court, he gave Yuri a cookie. And then after he'd opened the rear door to let her, Yŏndu, and Minsu out, he noticed she was sucking her thumb and took her hand.

"There's nothing to be afraid of," he said to her. "All you have to do is tell them what you know, tell them the facts. After we're done I'll buy you something yummy to eat, okay? But don't keep sucking your thumb—it's getting raw, see?"

Smiling sheepishly, Yuri tried to free her hand. Kang squatted and gently took Yuri in his arms. He could feel the palpitations of her heart, rapid like a bird's. Beside her, Yŏndu took firm hold of her hand the way an older sister might.

There were noticeably fewer reporters, but more parents and other citizens, than at the preliminary hearing. Kang, Sŏ, and Pastor Ch'oe, along with the three children, were seated in the first row of the gallery. The judge, perhaps responding to media criticism of his handling of the previous session, seemed calmer. His preliminary instructions to the courtroom were spoken gently.

"Today's session will involve examination and cross-examination of witnesses. I ask all present to consider the fragility of the witnesses and to maintain decorum throughout. To the prosecution and the defense counsel, I ask that in respect for the delicacy of the issues and the adolescence of the students, you phrase your questions appropriately, and if any witness requests it, we will proceed with the questioning behind closed doors. Interpreter, please convey this point to the witnesses."

Kang wondered if the judge was trying to emphasize that in removing at least three spectators from the previous session he was concerned with observing law and order, and it was not his intent to act prejudicial toward the disabled.

As always the faces of the brothers Yi were impassive. But their prison garb drew soft exclamations from Yŏndu and Minsu—to think that those two men were dressed like prisoners! Before Yŏndu realized it, tears had gathered in her eyes. She became aware of Kang's gaze and grinned, dabbing at her face, but the gesture was not enough to erase the vestiges of anger and fear in her gaze. Seeing this, Kang signed to her, *Go for it!* With a determined look, Yŏndu signed back the same message.

Witnesses for the defense were questioned first, beginning with Pak Kyŏngch'ŏl, surprisingly enough, the man who occupied the desk next to Kang's in the teachers' room at the school. He looked calm in his brown suit as he took the stand, not forgetting to nod discreetly to the brothers along the way. How could he do that with the children looking on? Kang wondered. Pak took the oath, and Hwang the attorney addressed him.

"Could you tell us, Mr. Pak, how long you have been with the Home of Benevolence?"

"This is my eleventh year."

"And during that time I presume you have had ample opportunity to get to know the principal and the administrator on a personal level?"

"Well, I'm not sure I can say I know them well, but as individuals I can say that they are two fine human beings."

A faint smile came to the faces of the brothers. Short exclamations escaped Yŏndu and Yuri when they saw the sign-language interpretation.

"Objection, your honor," said the prosecutor. "Counsel's question has no bearing on the case at hand."

The judge nodded. "Sustained. Counsel shall restrict his questions to the case at hand."

Hwang, short of stature and a bit stooped over, froze momentarily when he heard the judge. He was still getting his sea legs under him as an attorney in private practice, and his expression suggested he had never been corrected in public like this. Visible also was a tinge of regret, as if he had suddenly realized he himself was no longer a judge. But the next moment he was speaking again in a dispassionate tone.

"Would the witness please tell the court if he ever observed excessive displays of affection by the principal or the administrator toward the students? And were any of your students ever called to the principal's office or the administrator's office during class hours?"

"No."

No sooner was Pak's unequivocal response interpreted than outcries arose from the gallery. The girl who had fallen to her death the previous month had been in Pak's homeroom, and it was common knowledge that she had often been summoned from class to the administrator's office. A close friend of hers was one of those who had cried out in response to Pak's answer. The judge responded with a forbidding look, then considered a moment.

"Interpreter, please make it very clear that any further commotion will result in removal from this courtroom."

In the meantime Pak stared straight ahead, his face a frozen mask. For a long time afterward, Kang wondered if perhaps Pak had been looking ahead not to the courtroom but to his future.

Hwang waited for the disturbance to ease, then coughed importantly and resumed his dispassionate questioning.

"Is it safe to assume that if anyone had been taken to the principal's office or the administrator's office and had cried out, there would have been many people to hear the cry?"

"Yes, of course."

Before the prosecution could object, Hwang quickly said, "No further questions."

Yŏndu's face had hardened. Kang asked himself if perhaps the girl had assumed that every witness would speak the truth, in accordance with his or her oath, and that once the facts of the case were substantiated, truth would reclaim its rightful place at the scene of the events. And then he realized that he had entertained these same simplistic thoughts.

"Does counsel for defendant Pak Pohyŏn wish to examine the witness?"

A man in a light-brown suit, the court-appointed attorney for Pak Pohyŏn, rose and shook his head.

"No. The questions I prepared were pretty much covered by the honorable counsel just now. I have no additional questions."

Kang remembered seeing this man in the hallway earlier, nodding off over a tabloid weekly.

The prosecutor rose and approached Pak Kyŏngch'ŏl.

"You say you were posted here eleven years ago," he began. "Can you explain to this court how someone lacking a degree from a teachers' college ended up at the Home of Benevolence?"

The question brought Hwang to his feet. "Your honor, sir, the prosecution is asking a question that is irrelevant to the case at hand."

The prosecutor struck back. "Not so. All the teachers at this school have a disadvantage of one sort or another, and in sum these disadvantages are associated with the unfortunate events that have been covered up all this time at the school. Your honor, sir, it may very well be that the crux of this case lies here."

The prosecutor was a cold, blunt-looking man in his early forties who peered over the silver rims of his glasses as he spoke. But now that he was cross-examining, you could almost feel the heat radiating from his eyes. For the first time during the session, a look of relief came to the faces of Kang, Sŏ, and Pastor Ch'oe. Yes, they realized. At the core of this case was a cartel of silence.

The judge looked about the courtroom before pronouncing, "Objection overruled. You may continue."

Pak Kyŏngch'ŏl's face was if anything more rigid. He was no longer the man with the unsettling know-it-all expression who, while changing into his classroom slippers, had commented to Kang: "You're a determined fellow, aren't you. Didn't I warn you? Why are you so nosy, anyway? You have something in mind?" He looked instead a wretched, cowardly salaryman trapped by his contemptible behavior and a desperate need to cling to his lifeline, who on the witness stand was struggling to put his best face forward.

"I graduated with a degree in general studies . . . and then did graduate work in special education."

"With your background it must have been difficult to find a position elsewhere—same as now."

"I . . . wouldn't know."

Before Pak could add anything, the prosecutor asked his next question.

"Do you know sign language—not just simple greetings, but enough to communicate with the children?"

Pak, his face miserable, elected not to answer.

"No more questions."

Yŏndu turned to Kang, her face the picture of delight. Kang responded with a smile.

↜

To everyone's surprise, the next defense witness was the gynecologist who had examined Yuri at the request of the director of the Rape Crisis Center. What possible advantage could this witness offer to the defense?

Hwang delivered a document to the bench.

"And this is?" asked the judge.

"The medical opinion of the gynecologist who examined Miss Chin Yuri regarding claims of repeated sexual assault by the defendant."

The gynecologist was an obese woman who kept dabbing at the beads of sweat visible beneath the gold rims of her glasses.

"Did you have occasion to examine Miss Chin Yuri when she was brought to you by the director of the Mujin Rape Crisis Center?" began Hwang.

"I did."

"And what was your medical opinion resulting from the examination?"

"As indicated in the report, the vulva was infected, and the hymen was no longer intact. A one-and-a-quarter-inch laceration was found at approximately the five o'clock position; I noted the possibility that this wound was not related to sexual activity—that the laceration may have predated recent sexual relations—and advised subsequent examination of the laceration."

"It is my understanding that you have long been engaged in gynecology, that you are considered the godmother of the gynecological profession in Mujin. Could you tell us—is the hymen ruptured only as a result of sexual relations?"

The epithet of "godmother" brought a smile to the gynecologist's stiff face and a pause to her perspiration dabbing. Her answer sounded more assured: "No. It can also be ruptured by riding a bicycle or by violent masturbation—although such cases are not common."

A faint exclamation could be heard from the spectators. Kang checked on Yuri, who was observing the gynecologist, and noticed a trace of fear in her otherwise blank expression. He wished he could have shielded Yuri's eyes from the interpretation of this answer.

"It is my understanding that as the godmother of the gynecological profession in the city of Mujin you have had occasion to examine several patients who have experienced sexual assault. In general how would you describe their condition?"

Before answering, the godmother of the gynecological profession in Mujin squared her shoulders in a display of dignity.

"Usually, there is severe laceration to the vulva and mentally and physically a great deal of pain. Above all else, because of their shame they are on the verge of irrationality. And sexual assault is easy to distinguish because in many cases there are bruises or wounds to other parts of the body in addition to the vulva."

"Then in the case of Miss Chin Yuri, was she experiencing a great deal of pain when you examined her, and did you notice bruises or wounds to other parts of her body?"

The gynecologist pondered before answering. "No, she did not. And this made me wonder. All she did was eat cookies. As a woman and not just a doctor, I wondered how she could behave like this if she had just experienced a sexual assault. . . . And to the best of my memory, there were absolutely no bruises or wounds to other parts of her body."

"No further questions."

Sŏ, sitting on the other side of Yuri, bent low to mutter to Kang, "Oh no—Mujin Girls' High School."

"Meaning?"

"That doctor is the general secretary of the Mujin Girls' High School Alumna Association. And guess who the president is—Ch'oe Suhŭi. It never occurred to me—oh my gosh." She bit down on her lip.

Kang heaved a sigh and regarded her helplessly. "How many doctors in Mujin would you say didn't come from that high school?"

"Zero," Sŏ said with a smirk. "Except for the men, and of course they all graduated from Mujin High School. Why didn't it occur to me that she's an officer of the alumna group? How stupid I am."

"Counsel for defendant Pak Pohyŏn may examine the witness."

"The questions I prepared were pretty much covered by the honorable counsel just now. I have no additional questions," said the lawyer—exactly the same response he had given earlier.

Pak's head drooped. The judge considered the attorney, unable to hide his contempt.

"In that case, the prosecution may cross-examine."

The prosecutor leafed through some papers, then passed one of them to the judge.

"And what is this?" asked the judge.

"Also a medical opinion pertaining to Miss Chin Yuri." The prosecutor then addressed the witness. "The document I just handed the judge is the first opinion you wrote, is it not?"

At this question the gynecologist resumed dabbing at her perspiring face. The judge followed up before she could answer.

"Is it true that you wrote two opinions?"

Her shoulders tightened. "Well, it—"

"Please answer yes or no. From what I can see, you wrote two opinions, and they are not identical. In the first one you note, let's see, hymen is ruptured, in your judgment no recent sexual relations, treatment of vulva needed. What counsel submitted is the second one."

The judge fixed the gynecologist with his gaze before directing the prosecutor to proceed. The gynecologist looked imploringly toward Hwang, who looked straight ahead rather than making eye contact with her.

"First of all, can you explain to the court your reason for writing a second opinion?"

Before answering, the gynecologist looked again to Hwang, then lowered her eyes and considered. "I frankly didn't know that this case was so—"

"Do you mean to tell this court that a doctor's medical opinion is dependent on the magnitude of the case?"

"Well . . ."

"In your first opinion it was your judgment that there had been no *recent* sexual relations. Does that not imply that in your judgment there were *previous* sexual relations?"

There was no answer from the gynecologist.

"Your honor, sir. In my fifteen years as a prosecutor, I have seen numerous professional opinions that state a probable cause. And frankly this is the first time I have seen a professional opinion stating that something is *not* the cause."

"Yes, I too . . ." It sounded as if the judge was about to cite his years of experience before realizing they were fewer than the prosecutor's. He thought for a moment, then continued. "Yes, in my opinion it's a first." And then in a gentle tone he addressed the gynecologist. "Is it true that you changed the wording of your opinion because of the scope of this case?"

With a tearful expression the gynecologist finally explained: "No, I did not. I absolutely did not, your honor. But I did take into consideration the possibility of lifelong harm to an individual and that individual's family as a result of the grave implications of my opinion. I anguished over this, not as a doctor but as a human being. When the hymen is ruptured and the patient is brought to me right away, it is easy to distinguish. But in the case of Chin Yuri, the rupture appeared to have happened some time ago. But because the student was much too young at that time and is still quite young, I thought there was little possibility of the rupture being caused by sexual relations. Would that not be the case? She is fifteen years old now, but how could it have been possible for her to have had sexual relations five years ago? Physically—"

"That will be all," said the judge.

Hwang then came forward.

"Earlier you testified that with women who have experienced sexual assault, in most cases the woman is on the verge of irrationality because of the shame she feels—and you considered it strange that this particular victim was eating cookies. Did you realize that the victim had an intellectual disability?"

The gynecologist nodded. "Yes, I found that out later from the director of the Rape Crisis Center."

"If you would answer one more question for me. As a doctor, would you say that such children usually exhibit a sense of embarrassment?"

This question brought outcries and curses from the spectators. Before he knew it, Kang had drawn Yuri's face toward his bosom, his instincts telling him to shield the girl. Yuri didn't look up. Kang could feel her crying.

༄

"Order in the court! Order in the court!"

The commotion among the spectators brought a look of alarm to the gynecologist's face. She dabbed at the sweat under her glasses as she answered. "I really can't say. My diagnoses are confined to gynecological matters."

"Then let me ask you this. I realize this might be difficult, but for the sake of the truth, I hope you can answer. Just now you testified that the child is young, and you asked how it was possible for a girl that young to have sexual relations with a grown man. Even if it is possible, how could it take place . . . without the voluntary consent of the female?"

"Objection, your honor!"

The judge nodded. "Sustained. Next question, Counsel."

Hwang glared at the judge, his junior, clearly dissatisfied. "No further questions." And he took his seat.

Kang produced his handkerchief and dried Yuri's face. She was no longer watching the interpretation but merely laid her head against Kang. Would she and Yŏndu be called next? Worried, Kang kept patting Yuri's shoulders, waiting for the girl to calm down.

"Next witness," announced the judge.

Hwang rose to address the judge.

"Your honor, sir, the next witnesses are the three victims— students Chin Yuri, Kim Yŏndu, and Chŏn Minsu. In consideration of the embarrassment they are likely to experience, and to protect their privacy, we request that they be examined behind closed doors."

The suggestion was unexpected, and coming from the defense, it represented an offensive.

The judge nodded in response to this reasonable-sounding request and looked to the prosecution. How could the prosecutor object without seeming to agree with Hwang's implication, which had caused the disturbance in the courtroom just now, that children with intellectual disabilities had no sense of shame?

"Agreed," said the prosecutor.

"Spectators will please clear the courtroom," announced the clerks.

Even after Yuri saw the sign-language interpretation, she gave no indication of wanting to leave Kang's side.

"We shouldn't allow this, Pastor," said Sŏ. "Isn't there something you can do? You do understand: it's going to be too much for Yuri."

"Pastor, what would you do if Yuri were a six-year-old?" Kang added. "Granted, the children are fifteen, but they've been institutionalized much of their lives—they know nothing about the world. We can't leave them in an unfamiliar place with those creatures."

Pastor Ch'oe sighed. "Well, what can we do? Fortunately, Yuri is incapable of lying—we should trust in her. Mr. Kang, please tell Yŏndu to take good care of Yuri. And Minsu too."

Kang did as asked. Even so, Yŏndu and Minsu looked stricken with fear. Never in their lives had the children been in a place such as this courtroom. Kang gathered the three of them and signed: *Don't be afraid. We're not going away. We'll be right outside this door. Those gentlemen want to know the truth, and once the truth is known, nobody will do you harm—understand? You are representing the truth, you are representing your country—all right?*

The clerks repeated the order to clear the courtroom. Before Kang left, he placed one of Yuri's hands in Yŏndu's and the other in Minsu's. As he slowly walked out, three pairs of eyes followed him imploringly.

Kang found Pastor Ch'oe standing beside a window in the lobby, head down, seemingly in prayer. Kang had an urge to pray too. He approached and silently echoed the pastor's soft amens with fervent amens of his own.

⌒

Yuri took her place on the witness stand. Off to one side of the large chamber, all by themselves, sat Yŏndu and Minsu. On the opposite side sat Yi Kangsŏk, Yi Kangbok, and Pak Pohyŏn. While the children watched the hands of the interpreter with frightened faces, the smiling defendants were speaking with Hwang.

The judge addressed the defendants: "I have something to ask you. This courtroom has been cleared to protect the feelings of the witnesses. When you see these children, what are your feelings? Although you are confronting them in a court of law, are they not your students? Defendant Yi Kangsŏk, please speak first."

The principal slowly rose, rubbing his balding forehead.

"Now that I see her, I think I remember the child's face. I've always wondered who it was who said I did those awful things. So she's the one. Yes, the one who couldn't go home during school break, the one I sometimes gave money to so she could buy cookies. I absolutely despise those who would bring these poor children forth in order to tarnish my brother and me with this unspeakable slander. Do these people have no heart? Does blood not run in their veins—"

"Does the defendant mean to say," the judge broke in, "that you did not have a clear recollection of this child until now?" He sounded as if the notion were absurd.

"Now that I see her, I remember having seen her several times before, but . . ."

The judge pondered, chin cupped in his palm. Yuri, on the witness stand, was becoming unsettled, her gaze faltering. From where she sat, Yŏndu signed to her: *Yuri, it's all right. Don't believe what they say.*

"Yi Kangbok, Pak Pohyŏn, please speak in turn."

Yi Kangbok was the first to rise.

"It is as the principal said. I remember the girl now. Poor girl, her parents, too, are intellectually disabled. When I encountered her—at the entrance to the building, perhaps—I would smooth down her hair and tell her what a sweet girl she was."

The judge considered Yi Kangbok, who was gazing at Yuri as if he actually did feel sorry for her. Yuri lowered her head, uncomfortable with the attention.

"Pak Pohyŏn, have you too only now remembered this girl?"

Pak waited for the question to be interpreted and then, after a glance at the brothers Yi, began to sign in response.

No. I love this girl and the other children and have always treasured them.

As soon as he saw Pak using sign language, Minsu jumped to his feet and began signing violently. His face was red with anger, and practically all that could be seen of his bulging eyes were the whites. The interpreter paused, seeing that both of them were signing. He appeared to be at a complete loss. Yuri's face grew whiter.

"Interpreter, would you please calm the boy down."

The interpreter cautioned Minsu and then returned to his place.

The judge heaved a great sigh. "Let us continue. Prosecutor, you may examine."

"Miss Yuri, can you tell us which of these men took off your clothes and hurt you?"

The prosecutor was careful and prudent as he asked the question. Yuri indicated first the principal, then the administrator, and then Pak Pohyŏn. The judge noted this but did not see the three men glaring at Yuri with frightful intensity. Yuri's face hardened and lost all color.

"How many times?" asked the prosecutor, pointing at Yi Kangsŏk.

So petrified was Yuri by now that she was having difficulty understanding the interpreter. She kept signing back to him *Did you say, How many times?* Finally, she signed, *A lot.*

The prosecutor indicated Yi Kangbok and asked the same question. Yuri hesitated momentarily before signing: *Really a lot.*

The prosecutor pondered, then pointed to Pak Pohyŏn.

Really, really a lot.

The prosecutor turned to the judge. "No further questions."

And now it was Hwang who rose. By now Yuri was no longer looking at the interpreter but had fixed Yŏndu with an anxious gaze.

⌒

"It's absurd, Pastor. How could they kick us out and leave the children all alone with the perpetrators? And whatever got into the prosecutor? I think I know—it's because he's a man. I mean, I'm an adult and it would be hell if they confronted me with a man who'd sexually assaulted me. I think if the prosecutor were a woman, she wouldn't have allowed this."

Having vented her indignation to Kang and Pastor Ch'oe, Sŏ fell silent. Perhaps it was more than just a matter of gender: thinking of Chief Inspector Ch'oe and her haughty brazenness, she decided the prosecutor wasn't so bad after all.

Just then one of the court clerks rushed into the lobby, shouting, "Is Chin Yuri's guardian here?"

All three responded and followed the beckoning clerk back into the courtroom.

"Miss Yuri has had some kind of seizure, and the judge called a short recess. Do you think we should call an ambulance?"

Kang rushed to Yuri, with Sŏ close behind. Yuri's face was buried in Yŏndu's bosom, and she was trembling like a bird that's flown in through an open window by mistake. Kang's attempts to soothe her brought no response. Yŏndu looked up at him, her eyes wet with tears.

The attorney kept calling Yuri a liar. He wanted to know who told us to lie. Teacher, we just want to go back to the dorm. Didn't you say that if we told the truth they would listen to us? But it didn't happen. The grown-ups are the ones who are lying, not us, and no one stopped them. This place is just like the school.

Once the children were more composed and Yuri had stopped trembling, Kang reached for her. She struggled momentarily, reluctant to let go of Yŏndu, but then nestled herself against him. With Yuri in his arms, he couldn't sign to her. Instead he patted her back and muttered:

"It's all right now. You had a hard time, didn't you? But you did well. We won't let them do that ever again. Yuri! Our little Yuri . . ."

The gentle, rhythmic play of his hands on her back brought to mind a line from Yŏndu's letter: *Yuri said she was thinking it would be really nice if you were her dad, Teacher.* Suddenly, Kang recalled the address of Yuri's home, a place name he wasn't familiar with. He thought about this child whose parents supposedly never visited her, who during school vacation, when all the other children had gone home, was left alone to look out the window of a vast, cold dormitory and wait in vain for someone to come. And he thought about how a teacher must have come and taken her in his arms like he had just done. He wondered if at that moment, just before that teacher's beastly hand had removed her panties, she'd had the same thought she'd later express to Yŏndu—*It would be nice if he were my dad. . . .*

∽

Kang felt a surge of heat, a sensation he thought would never end. It was anger, but more than that; a determination to emerge triumphant from this trial, but more than that; compassion for the children who had to endure this fate, but more than just compassion. Lurking behind the pain and sorrow of these children was a vast concealed world—a world of darkness and fear, a world of hypocrisy, abomination, and violence. Kang had come to realize that he was already one with these children, that his fate was theirs and was not without value. He now realized, he who had come to Mujin as if driven there in search of sustenance, that a light glimmered within him. That light was warm and bright, and it invested his very existence with dignity. Along with the light he thought he could hear a voice: *You are not simply an animal prowling for prey.* With Yuri resting against him, he took Yŏndu's hand and looked into her eyes.

Yŏndu, your turn now. I'm going to be frank—you have a tough fight ahead of you. To establish the truth you have to throw yourself into the struggle. You have to gather yourself together and be strong. But if we think that truth is worthless and we are powerless, then we have already lost our power. Yŏndu, you have to be brave. For the sake of truth, for the sake of Yuri . . . you can do it.

Yŏndu's tear-filled eyes remained downcast, Kang looking in vain for signs of confidence.

↬

Pastor Ch'oe returned from his meeting with the prosecutor with delight written all over his face. "Children, it's better now. We can be with you when you testify—you won't be by yourselves. And Yuri doesn't have to testify further."

The next moment Yŏndu's face had brightened as well. Kang followed her gaze and saw her mother approaching them, accompanied by a man with a sallow face who looked on the verge of collapse.

"They finally fixed the date for his surgery," the woman announced to them. "We should have gone up there yesterday. But the girl's dad absolutely insisted on seeing her, and here we are, Teacher."

Yŏndu's father nodded to Kang and Pastor Ch'oe before embracing his daughter. He remained silent, eyes closed, trembling. Kang realized that if Saemi were in Yŏndu's position, even if he himself fell ill and received a death sentence from cancer, even if he lost his job, even if his wife looked sickly and emaciated, he too would come here as long as he had a single breath to breathe. He too would come here to take his daughter's hands and show her his never-ending love and support. With this realization Kang felt an immediate connection with this man he had never met. He felt Yŏndu's father's pain and wanted to comfort him in the name of all the fathers in the world.

8

Yŏndu measured up to all expectations. She was articulate and precise in answering the prosecutor's questions about the indecencies perpetrated by the principal in the women's bathroom as well as the sexual assault of Yuri that she had witnessed. During her testimony two graduates of the Home of Benevolence school were removed from the courtroom after crying out. Many other deaf spectators covered their mouths to block outcries they might make in spite of themselves.

The judge's expression grew more grave as he listened to the interpretation of Yŏndu's testimony. When the prosecution's examination came to a close, Attorney Hwang rose. He glared at Yŏndu as he approached. Before Yŏndu realized it, her gaze had fixed itself upon her parents. A smile came to her father's sunken face, and he held up a clenched fist. Yŏndu's mouth clamped shut in a display of determination, and by the time Hwang arrived in front of her, she was looking straight at him, her eyes like points of light. The spectators, having witnessed the brilliance of Hwang's verbal dexterity, fell silent.

"Miss Yŏndu, you have testified that the principal took you into the bathroom, is that correct?"

Yes, it is.

"Would you say that you were pretty well acquainted with the principal?"

No. The principal occasionally came to our classroom when parents were visiting, and so I only occasionally saw him, and never close up.

A tinge of color came to Hwang's expressionless face.

"I see. Then how did you know that the man who took you into the bathroom was the principal?"

Yŏndu cocked her head skeptically before replying. *Because he had just come out of the principal's office when he saw me, and he took me into the principal's office.*

"I see. And so, Miss Yŏndu, is he here now?"

Yŏndu nodded as soon as the interpreter signed the question.

"I see. Now Miss Yŏndu, where is he? Which of those two is he?"

Yŏndu regarded the brothers. Everyone's gaze followed hers. And all realized then that the twins were wearing identical prison garb. At the school it was possible to distinguish them by their clothing—not so here. Yŏndu blanched, along with several of the spectators.

"Objection, your honor. It is meaningless for the witness to be asked to identify those who have already been indicted."

Hwang's voice was higher in pitch when he responded.

"I disagree. This is a crucial point. All that has been established by the witness's testimony regarding Principal Yi Kangsŏk is that a man came out of the principal's office and took the witness into the principal's office. It might therefore be the case that it was the defendant Yi Kangbok who committed the crime in question, for his face is identical to the principal's. In which case one of these two could be innocent."

The spectators began buzzing. Here was a surprise that could only have come from the man once described as the Genius of Mujin.

"Objection overruled. Counsel may proceed."

Hwang advanced a step closer to Yŏndu, a sharp look in his eye. The interpreter necessarily had to follow, with the result that Yŏndu was practically screened from view by the two men.

"All right," Hwang pressed on, "which of the two is he?"

There was a long silence. Yŏndu's response would be telling, for the distinction would also be necessary when she testified about the sexual assault of Yuri. Had the defense decided that one of the brothers would shoulder the blame for everything?

The interpreter turned from Yŏndu to the judge.

"Your honor, with the court's permission Yŏndu requests to see the defendants close up."

This drew another tremor from the spectators.

The judge nodded. "Permission granted."

Yŏndu came down from the witness stand and deliberately approached the defendants. The brothers' oblong eyes bored into Yŏndu. The girl was trembling almost imperceptibly. She took another look at her father, then turned back to the brothers and quickly moved her hands in front of them—one movement, a second movement, and then, more vigorously this time, a last movement. From where he sat, Kang couldn't very well make out what Yŏndu was signing.

After she had repeated the signing sequence several times, with the same intensity, she spread her fingers—and pointed to one of the two men with the same receding hairline, the same white face, the same oblong eyes, who wore the same prison uniform.

The interpreter spoke as if he were in a trance.

"She says it's . . . him."

The judge looked back and forth from the defendants to the papers before him, then nodded. Hwang scowled.

"Would the witness please return to the witness stand. Yes, you have correctly identified the principal. Now I will ask you a related and equally important question. Does the defendant Yi Kangsŏk have a distinguishing physical feature? That is to say, on what basis did you decide it was him?"

Yŏndu began signing, the interpreter turning to the judge to put the signing into words.

Frankly, I did not know which man is the principal and which man is the administrator. I only know that the man who took me into the bathroom and did those awful things to Yuri in the principal's office knew some simple sign language. So I went to them now and used sign language, and one of the men's faces got red. That man is the one.

A collective gasp came from the courtroom. The judge cocked his head inquisitively.

"What did you say to them in sign language?"

That man told me in sign language that if I told anyone about what he did with Yuri and me, he would make me pay for it. And so I repeated that to those two men in sign language—that he would make me pay for this. One of them understood, and he glared at me. He's the one.

Applause burst out from the spectators, and this time the judge was indulgent. A faint smile escaped him, the delight with which one wise person recognizes another.

"Counsel, from this point on you shall waste no more of the court's time with questions concerning the fact that those two are twins."

Yŏndu looked to her parents and saw her father holding his clenched fists high. She broke into a broad smile.

↩

"This is taking longer than we anticipated," said the judge in a gentle tone. "But since Yuri is not well, we will hear your testimony in her place, Miss Yŏndu. Is that all right?"

The interpreter signed the question and Yŏndu nodded.

"The prosecution may redirect."

The prosecutor rose.

"You testified that on a certain evening last month you brought cup ramen from a store near the school, and when you didn't see your friend Yuri waiting for you, you went looking for her and happened to be near the principal's office, where you witnessed Yuri being sexually assaulted. Is that correct?"

Before the prosecutor had finished, roars of "Lies!" and "Stop that!" rose from the spectators. The judge's face stiffened, and the court clerks approached those who were shouting—members of the Mujin First Church of God's Glory.

Yes.

"Your honor, the particulars are outlined in the indictment. Considering that these students are minors, I wish to use the indictment in lieu of further testimony by this witness."

"It is so noted."

Now it was Hwang's turn. Glaring momentarily at Yŏndu, he approached her, a sheet of paper in hand. The interpreter joined him. The attorney drew himself up and began.

"From the beginning I have been struck by how strange and peculiar this case is. How could this slander—and it is the ugliest kind of slander—be brought against the offspring of a respected family, the family that founded the Home of Benevolence and have devoted long years of service to the disabled. In my questions to you now, Miss Yŏndu, I would like to clear these innocent noblesse of slander. And by the end of this cross-examination, the dark forces behind this slander will become known."

Hwang finished his preamble with the judge seemingly poised to cut it short. The faces of Kang, Sŏ, and Pastor Ch'oe were tense.

"Miss Yŏndu, according to the indictment you returned from purchasing cup ramen to find Miss Yuri gone. You thought she might have gone to the dormitory, is that correct? Why, then, did you go to the principal's office rather than the dormitory? Interpreter, please interpret this carefully. According to the indictment, Miss Yŏndu, you were headed for the dormitory, but when you heard the faint sound of music, you went in a different direction, correct?"

Yŏndu nodded. For the first time Hwang's expressionless face became animated. The pitch of his voice rose.

"Your honor, sir, this is precisely the point—the faint sound of music! Miss Yŏndu is hearing-impaired. And yet she says she heard the faint sound of music?"

The prosecutor rose.

"Your honor, Counsel is insulting the witness by bringing up matters that have no particular relevance considering the magnitude of this case."

"Overruled," said the judge. "In cases involving sex, because there is a victim and a perpetrator, it is crucial to establish the particulars. The question is reasonable. Counsel, you may proceed."

Shouts of "Hallelujah!" rose from the gallery.

"Was that part of her statement?" whispered Sŏ to Kang.

Kang couldn't rightly recall; he could remember only that the events the children had described in their statement were shocking. But now that he thought about it, he did seem to remember Yŏndu saying something about music. And he recalled that later, when he and Sŏ had read the indictment, something had caught his attention, only to be forgotten.

"But why would she include it in her statement if it made things difficult for her? What if she hadn't mentioned it?" So saying, Sŏ gnawed on her lip.

⌒

While the interpreter was signing to Yŏndu, Hwang addressed the judge.

"This hearing-impaired child has testified that she followed the sound of music. Your honor, sir, they have slandered the educators of this excellent family, accusing them of unspeakably filthy sexual crimes. If in the name of the laws of the Republic of Korea we cannot protect these men, if we cannot expose the hidden forces of harm, then our country should be absolutely ashamed of itself."

Hwang was becoming agitated. His voice was filled with pride, as if he were the apostle of truth pulling the carriage of slander up the hill of righteousness. He was pulled up short by the judge.

"Counsel, you will restrict your comments to the cross-examination of the witness."

Just then the interpreter spoke up.

"She heard the music. It was a song by Cho Sŏngmo."

A ripple of realization passed over the faces of Hwang, the prosecutor, the judge, and all in the courtroom, and then there was silence.

"What?" said the attorney.

The interpreter checked with Yŏndu, who signed in response.

I heard the faint sound of music. It was a song by Cho Sŏngmo.

There was a stir in the gallery.

"Order in the court!" shouted the judge, who was scowling as if from a splitting headache. The next moment he addressed Yŏndu: "I want you to think carefully about this. You are hearing-impaired. And yet you say you heard a song?"

The gleam in Yŏndu's eyes testified to her self-assurance. She nodded deliberately. Hwang conferred with his young assistant and then approached the bench.

"Your honor, sir, in the presence of the citizens of Mujin and the ladies and gentlemen of the press, we would like, with your permission, to conduct a little experiment. We will play for Miss Yŏndu a song by Cho Sŏngmo and see if indeed she can hear it. In order to do this today, we will need to make a few preparations. If the court will indulge us briefly, we will be able to start right away. And then we will identify who is responsible for this unspeakably disgusting disturbance that has affected all of Mujin."

The judge hesitated momentarily before replying. "Permission granted. The witness shall remain on the stand."

↩

Hwang returned to the judge and made what appeared to be an involved request. Whereupon a CD player of modest size was produced from among the spectators and Yŏndu positioned so that she faced the judge, with her back to the courtroom. The interpreter took his place in front of her.

"Miss Yŏndu, we will now test you to see if you do in fact hear music. If you hear the music, please raise your hand. If you don't hear the music, then do nothing."

"Mr. Kang," said Pastor Ch'oe. "What's going to happen? Can these children hear? If so, how can they be hearing-impaired?"

Kang shook his head, unable to understand why Yŏndu had fearlessly testified to having heard the song. Pastor Ch'oe lowered his head and closed his eyes.

Unable to see Yŏndu from the front, Kang grew unsettled. Even if she were able to distinguish sound, here she was staking her future on the weighty testimony she was giving in this unforgiving courtroom. At this moment all she could see was the judge—how could she possibly hear anything? How could a fifteen-year-old girl possibly withstand the isolation and the pressure? If only he could stand beside Yŏndu and take her hand. Instead he felt for the trembling hand of Yuri beside him and held it.

"Let us begin. If you hear the Cho Sŏngmo song, please raise your hand."

The interpreter signed Hwang's instruction, and Hwang pressed the play button. A high-pitched plaintive voice rose throughout the courtroom. Seeing Yŏndu's small shoulders tremble, the shoulders of this girl who had to testify all alone about all the crimes, Kang could almost feel trembling in his own shoulders. And then Yŏndu's hand slowly rose.

Exclamations were heard from various quarters. After another
short interval Hwang pushed the stop button. Dead silence
fell over the courtroom and Yŏndu's hand dropped. There
were more exclamations, softer this time, and brief applause.
Hwang's face clouded over, and the brothers looked distressed.
Glaring at Yŏndu's back, Hwang pressed the play button again.
The judge was fixated on Yŏndu lest he overlook the slightest
reaction. Cho Sŏngmo's high-pitched voice again filled the
courtroom. And again Yŏndu's hand slowly rose. Quickly this
time Hwang pressed the stop button. Yŏndu cocked her head
thoughtfully, then lowered her hand.

Hwang broke the silence. "We'll try once more," he said in
an irritated tone. "Interpreter, please inform the witness."

The interpreter did so, whereupon Hwang did nothing
further.

"That's not fair," called out one of the spectators.

Biting down on her lip, Sŏ regarded Yŏndu. Kang released
Yuri's hand and wiped his own sweating palm against his
pants. Yŏndu's hand remained motionless. Kang almost
expected her small, taut shoulders to split apart. But Hwang
had been foiled, and his face began to show it. All in the
courtroom were holding their breath. Still, Hwang remained
motionless. As did Yŏndu's hands. The silence in the court was
deafening. Finally, it was broken by the judge.

"Let the record show that the court accepts the testimony of
this witness. The prosecution is hereby instructed to obtain the
professional opinion of a specialist in audiology and submit it
to the court."

༄

"Miss Yŏndu, thank you for your cooperation. You may return
to the witness stand."

Yŏndu remained motionless.

"We're done," said the judge. "Now back to the witness
stand."

The interpreter broke off in the middle of his signing and rushed to Yŏndu, who slumped against his arm like a damp towel. Her parents cried out in alarm.

"It's cruel to put her on display like that," said Sŏ to no one in particular. "The crimes are obvious, she's the sacrificial victim, and they're just making it more difficult for her."

Pastor Ch'oe motioned to the prosecutor, who then rose and addressed the judge.

"Your honor, we believe that this is too much for these young witnesses to handle. We ask that the court treat them with proper discretion."

The judge gazed at Yŏndu, unsteady on her feet, a blue tinge to her face, the interpreter with an arm around her, before answering. "We will stop for today. Court is adjourned until next Friday. Prosecution and counsel for the defense will register the names of any remaining witnesses with the court."

As soon as the judge had spoken, Yŏndu's parents hurried to the witness stand. Yŏndu came down and sank into her father's arms. By the time Sŏ, Kang, and Pastor Ch'oe arrived at her side, she was crying.

Well done, Yŏndu, Kang signed. *Nobody could have done better. It must have been difficult.*

Yŏndu managed a wan smile.

"But how could Yŏndu . . . ?" said Pastor Ch'oe to her father.

"It's not unusual," said Yŏndu's father, his daughter nestled in his arms. "We noticed way back when that she responded to music, and we took her to a doctor, thinking maybe she could regain her hearing. According to the doctor, even the hearing-impaired respond to sound, but each person is different—it depends on the frequency. Some people hear only low-frequency sounds, others hear only high-frequency sounds. It all depends on the frequency and the type of impairment. The music playing in the principal's office must have been at a frequency Yŏndu could hear. What gets me is that those people brag about establishing a school for the hearing-impaired, they brag about all the years of service they've put in, and they don't even know that hearing disabilities differ from person to person. Those people are unfit. Doesn't this tell you how little concern they have for the children?" And then he lowered his voice. "But I'm grateful it was music Yŏndu could hear. It makes me feel that heaven has decided to punish those people."

⤚

Early that Saturday morning Kang was hand-washing laundry when his doorbell rang. He opened the door and there was Sŏ.

"I'm sorry, I should have called, but I was afraid you'd say no. I got to thinking I haven't shown you the reed fields since you've been here, haven't even taken you out for fish hotpot. So I thought we'd have ourselves a date today. But on one condition—no bringing up the past." She punctuated her proposal with a mischievous giggle.

Kang displayed his rolled-up pant legs and wet hands and made a face.

Sŏ turned serious. "I had a call from one of the teachers at the home. Apparently Yun Cha'ae and the new administrator went to visit Yuri's and Minsu's families. We should go too—before it's too late."

"What's happening?" asked Kang.

"It's just like we talked about." Sŏ nodded to reinforce the point. "So why don't we go. I thought about going alone, but since you're their homeroom teacher I think it makes much more sense to go together."

And with that she went out the door and skipped down the stairs. Kang hesitated a moment, then changed quickly and threw on a jacket. As soon as he arrived at the foot of the steps, Sŏ started her car.

"Our staffers have been trying to reach Minsu's family by phone," said Sŏ. "There's a storm warning out, so the ferries aren't sailing. Sounds like that bunch barely made it there and back. Times like this make me wonder if there's really a God. The filial daughter Shim Ch'ŏng had to die before God would calm the sea. Think about it—the bad guys on the boat who sacrificed her got to ride those calm waves—shit! But Yuri's family, we can reach them by car in an hour and a half."

"There's no end with those sick bastards," Kang grumbled. "How can they go to the kids' parents with their pockets full of money and ask them to sign off? They must be out of their minds. You said things are—how did you put it—like a crucible of frenzy. I can't believe they'd do this."

"But you remember, don't you—when a kid below the age of thirteen is sexually assaulted, either the child or the guardian can withdraw the complaint and sign an agreement, and then the charges get dropped. The parents who are poor and intellectually disabled will need some persuading from us. . . ."

And off they went.

"What sort of agreement would they sign if their children were being sexually assaulted?" growled Kang in between puffs on a cigarette.

"That's what I'm saying! Yuri has an intellectual disability, so I'm not sure what the agreement would be in her case, but if Minsu's parents sign an agreement, the accusation will be dropped. From what I can see, the way that bunch from the school are going about it, they're assuming that even Yuri could have resisted the assaults—and that having a hearing disability doesn't mean a person couldn't resist. It's hard to believe they actually consider the children capable of resistance. Anyway, if Yuri's family sign, that would leave only Yŏndu's parents, who definitely won't sign, and then there's only one guilty party—the principal, for his assault on Yŏndu. Which means the administrator and Pak Pohyŏn go free."

Kang felt stifled and lowered the window. But instead of a refreshing breeze, it was thick mist that surged in, practically dripping with moisture.

"And there's more bad news. Yŏndu's father collapsed last night."

Kang lowered the window all the way. He felt something from far off growing close enough to wrap itself around his neck.

"Before we do anything let's eat. As promised, I'm going to treat you to some hotpot. I've got a place in mind, but it involves a bit of a walk. Is that all right?"

Instead of answering, Kang asked a question of his own.

"Don't tell me—you went on another bender after court yesterday?"

Sŏ grinned in response. She parked at a breakwater and they got out. The sun was rising, and the warm light looked like it might melt the haze. Shining through the film, the sun looked like it had a cataract, its pupil bright yellow and festooned with wisps of fog that resembled the pale locks of a sorceress.

"I guess Yŏndu's mother rushed him to the hospital in Mujin, but his condition must be deteriorating drastically—last night the doctor told them to expect the worst."

The reeds were drying in the warmth of the sun, their wet tips shaking moisture free. They extended along the breakwater out to a sea wall. Sŏ and Kang followed a path through the milky expanse.

"Did I ever tell you about my father? I was a little girl near the end of the Park Chung Hee regime, when the Yushin Constitution was in effect. We lived on the outskirts of Seoul, right next to a small church where my father was the minister. Black locust trees grew all around the church. One day—I think it was spring because the scent from the trees was really strong—he didn't come home. He'd been taken into custody. They said he'd sheltered dissident students and criticized the government during his sermons. When he came back . . . even in my little girl's eyes, he looked like a rag doll. He was in bed for three months, and then he passed away. From that time on, there wasn't a day when we didn't struggle with poverty. There were occasional visitors, people who had known Father. They all said he had a good heart and was a wonderful minister. And then in adolescence, whenever I heard someone talk about Father, I got to thinking. Why do all the good people end up getting beaten, tortured, and jailed and then dying a miserable death? Doesn't that mean the world is hell? Who could possibly answer those questions for me? Well, someone did answer—maybe it was my mom, maybe it was my teachers, maybe it was the ministers who were close to my father, or maybe it was all of them, and the message was study hard, and when you're grown up you'll learn. Well, I believed them. But I really didn't learn the answer until I got involved with what was happening at the Home of Benevolence. Instead of finding out the answers when I grew up, I forgot the questions. But now I really want to answer those questions for myself. Because if I don't, then my father's life, those of Yŏndu and her father, your life and mine, will have about as much meaning as a stone-cold hunk of rice cake. I'm not afraid of poverty, and suffering doesn't scare me. Those who want to judge me and spread rumors about me—they can blab to their hearts' content. But for me, losing meaning in my life . . . I guess what I mean is, there has to be more to life than just putting food in one end and passing it out the other end, more than saving money and buying clothes—and I want to find that something before it disappears. Because if I can't, then I don't think I can keep going."

The offshore breeze came up, and quickly the fog began to swirl and dissipate. They walked in silence until they reached the humble eatery where they had their hotpot.

ᑌᑎ

By the time they arrived in the vicinity of Yuri's home, the sun was well past its zenith. They had driven along an unpaved road, the car rattling so much the GPS kept falling off the windshield. When they finally managed to find the home, they were both a bit dazed. The slate roof of the dwelling listed

at a slight angle. It was reinforced by a sheet of plastic held
down by rocks and other makeshift weights, and it flapped
in the faintest of breezes; a stronger wind might carry it
away entirely. A scrawny yellow dog, a row of withered teats
swinging between its legs, came across the yard toward them.
It seemed not to have had much contact with strangers and was
not wary of them. It merely circled Kang and Sŏ a time or two,
sniffing at them, then produced a great yawn and went back to
its place and lay down.

"Is anyone home?" Kang called out before leaning forward
to open the door. He was hit with the rank odor of a person
long bedridden. Through the interior gloom he made out a
quilt-covered shape on the floor. Just then an old woman with
an aluminum bowl full of young squashes entered the yard;
her back was bent at a ninety-degree angle to her waist. Kang
and Sŏ introduced themselves, and an awkward look came to
the woman's face—for Kang a bad omen. When the woman
was seated, Kang and Sŏ offered gifts of pork and cookies,
then perched themselves on the edge of the narrow wooden
veranda.

"Perhaps you'll remember one of our staffers coming here
for a signature for the complaint form we filed for Yuri. You
must have had a lot of heartache over what happened to her."

The woman listened to Sŏ, then lifted her skirt and
produced a pack of cigarettes from her bloomers. Kang was
quick to offer a light. The back of her hand was wrinkled like a
silkworm larva. She took a long drag on her cigarette.

"I'm Yuri's homeroom teacher and I wish I had the words
to explain what happened," said Kang. "But Yuri is getting
better . . . In any case, I'm very sorry it's taken me until now
to visit."

"Well, you see my boy in there—he was an only child, and
his wife went and delivered a deaf baby and run away. He was
still able-bodied then, and the two of us had a little eatery in
town and managed to scrape by, but then he come down sick

and couldn't get out of bed, so we moved out to this here neck of the woods. We never had a day of comfort, but I have to say that the day that youngster come and told me what happened to Yuri and asked for me to sign that complaint form—that was the most godawful, the most sickening day of my life."

The lips sucking on the cigarette began to quiver. The old woman's drooping eyelids, yellow as nicotine stains, almost covered her small eyes. The tears forming in those eyes looked like fish scales. "Of all the bastards beneath heaven . . ." She dabbed at her eyes with the hem of her skirt.

"We know this isn't very pleasant for you, but have you by any chance had a visit from the wrongdoers? The people who victimized Yuri are now on trial, and if by chance you signed an agreement with them, then it's like the incident never happened. And I'm sure you know this, but Yuri would then have to go back and live with those evil people who treated her so horribly."

To their surprise the old woman produced a faint snicker. She regarded Sŏ momentarily before speaking.

"Yeah, they visited all right, and what they said was, if I wanted, they would give us a heap of money so Yuri could go to college, and we could pay her dad's medical bills."

It was as they had feared. And then the woman produced another incongruous snicker. "'So how much you want to give me?' I asked them. 'As much as you want, Grandmother. Enough for you and your family to get along for years without any worries.' I tell you—of all the bastards beneath heaven."

Kang felt a chill run down his back. The face of this old woman who was talking about the sum of money offered by "the bastards beneath heaven" contained more than just anger. It also held the dreamy look of a person talking of a distant location she would never reach during her lifetime.

"You're right, they really are horrible," Sŏ said, echoing her words. "Grandmother, I can imagine how sick to your stomach you must be."

Kang gazed out at the cornfields spreading beyond the remote dwelling. The tall, withering stalks had the ghostly look of a band of spiritless, defeated soldiers. Again the woman lifted the hem of her skirt, this time to blow her nose.

"I worked myself to the bone my whole life and still it's hard to lift a spoonful of rice to my mouth without worrying. The only thing we get more of is debt. Damn disease only hits poor folk like us, and those bastards at the hospital, all they care about is raking in the money. They sure as hell never cured him. And then Yuri . . . sir, ma'am, I ain't had no schooling, I don't know nothing, but when I think about that little girl, how it must have hurt her, how sad and scared she must have been, I'd like to go right this moment and rip the balls off those bastards, even if it's the death of me. But no matter how poor and ignorant I am, and so wretched my son turned feeble, and if that weren't enough my grandkid is born defective—still, I know what they're fixing to do."

As he listened to the old woman, Kang heard the sheet of plastic flapping on the roof and the rattle of the rocks and other objects anchoring it. These noises, jarring as they may have been, couldn't compare with the poverty to which Yuri's family had been condemned. He recalled the storm warning, the ferry, and the island where Minsu's family lived. Then considered what Sŏ had said—you don't know if there's a God. And thought finally of what his mother used to say when he was a boy: "Don't they ever wonder if God's looking?" And concluded that the frightening thing now was that this frightening God wasn't there.

"How could I sell my grandkid to pay for her dad's treatment? People ain't capable of such things. They shouldn't be. But, sir, what those people said—I know it's water over the dam, but wouldn't it be nice if we could take the girl's dad to a hospital in Seoul and then put her through college? Sir, ma'am, I told those people 'No way!' But after they left, what they said . . . I keep hearing those words, you know what I mean?

Sir, ma'am, my son and my grandkid, they can't hear those words. But these ears of mine *can*—they keep hearing them."

On their return trip it quickly grew dark, the dusk blanketing the hamlet like an eagle swooping over a nestling. Sŏ's small car lurched back and forth on the unpaved road until finally they came out on the highway. Neither of them said a word all the way back to Mujin.

⌒

It was Friday, the day the trial was to resume. Minsu and Kang were scheduled to testify for the prosecution. Kang had just returned to the teachers' room from his morning classes when the flashing display of his phone told him he had a call from Sŏ.

"You don't need to bring Minsu."

It was as if a black curtain had dropped before him.

"Even if they're poor, does that make it right?" Sŏ continued. "With one of their kids dead and the other so badly damaged? Signing off and taking money from the abusers? So if you're poor, you don't need to do a parent's duty, and that's it? Kang, think about it. Growing up under such parents, maybe the boys just accepted things the way they were. I'm so vexed I could die. . . ." Sŏ's voice was breaking up.

Kang found it odd. In Minsu's case, the defendant was Pak Pohyŏn. So why was the school intervening on Pak's behalf? Pak, who had to settle for a dozy public defender, couldn't have put the payoff together himself.

"Let's calm down," said Kang. "First of all, it's very strange, why Minsu . . . he didn't have anything to do with the twins, right?"

"We're wondering about that too. Maybe they felt the death of Minsu's brother was a loose end. Otherwise why preempt the hush money? Either way, what do we do? If Yuri's grandma signs off too, then they're off the hook! I just can't believe it."

After the call ended, Kang stared out the window. Poverty— he himself had never experienced it in any tangible way. His father, a grade school teacher, was an honest man, and his mother was thrifty. Kang hadn't always gotten what he wanted, but he had never gone hungry and had never been disdained by others. He had always wondered if the shabbiness associated with poverty was the result of people's propensity to substitute cash and food for human dignity.

Kang turned away from the window to see Minsu approaching. The boy was expecting to testify in court. Minsu came to a stop when he noticed Pak Kyŏngch'ŏl. The next moment Kang shuddered at the thought that for years people such as Pak had been inflicting brutal violence on these fawn-like children. The rage that followed overcame the indignities from Pak over which he'd been brooding. But now he had to tell Minsu that his parents had signed an agreement—they would never file for civil or criminal damages. Off he went with Minsu toward the cafeteria.

As they walked down the hallway, side by side, Kang caught Minsu looking up at him. The boy flashed the calm, gentle smile that Kang had come to associate with hearing-impaired children, a trusting smile that told Kang the boy was relying on him. Kang felt a surge of emotion that made his eyes smart. He clenched his teeth but the hotness pushed up through his throat. And then it hit him—he absolutely could not betray these children's trust in him. Again he shuddered, this time because he realized that _absolutely could not betray_ was premised on the notion of _possible to betray._ Kang rested a hand on the boy's bony shoulder, squeezed it once, and began to sign to him.

Minsu, I'm sorry to tell you this but . . . your parents have forgiven Teacher Pak.

The boy's face hardened in disbelief. He kept blinking in confusion. And then he signed, _My parents can't read. There's no way . . ._

Kang looked directly at Minsu. He knew the boy's parents were not only hearing-disabled but intellectually impaired. He had heard that the father's brother, who lived in the adjacent home, looked after them. Kang wondered how he was going to explain to the boy that it was possible for his parents to have signed an agreement they couldn't read. After all, this peculiar document didn't require the people signing it to be literate; instead, it was executed with an exchange of money and the stamping of one's seal.

Apparently, those people visited your parents and begged them— got down on their knees and begged them for forgiveness. And your parents are good-hearted people, aren't they? They aren't the kind of people to hate others, are they?

It was difficult for Kang to relay this. Minsu slowly shook his head and signed back.

Those people are in jail, aren't they? And it's me and my brother they should be begging to. They should be telling us they did wrong. Shouldn't they? This is not forgiveness. My brother died—how could they be forgiven!

A spark burned in Minsu's eyes. Kang hung his head. No, this wasn't forgiveness—no way was it forgiveness. Because forgiving was done not from feebleness but out of heart. Forgiveness was not a matter of closing your eyes to sin, corruption, violence, and humiliation. Rather, condemnation of such acts was necessary beforehand. But how could a teacher explain this to a student?

Minsu signed again, this time more vehemently.

No way! That bastard, he killed my brother. I was going to speak up in court, whether anyone asked or not. . . . I was going to tell that he did it in the shower room, he did it in the bathroom, just at the sight of us he beat us, and he took my pants off, and my brother's pants—

And then he howled and pulled up his shirt sleeves to reveal the bruises still visible on his forearms. Kang took the boy's hands. The way he was thrashing, Kang was afraid he would run out to the playfield and throw himself over the cliff. Tears streamed down the boy's cavernous cheeks, and still he wailed.

Finally, Kang gathered the squirming boy in his arms and held him tight.

"I'm sorry, Minsu," he mumbled. "I'm so sorry. But it's not your parents' fault. No way is it your parents' fault."

And as he said this he could almost hear the words of Yuri's grandmother: *Sir, what those people said—I know it's water over the dam, but wouldn't it be nice if we had an opportunity to take the girl's dad to a hospital in Seoul and then put her through college? Sir, ma'am, from where I stand I know for sure it's out of the question, but after those people left, their words . . . I keep hearing them, know what I mean? Sir, ma'am, my son and my granddaughter, they can't hear them. But these ears of mine* can—*they keep hearing them, do you know what I mean?*

Held in Kang's embrace, Minsu sobbed and sobbed.

⌒

The courtroom was sweltering in spite of the air conditioning. It was past mid-October, the weather unseasonably warm.

As Kang went up to the witness stand, he saw Yun Cha'ae, out of the corner of his eye, shooting him a look from where she sat. Where had that unwavering hostility come from? The next moment he was swearing to tell the truth, and then he was questioned by the prosecution about the events he had witnessed.

Now it was Hwang's turn. The attorney was straight-faced as usual, but he looked supremely confident as he approached the stand. Kang noticed the faintest of smiles on his thin lips.

"Starting in March 1997 you were a member of the National Teachers' Union, is that correct?"

The question hit Kang like a blitz.

⌒

The National Teachers' Union? What was this about? And what relation could the NTU possibly have to this case? Kang hadn't a clue.

"Is it not the case that you were active in the NTU as of March 1997, at which time that union was illegal?"

Hwang's penetrating gaze made Kang feel like a fish on a cutting board, about to be filleted. A frigid sensation rose to his head, which began to feel fuzzy and frosty; he felt cold sweat in his armpits. *Get a grip on yourself.*

"I have no recollection of that."

The next moment Hwang was flourishing a document.

"According to this, you joined the NTU in 1997 and were an active member until December 1999, when you left your teaching job—"

"Objection, your honor," broke in the prosecutor. "Counsel is making an issue out of the witness's past, which has no bearing on this case."

Hwang shot Kang another stony look before turning to the judge.

"Not so. Among those at the Home of Benevolence, the witness was the primary instigator of the criminal charges against the defendants, and he is the principal eyewitness of the events there. In the absence of any other eyewitness, I believe it is crucial to establish his integrity. This witness is now denying what is clearly written on this document, which includes his own name. I present for the court's perusal this roster of the NTU membership at the time in question."

The judge examined the document, hesitated, and, after sustaining the objection, addressed Kang.

"Although the NTU was illegal at that time if memory serves me correct, it shouldn't be much of an issue now. And so I can't understand why you would insist on denying you belonged to it. The name Kang Inho appears here, and counsel is correct—you are listed as having joined in March 1997."

Kang's face had turned bloodless. There was a stir in the gallery. He searched his memory but turned up nothing about either joining the NTU or participating in its activities. First of all, he had had little interest in such organizations. He had been a teacher in 1997 and at the end of that year, before the semester was over, had joined the army.

"I'm sorry but I just don't remember. And I wasn't long at my teaching post before I had to go in the army, so . . ."

The judge fixed Kang with a dubious gaze. Hwang's smile was more obvious now.

"Next question. Is it not true that around that time you sexually assaulted Miss Chang Myŏnghŭi, one of your students at Mihwa Girls' High School in Sŏngdong District, Seoul, leading to her death?"

If the previous question had felt like a series of slaps to Kang's face, this one was a hammer blow to the back of his head. The judge regarded Kang as if he were approaching the climax of a suspense novel. As the prosecutor rose to lodge another objection, the judge spoke.

"Counsel is not digging into the witness's past; rather we have here a matter of character and morals that is important in this case. Counsel may proceed."

The gallery was still. Rather than the trial of Yi Kangsŏk, Yi Kangbok, and Pak Pohyŏn, the spectators were in essence witnessing a fact-finding committee focusing on Kang Inho's past.

"I did not sexually assault her, and I did not learn about her suicide until after I was discharged from the army."

"So you did not sexually assault her—all right. But at the time you were involved with Miss Chang she was a minor. And a former student of yours. So was this sexual relationship . . . consensual? And would you say it reflects your morals?"

The courtroom was still. Kang, in the witness booth three feet above the spectators, felt even more of a stillness. Underwater stillness, as Yŏndu had phrased it in her letter. The stillness of being immersed deep beneath the surface. Still . . . ness.

"I didn't realize she was a minor. She had graduated from the high school, and there wasn't that much of a difference in our ages, and it's generally accepted that once a girl graduates from high school, usually . . ."

Kang felt beads of perspiration at the corners of his eyes.

Hwang turned his faintly smiling face toward the judge.

"I present for the record the will of Miss Chang Myŏnghŭi, submitted to us by her parents. The parents saw the coverage of the Home of Benevolence matter and realized that the man who lodged the complaint against the defendants was Kang Inho, the man responsible for their daughter's death. They then sent us the will left by their daughter more than ten years ago. They said they had wanted him punished, but their daughter's death was a suicide, and no evidence connected him to it, so he was never prosecuted. Your honor, sir, this man who flatly denies he was a member of the NTU for some three years, this man who under the pretense of wholesome teaching was active in an illegal organization, this man who sexually assaulted a girl who was his student when he taught at a girls' high school, resulting in her suicide—is such a man qualified to accuse these defendants, whose family has over the course of two generations, beginning with their late father, bent every effort in service to the disabled? Shall we believe the testimony of this man who denies even the fact that he was an active member of the NTU? Must we smear the reputation of the defendants' family and the fifty years of history of the Home of Benevolence? No further questions."

Kang slowly stood as if glued to the witness stand. The curtain of time began to lift from his frozen mind, allowing fleeting glimpses of the past. Only then did the actuality of his activity in the NTU appear faintly. He had graduated from college, and due to an administrative error on the part of the Military Affairs Administration, he would spend almost a year waiting to be inducted. Knowing this, a fellow alumnus who had graduated ahead of Kang asked if he wanted to teach during the interim at the private girls' high school where he himself taught. For Kang it was an amazing stroke of luck. And then one day the teacher urged Kang to join the NTU. As the judge had said, the NTU was illegal at that time, but it was clear to all that it would soon be legalized. The overture wasn't based on an impassioned ideology the two men shared, and Kang had no feelings of opposition so he signed on.

He was twenty-four at the time, the education of the girls not his primary concern, and he himself had not yet outgrown the last vestiges of adolescence. With his teacher's salary he could invite friends out to drink whiskey, and he had one-night flings with anonymous women he met at night clubs. When he arrived at class after a night of heavy drinking, the girls—who looked all grown up to him—would hold their nose and, disguising their interest and affection for their young bachelor teacher in a tone of antipathy, say, "Wow—Teacher smells like booze!" He could still remember how they cackled. . . . During that time in his life, he didn't enroll in a savings plan, nor did he buy a car. He felt like an expensive tutor. And then a year later, he went into the army. He learned sometime later that the school was keeping his teaching job open and had placed him on temporary leave. This, too, was a stroke of luck.

But after his discharge, instead of teaching he helped out an older friend from college in a clothing-export company, and armed with that experience, the two of them started their own small garment business. And so it was true that until he left teaching for good, he would have been listed as a teacher for three years, and for the same period he would have been on the NTU roster. But other than a piece of paper with his name typed on it, he had had no connection with the NTU.

"All right, I remember now," Kang called out. "About the NTU . . ."

The judge glanced at Kang, leafed through the documents before him, then pronounced in an icy, officious tone,

"That will be all—the witness may step down. Counsel, next witness."

Yun Cha'ae rose and approached the witness stand with Kang still standing there. Her scornful gaze felt like a pair of tiny needles. And then he sensed the penetrating gazes of the three defendants, first on his cheekbones, then his cheeks, his hair, the nape of his neck, the backs of his hands. He felt stung by the trio and then by a swarm of pointed looks from the gallery. He tried to remember where he had been sitting but lurched toward the exit at the back of the courtroom. It was such a long way. Outside, the ground felt unsteady, and the air was throbbing. Perspiration had soaked his dress shirt, permeating his lightweight suit jacket so that he appeared to be bleeding.

9

The phone in Kang's pants pocket had been vibrating, but he didn't notice it until he arrived at the plaza below the steps to the courthouse. It was his wife.

"Dear . . ."

She said just the one word and then, silence. Kang knew intuitively that bad news was on the way. He hesitated before replying.

"Unless it's urgent, could I call you back in ten—"

"It's not urgent but it's important."

Was there no end in sight? Kang asked himself.

"Dear . . ."

Kang could almost feel his wife trembling.

"Dear, your student Chang Myŏnghŭi . . ." And now she was crying. "Are you—did this student of yours kill herself because you sexually assaulted her?"

Kang's vision grew fuzzy. How in God's name had his wife found out about the particulars of his testimony just now?

"Dear, what—" And then she was screaming incoherently. Finally, she managed to speak again. "It was posted on the Mujin First Church of God's Glory website. My friend called me. How far do you plan to go before you destroy yourself?"

"Dear, I'm now—"

"Yes—now what? And who is this Sŏ Yujin? She's been seen several times coming out of your apartment at dawn. It says the two of you live in the same complex—is that right? Is that why we haven't seen your shadow since you went down there? How could this happen? I can never forgive you, I mean it. And what's to become of Saemi? Tell me. How could you do something like this? I begged you to let go and now look—this is how it turns out!" And then she burst out crying.

Kang felt heat surge up from his gorge and cold run down his spine—his body's thermostat was out of whack. He went weak in the knees. The ghastly chill on his back duplicated the sensation he had experienced when Myŏnghŭi's face had appeared during his trip here from Seoul.

"How can Saemi and I show our faces in public?" his wife said with a sob.

"Dear, listen to me, it's not like that, it's—"

"I'm not interested in your excuses." Her tone had grown cold. "The problem now is that once this is on the Internet, it makes no difference what's true and what's not. If these are simply wild accusations, then you can file a complaint. But you have to decide about Chang Myŏnghŭi and about Sŏ Yujin, both of them. If none of it's true, you have to file a complaint, see?"

Kang slowly lowered himself into his car, then yanked the door shut. The stillness in the interior left him strangely composed.

"Dear, could you please calm down and listen. About Chang Myŏnghŭi—yes, we knew each other for a time . . . and yes, she was my student. And yes, she committed suicide. But I never . . . and Sŏ Yujin—yes, she lives in the same apartment complex but—"

With one last shriek from his wife, the line went dead. Kang loosened his necktie and lowered the window partway.

On the facade of the Mujin District Courthouse were inscribed three words. Only now did they register: Liberty, Equality, Justice.

～

Yun Cha'ae looked fierce as she took the witness stand. Apart from her role as one of the strongest supporters of the principal, it wasn't immediately clear to Sŏ and Pastor Ch'oe why Hwang had called her to the stand. It had never been confirmed that her name Cha'ae, "benevolence," had been given to her because she was the foster daughter of the Home of Benevolence founder, Yi Chunbŏm, but it was rumored that she was the principal's lover. Perhaps the anger lurking beneath the common-sense exterior of this woman who had applied vigilante justice to Yŏndu harbored a monstrous envy because of her background.

"You work as a guidance counselor in the Home of Benevolence dormitory, is that correct?"

"Yes, that's correct," Yun answered in her clipped tone.

"And how long have you been serving in that capacity?"

"This is my eighth year."

"A not inconsiderable amount of time. And regrettable though it is, I understand that among all who work at the Home of Benevolence school and dormitory, it is you, someone who is not hearing-impaired, who is the most skilled at sign language—is that correct?"

"It is. Because I was raised as the foster daughter of Teacher Paesan, Yi Chunbŏm, founder of the Home of Benevolence, I spent my childhood there, so I've spent more time than anyone with the hearing-impaired."

"In that case you must be knowledgeable about the attributes of the hearing-impaired and the characteristics that differentiate them from other disabled individuals, and you must have long observed the students who claim to have been victimized by the defendants."

"Objection, your honor," said the prosecutor, rising to his feet. "Counsel is examining the witness about facts that are not relevant to this case."

Hwang was ready with his response.

"Not so. All the children who have accused the defendants are hearing-impaired and have spent their childhood at that facility. They are not children we would encounter in everyday life. They have been isolated, and it may be that they have a completely different set of values than we do. And this could be a key to the present case because they are all from that facility, and they are claiming that the defendants committed crimes."

"Objection overruled. Counsel may continue with his examination."

"Pastor Ch'oe," whispered Sŏ where the two of them sat in the gallery, "don't you think the judge is acting kind of peculiar? I think he's too lenient with the defense attorney."

The pastor was deep in thought and didn't answer.

"Deferential treatment . . . should we be worrying about this?"

The pastor was silent a moment longer, then sighed quietly. The exposure of Kang's past had been a surprise, and the judge had indeed begun to extend preferential treatment to the defendants. Both Sŏ and Pastor Ch'oe had a bad feeling about these developments but couldn't as yet reveal that sentiment to each other.

"In my view," Yun was saying, "among all the disabled, the hearing-impaired are the most difficult to deal with. As we often say, they don't hear others. And so they believe that they alone are right. Even when they feel they've made a mistake, they don't think to correct themselves."

The interpreter turned toward the gallery with a pained expression. Sure enough, as soon as he began signing, catcalls broke out. The court clerks rose and the judge glared at the spectators.

"What's more, they've ended up a people unto themselves, using the same language, forming a closed society of the deaf. Their regimentation is extraordinary. With these children now, only the body is maturing, not the mind, so they tend to be promiscuous. This is what I focus on the most in the dormitory. And it's not just what they do among themselves. Sometimes the boys will make blatant demands of me, a female teacher, and the girls will blatantly tempt the male teachers—going around only in their underwear, for example, in front of these two gentlemen, the principal and the administrator, and anybody else—"

The catcalls from the gallery grew louder, and then a shoe went flying toward Yun. The man responsible was a member of the Home of Benevolence Alumni Association. The court clerks rushed toward him as the judge fixed him with a glare.

"I hereby charge you with disruption of a court of law. Take him into custody."

As the deaf man was led out, his weird outcries plunged the courtroom even deeper into silence. Several deaf women were wiping their teary faces. Unable to hear, unable to speak, they had to look on helplessly as others disparaged them.

Next to Sŏ, Pastor Ch'oe was rubbing his eyes; he looked tired.

⌒

Sŏ had long been considering: if someone were to ask what the most frightening thing in the world was, her answer would be lies. If the world were a lake, then a person's lies are like black ink spilling into the lake and dyeing everything around it. To restore the original clarity of that lake would require an infinite amount of purity.

She had once been told that the haves use twice as much energy to keep their possessions as the have-nots spend on taking those possessions. This is because the haves know both the pleasure of having and the fear of not having. And so the chorus of lies of the haves, who try to prevent their possessions from being taken, contains enormous energy, enough to call down lightning and thunder from clear skies.

This chain of events had taught Sŏ a different way of looking at the world. She had learned that there were those who inflicted scars on others in order to hide their own imperfections. And that the more the haves had, the more indiscriminate and cruel their abuse of others. She felt that for some time here in Mujin the voices of principle, morality, and conscience had been thrown in the trash, sorted out, and then recycled into anomaly, private gain, and compromise.

While she was absorbed in these thoughts, Yun's testimony continued.

"The intellectual capacity of the hearing-impaired is noticeably less than that of other groups of disabled. The primary reason being that they have no ear for language, and language is the source of thought. In other words, they have multiple handicaps. If we can say that those who are vision-impaired have just that one disability, then these people have a dual disability—both in hearing and in speech."

The interpreter's face was more contorted than when he had heard the children's statements about the sexual assaults. No sooner had he interpreted Yun's statements than shouts broke out again from the spectators who were deaf.

"Order in the court," the judge called out. "Anyone causing a commotion will be taken into custody immediately."

That day five people were detained.

⌒

With the onset of darkness, the fog pushed in from the sea, infiltrating the spaces between one person and the next so that even those near each other felt isolated. Dark, damp air layered the streets; the windows of all dwellings were closed. Shop owners hastened to illuminate their signs, but the mist soon blurred them. People hurried for home. Drivers honked more than usual, wanting to reach their destinations before the fog thickened.

The fluorescent lights flickered above those gathered in the office of the Mujin Human Rights Advocacy Center. The phone kept ringing, the callers all criticizing Kang. The staffers, men and women alike, took turns answering and attempted to offer clarification, but the callers obviously had another goal.

Kang's clouded face reminded Sŏ of tarnished copper. The posting on the First Church of God's Glory website, in particular the word "shocking," had spread like the wind to various other websites. The staffers all sensed that someone was orchestrating a kind of cyber libel, but they knew not how to block it. It was only a matter of time before the children at the Home of Benevolence saw the church website posting—and what then? It was a nightmare—as if every billboard nationwide contained photographs from Kang's past, as if every top-story newscast was about Kang, as if playing on every computer was a video clip from his past. Kang was baffled. Perhaps he should walk into the misty sea and sink into an eternal abyss?

Sŏ broke the silence. "Someone's been stalking us but for God's sake who?" She turned to Kang. "That night you got drunk and then mugged and I took you home way past midnight—wasn't that right after this case was filed with us? Oh my—was the cover-up already under way then?"

She delivered this dramatically, at the same time keeping watch on Kang out of the corner of her eye. The priority was to focus the discussion on *her* role in this case; only then could she deflect attention from Kang's terrible memory gaps.

Pastor Ch'oe spoke with an effort. "Not necessarily—perhaps they're just prodding us to see how we react. After all, you're still young and so is Mr. Kang, and the two of you knew each other in college. So they pick up on the fact that a man and a woman are involved and assume there's an affair—you can find that tunnel-vision breed everywhere, right? It might not be a bad idea for us to file a complaint that someone's circulating misinformation. The issue is . . . what happened in the past. . . ." Pastor Ch'oe was about to bring up Chang Myŏnghŭi and her suicide, but thought better of it.

Finally Kang spoke, his face wooden. "First of all . . . I'm going to leave the school and leave Mujin. I think that's the best way to prevent trouble for the children and all of you."

Sŏ's eyes met Pastor Ch'oe's. There was a brief silence.

"It's natural for you to feel that way," said the pastor. "This news is libelous and it's overblown. You and Chang Myŏnghŭi, after all, did have a love relationship, and there was only five years' difference in your ages. I think I understand how you feel, but you can't just run off. You have to explain to the children, I'm not sure how, and then you have to stand up to those people."

"That's right," said one of the staffers. "And our first step now is to get on the Internet and post a rebuttal. Please don't be overly concerned."

"A rebuttal?" said Kang, flaring in anger. "And what are you planning to say? That I was twenty-five and I was going around soul searching? That I was no longer teaching and she'd graduated and so I was free to do what I wanted with her? That I didn't know she was a minor and we slept together? That there were a couple more women I had relations with, we slept together, we went our separate ways, and they didn't kill themselves and they lived happily ever after? That it wasn't those women I married, that I live with my wife and a daughter named Saemi? That I've known Sŏ Yujin since we were in college and that we're merely friends, nothing for anyone to worry about—is that what you're going to say? That if I was ready to accuse the principal and those under him of repeated acts of sexual assault against those poor children for ten years or more, I should first have had a press conference to lay bare my life and my love affairs and my old flames, who should have said they had fond memories of Kang Inho and who definitely did not die or kill themselves and who should have lived happily ever after, but unfortunately . . . and I'm sorry about what happened—is that what you're going to say?"

Kang's eyes were bloodshot. Again Pastor Ch'oe seemed about to speak, and again he demurred.

"I'm sorry. But at this point how can I keep fighting? I'm thankful to all of you. But I'm not sure what more I can do . . . I'm sorry."

Kang left without saying anything further. Outside, dense fog draped the streets. Kang remained at the entrance to the building. Very gradually, he began to have trouble breathing. And then he was seized by an illusion that he couldn't breathe at all, and he clutched at his chest. Was this the last scene of his earthly life, his soul being sucked into a despair of utter blackness?

～

A note appeared in front of Sŏ. She looked up to see one of the women staffers.

"Hanŭl is sick. They've taken her to the emergency room!"

Focused on Kang's distress and on their next move, she didn't immediately grasp the situation.

Hanŭl—yes, Hanŭl. Sick—Hanŭl's sick!

She showed the message to Pastor Ch'oe and rose. Hanŭl had been well the past few months, hadn't come down sick, but now she was in the Mujin University Hospital emergency room—not good. Was it her heart? Medical science could treat but not cure her. Each new day she lived was a miracle.

Outside the office she turned on her phone. It had been off all day, what with her shuttling between the center and the courthouse. _Ding-dong._ She scrolled through the voice messages and finally heard her mother.

"She's all right—she's being looked at now in the emergency room. She had a really high fever and was going into

convulsions . . . but she's going to be all right. You don't have
to rush. But Mom does need to be here, the doctor said. You're
the one who has to make the important decisions."

Her mother sounded exhausted. She must have been past
the point of fear and confusion and had simply resigned
herself.

With the phone to her ear, Sŏ rushed toward the parking
lot. At the thought of her daughter, all color drained from her
face, she grimaced, and tears oozed from her eyes. In a way it
was laughable—at work, no matter how difficult a problem,
she never cried, but when her daughter was sick she wept more
often than not.

Arriving at her locked car, she could feel her own face
draining of color. Wiping the mist-covered window just
enough to see inside, she noticed her car keys in the ignition.
Off she ran to the street. As always, there were no taxis when
she needed them most. And traffic had slowed to a crawl
because of the fog. Her time in Mujin had told her that on
days such as this it was practically impossible to flag down a
cab. What if something happened to Hanŭl because she was
late getting to the hospital? And here she was, all alone on the
street, wiping her tears. Nobody else was out walking around
in the fog.

"Help me. For the love of God, help me."

She hadn't been inside a church for a couple dozen years,
and now her desperation over Hanŭl urged her to latch on to
any source of help.

Just then a pair of milky headlights pierced the mist, and
an old silver-colored sport-utility vehicle pulled up beside her.
The driver's-side window rolled down.

"Need a lift?" Sergeant Chang gestured with his chin for
Sŏ to get in. As she regarded him in surprise, he repeated the
gesture.

Sŏ quickly climbed in, even as she wondered what he was
doing here.

⌐

"What I don't get is, how can you be so calm and collected on the outside but always run around half cocked? You locked yourself out that time at the police station too, didn't you? How can an itty-bitty lady going around like a chicken without its head stand up to the movers and shakers here in Mujin?"

Instead of responding, Sŏ strapped on her seat belt and said, "Mujin University Hospital—please." And then, more cynically, "So, with the new administration the police are back to tailing people?"

Chang smirked. "Oh, let's go easy on the police—we're walking sticks for the public, after all. This here's my golden opportunity to serve the citizenry—and at my expense."

He operated the vehicle with the ease of someone who had been driving for most of his life. When a light turned red ahead of him, he turned right and detoured around it. But one of the red lights he didn't see, and he narrowly avoided hitting a car that had turned left in front of him.

He must have been the only one in Mujin speeding through the dense fog, Sŏ told herself.

Chang glanced at Sŏ and saw her clutching the handgrip. "Don't be alarmed—I've been driving twenty years without an accident. You should give me some credit—not everyone in Mujin can say that. When people ask me how I manage, this is what I say: even with fog, if you've experienced it long enough, you can *see* in it. To people who think the world always has to be clear and transparent, the fog's an obstacle. But if you've always thought of the world as something foggy, then the days that aren't foggy are a windfall. Now think about it— non-foggy days are actually in the minority, aren't they?"

Forward they went, Chang narrowly beating one red light after another.

"I can drive like this and still catch the lawbreakers, you know. The ones who pretend to be law-abiding but aren't—now that's a different story." Then, uneasy because of Sŏ's persistent silence, he added in a sheepish tone, "Actually I'm driving like this because I'm guessing there's an emergency—a sick daughter or something like that."

To Sŏ he sounded unexpectedly meek. For the first time she regarded him. "And how did you find that out?"

"In this neck of the woods old Chang Hamun knows everything there is to know about anyone who lives, breathes, and walks."

"I'm afraid I'm not that important in Mujin." Sŏ left it at that and returned her gaze to the street ahead.

Chang managed a look at her. "There's something I've always wanted to tell you: you should do what you have to but know when to stop. Do you know what you've gotten yourself into here? Who you've picked yourself a fight with, I mean. I've heard your father was the estimable Pastor Sŏ Kaptong, a legend during the Yushin regime. . . . I used to have a great deal of respect for him in high school. It was so long ago I don't remember all that much, but there was an article he wrote for a magazine called *A Grain of Wheat* about the battle between David and Goliath. I'm not sure I remember it correctly, but I think he said that if you keep hitting a rock with eggs, in the end the rock will break—something to that effect. I'm wondering if you have some strange notion about that battle. Everyone knows about it—it was the only battle of its kind after the creation of heaven and earth. Do you ever think about that?"

Sŏ listened, arms folded. Maybe it wasn't such a good idea after all, accepting a ride from Chang. But with this fog . . . "Listen," she finally burst out. "I'm fighting with liars. Children were hurt, and we filed charges against those who hurt them—that's it."

Sergeant Chang smirked again. "In that case you might just have to fight everyone in Mujin. Because everywhere you look they're lying and turning a blind eye to one another. A City

Council member and the brother-in-law of a builder; a Department of Licensing test site clerk and a hospital director's wife; the police chief and a room salon madam; a lonely missus and an obscure night-club singer; a married woman and a minister; a professor and a textbook publisher; the Bureau of Education and a cram school director—they all look the other way and lie, in the name of taking care of each other. It's not integrity or justice they want. And sometimes they'll give up some of their wealth, and that's fine with them. What they really want is for nothing to change. Just for once you close your eyes and everyone's happy. One or two people give in—the buzzword is "concession"—and all is quiet. But then you come barging in and stirring things up and wanting to make changes—and change is what they hate most."

"What do you want from me?" Sŏ asked, more politely than necessary but shooting him a look. "If you keep this up, I'm getting out."

"Please listen," said Chang. "Do you really think there's any justice to be salvaged from this trial? Do you know the saying 'deferential treatment for past service'? Hwang the attorney came down here in return for a promise of an office in Kangnam, Seoul, complete with all the fixtures. You can guess what a pile of money that involves, right? Unless he's an idiot and not the Genius of Mujin, do you think he doesn't know what those animals did to those deaf-mute kids? Come on! Oh, I'm sure Attorney Hwang did some soul searching, and then for the sake of social justice, for the sake of regional development—in other words, on behalf of the great cause of justice—he probably decided it was right to sacrifice a few deaf-mute kids. And what about the judge? Well, he along with the others went to the same university and took the bar exam together, and he's connected to somebody's wife's uncle and to somebody else's high school classmate's in-law, and he's the beloved mentor of somebody's son-in-law. Next, the prosecutor. He's only got six more months in Mujin, and his posting is over. If he lets this trial drag on and ends up rubbing someone the wrong way, that could ruin his plans to return to Seoul and rejoin the wife and children. These people, from the time they're born, all they hear is 'grades, grades, grades, competition, competition, competition,' and now here they are, and everyone else has been left behind. Two friends take an exam and the difference of a single point on their score decides who ends up a vagrant and who gets to be a judge or a prosecutor. Do you think these people, on account of a few handicapped kids, will restore justice and truth—whatever that means— and in the process publicly embarrass the wife's uncle, the college classmate's in-law, the son-in-law's beloved mentor, and the father-in-law's fellow alumnus? Do you really think they believe that a school principal and a disabled kid are on the same level when it comes to human rights?"

Sŏ regarded Chang with a look bordering on consternation. The sergeant for his part realized he had been talking a blue streak and fell silent. Then bit down on his lip in self-reproach.

"Are you . . . trying to give me some pointers?" Sŏ probed.

Chang toned down his approach. "Well, I guess that's how it sounded. I'm sorry if I crossed the line. I know this sounds strange, but you were born the same year as my youngest sister—she died a long time ago—and then I just recently found out your father was Pastor Sŏ Kaptong. . . ."

Sŏ had never expected this. What did it all mean?

"This business you're wrapped up in is so—how can I put it? There's an easy way, and yet you choose the hard path. It's just plain stupid. Stupid thoughts, stupid behavior—let me give you an example. If you join the police force, in a year and a half you've gotten all the stupidity out of your system. By the time you're twenty-something, stupidity should be done and gone. You get married, you have children, and your parents start breaking down—that's when you have to stop being stupid. But here you are, divorced, sick child, parents not doing well, and

you're doing _this_. . . . It's _crazy_. And you're not a man, you're a
woman!"

When there was no rejoinder, Chang continued. "Frankly,
I like women, and when I see a pretty one I get all weak in the
knees. But the only times I ever see women get involved with
criminal matters, it's because of a guy they fell for, nothing
else. I'm curious—you're not very pretty, so where do you get
the spunk to live the way you do? I stopped respecting women
in first grade—my family was poor then—because my teacher,
a woman, was always humiliating me and slapping me because
my mother couldn't afford to give her a 'gratuity.' And so I've
always wondered—I don't really know you, but you don't seem
all that interested in politics—why are you intent on changing
the world in such a juvenile way—"

"We're here," Sŏ interrupted when she saw Chang brake for
a red light. She looked down momentarily, then out at the fog
soup of the streets, before continuing, slowly and distinctly.
"Whatever thoughts I had about changing the world, I put
away when my father passed on. I'm fighting now so that _they_
won't change _me_."

꙰

Ripples slapped against the sides of the boats anchored in
the inlet that extended through the reed fields far into the
mainland. That sound was the only indication of the ocean's
presence. In the moonlight, everything before Kang was a vast
expanse of reeds. But beyond those reeds was the ocean, the
largest natural feature on the face of the earth.

Beside Kang, all by themselves, sat two empty soju bottles.
The evening breeze had turned chilly. It whooshed toward him
through the reeds, and every time it brushed the nape of his
neck, he could feel gooseflesh and other sensations coming
back to life. He found his pack of cigarettes, heard it crinkle in
his grasp. One left. He had smoked the rest—that was how long
he had been here.

Every once in a while, he had endured an experience like today in court, an experience that turns existence on its head the way a tidal wave stirs up the ocean floor. The past he thought he had forgotten was summoning him like a ghost, and no matter how drunk he became, and even if he passed out, he could still hear inside him, persistent until the end, someone posing questions to him. Every step along the way had left vivid, blood-red wounds, and those wounds, untreated, now produced a stench.

How was he going to face the teachers and the students the next day? In spite of the cold wind, he felt a fiery sensation starting from the soles of his feet, as if he had stepped onto hot asphalt. All day and all this evening, he had confronted the flickering image of a finger pointing him out as the teacher who had sexually assaulted his former student and driven her to her death. It was terrifying to think of having to face up to precocious Yŏndu and her parents, and to Minsu. And then there were the jagged, hostile eyes of Pak Kyŏngch'ŏl—just the thought of those eyes made Kang feel he was being minced. Enveloped in darkness, stickiness, dampness, he wanted to curl up tight and make himself as small as possible.

It remained only for him to go back to his apartment, pack his belongings, load them into his car, and take off. But once he had left, where would he go? If he went home, it would be with the baggage of his time in Mujin, and there would be arguments with his wife. And if he had to offer a clarification of his past, he might as well do it here in Mujin. But his attempts at vindication would be humiliating, and the facts would remain clear. He couldn't go forward and he couldn't go backward. Now that darkness had suffused him, why not walk out to sea, to a comfortable, eternal sleep? This whispered question had been tickling his ear for some time.

A day began to replay itself in his mind. Late spring, or was it early summer? Either way, the temperature had suddenly climbed, and it was very hot. He was in the army, and again the red alert order had come down and with it, the ban on outings day or night, on telephone calls, on any contact with the outside world. Myŏnghŭi had arrived to see him—she had failed the college entrance exam the previous year and was preparing to take it again—and Kang knew she was waiting for him. But what was demanding all his energy just then was the master sergeant who had been harassing him, and it was all Kang could do, from one day to the next, to suppress his urge to kill the man. As they marched along beneath the blazing sun, he debated with himself—*Kill the son of a bitch? No! Kill him? No!* The letter he received from Myŏnghŭi a few days later was depressing. Every day she was on the receiving end of blatant contempt from her parents for not getting into the school of her choice. Her older brother and older sister, both of whom had been admitted to elite universities, also disdained her. During her most recent clash with her parents, she had dropped a bombshell—she was giving up on college and would get married instead. And then to her dazed parents she released another thunderbolt: her husband would be her former teacher Kang Inho. Please, she wrote in her letter, could Kang meet her parents the next time he had leave? The question left him as stunned as her parents. How could he, a twenty-five-year-old infantryman, plan his future at that point in time? What's more, the prospect of fitting Myŏnghŭi into that future was too burdensome to consider. And so when she arrived the following weekend, he begged off seeing her on the pretext of illness. The following weekend she visited yet again. And again Kang did not go out to meet her. Her letters became more frequent—the sad, weighty letters of a would-be entrance-exam repeater. He didn't write back. Eventually, it was all he could do to give them a quick scan before he shredded them and threw them into the bathroom wastebasket. And then one day he received what would be his last letter from her. She had failed the college entrance exam a second time, but the tone of the letter was surprisingly reserved. Seizing on the opportunity presented by that reserve, he decided it was all right to forget about her, and his feelings of guilt lessened. After that he threw in an occasional prayer that she would find happiness. And that was that—or so he thought. When he was discharged, a fellow teacher from the girls' high school delivered the news: early that winter she had taken her own life.

A gust of wind raked his neck. He looked out into the murk, his empty pack of cigarettes crumpled in his hand. A form took shape in the darkness. Now that he was thinking about Myŏnghŭi, the face he saw was as young as those of his students now—maybe that was how he had looked at the time. That face, bordered by the cropped hair of a schoolgirl, rose slowly in the darkness, a face the size of a balloon. He observed that image, kept observing it. He put his lips together to utter her name, and at that instant an ache came over him, seized him, wrung him. And that's when he finally realized that ever since he'd heard the news of her death, the guilt feelings buried deep inside him were a huge, living growth. A long-lived, mold-colored growth that had settled among his innards, a growth named Chang Myŏnghŭi. That name now rose inside his abdomen, glancing against his rib cage, searing his throat, and finally issuing from his mouth: "Myŏnghŭi, I—I'm sorry, I'm so sorry."

↶

Sŏ was sitting on the steps outside Kang's apartment. She wore a beige trench coat, and the ends of her white scarf fluttered in the wind like a white flag signaling surrender. Seeing Kang approach, she rose to greet him.

"You all right?"

"Mmm" was all he said. He made for the entrance to his apartment.

"Hey. Inho, let's talk."

"I'm tired—how about later?" He came to a stop on the steps, sensing she was following him. "You want to be in a photo on the Internet with me?" There was no reply from her. He felt a sudden surge of anger. "So my wife can divorce me?" His voice burst out louder than he'd intended, loud enough to echo against the walls of the modest apartments, from which the paint had flaked off.

When she didn't answer, he finally looked back, and there she was two steps below, looking up at him. Her expression was a mix of dismay, disapproval, and sadness.

Sorry to have shouted, he reluctantly retraced his steps to the open area in front of the building. That area, too, had not escaped the fog's cool, damp breath.

They sat down on a bench. Overcome by the mist, the single streetlight shone only faintly, the lamp seeming to say, "Hey look, I'm a light too."

"My father was a grade school teacher," said Kang. "I wonder how much injustice he had to turn a blind eye to and how much pride he had to throw in the garbage in order to put me and my sister through college during the Park Chung Hee regime. And here comes Kang Inho to Mujin— for whatever table scraps he can gather and not because he's dedicated to teaching—and it's just his luck that out of the blue he's turning into a fighter. I guess my father was cowardly in his own way, but that's what made it possible for me to get through college and reach this point in my life without too much trouble. But your father, Pastor Sŏ, had a spotless reputation; he was upright, he was renowned, and you said that after he passed on, you had a hard time because you were so poor. I don't know—if it were only me, I could fight. But there's Saemi . . . and her happiness and good fortune are too big a price to pay for maintaining my fine and dandy standards of justice. I'm sure she'll see what's gone up on the Internet. As her dad, if I were to do like your father—"

Sŏ broke in, wanting to change the subject. "Right after you left I got a call from my mother that Hanŭl was in the emergency room, so I went to the university hospital." Her tone was resigned.

Kang had lit another cigarette. When he heard this news, his fretful expression hardened.

"Usually, if she goes to the hospital, she ends up spending three months there. Luckily, this time it was just a cold. She got a shot and took some medicine, and her fever went down. You know my mother—once burned, twice shy. So when I saw Hanŭl with an IV, I asked the doctor to hook my mother up too. Just now they were both sleeping, so I came here thinking dinner or something. I saw your lights were off and decided to wait."

"Good news about your daughter. But I'm really sorry—I just don't think I could handle dinner now. . . ."

She smirked. "I understand. It's the same with me." She stared off into space before continuing. "Inho—I heard that Yuri's grandmother signed the agreement."

Kang almost dropped his cigarette.

Sŏ silently watched the fog spreading and lifting, spreading and lifting in long, murky strands.

Images from Yuri's family's rustic shack passed before Kang's eyes—the vinyl-covered roof, the rank odor of someone long bedridden, the grandmother's rake-like hands . . .

"But we can't very well resent her for it."

Kang passed a hand wearily down his face.

"The prosecutor told us," Sŏ slowly added. "For better or for worse, Yuri is intellectually disabled, so the indictment stands even with the signed agreement, but that agreement will influence the verdict, so we should be prepared for the worst. I was going to make an issue of it—the children have been horribly ill-treated all this time, and now he'll go easy on those criminals just because of a signed agreement? But I didn't. The prosecutor didn't do anything wrong. He didn't ask anybody to

sign an agreement, and he didn't make the law that there's no
punishment if an agreement is signed. He's just doing his job."

She thought a moment, then smiled as if incredulous. "Isn't
it ridiculous? How did everything turn out like this? Doesn't
someone have to take responsibility for this crazy situation?
Sergeant Chang delayed the investigation just enough. Instead
of doing nothing, he dragged his feet and went about it
passively. Attorney Hwang, for once in his life, gets deferential
treatment—like all his classmates and fellow alumni, he cashes
in just this once. They say he was an excellent judge. Man of
integrity that he is, he didn't pocket or save much money, and
he opened his practice across from the Kangnam courthouse,
and the cost of _that_ is beyond the means of a former judge
of integrity. Instead of the perks of his position, he devoted
twenty years to his government, and he probably figured that
by now he was entitled to a bonus. And perhaps in addition
he wanted to protect the Yi brothers, who have been responsible for fifty years of public welfare in Mujin. Maybe he came
to the conclusion that here was an excellent opportunity to
work on behalf of Mujin—after all, it's the ancestral home. He
didn't want the long service of the Home of Benevolence to go
up in smoke, didn't want Mujin's upper class and its honor to
be tarnished. And it's probably the same with the gynecologist. Only she had more time to sort things out. Time to think
about the husbands of her classmates, the couples she runs into
at the Mujin Golf Club, the families of whom live nearby and
about whom she knows practically everything. How could she
shovel them all into a pit of disgrace just because of a dim-wit-
ted girl with a ruptured hymen? She never bothered to see for
herself where the rapes took place, she never had to rush to the
hospital with the bleeding girl. As for Pak Pohyŏn and Yun
Cha'ae, they actually liked the principal and the administrator, those men of such lofty character, and probably decided
the two gentlemen were being slandered. At least I'm trying to
think of it that way. But you know what's really preposterous?

The prosecutor is not the one who made the law that if the parents sign an agreement then the indictment is automatically nullified, and what's the judge supposed to do in a case where the prosecutor doesn't file charges? And here's where *you* made a mistake! You sexually assaulted your student—regardless of the actual truth of the matter—and drove her to her death. And you and I were often together in the same apartment late at night, so there's probable cause for adultery. This was a grave mistake. And so the only truth that comes to light in this case is that Kang Inho is in fact a bad guy."

She giggled. But not Kang.

"What I'm finding more and more difficult to understand is that there's no ideological issue here, nothing philosophical, just a messy case of sexual abuse. But why then are so many bright people jumping into the fray as if their life depended on it?"

"I misjudged the situation myself," Kang answered. "I thought it was obvious. I thought what we did made perfect sense. It seemed perfectly simple. . . . Who would have thought it would turn into a senseless battle?"

Sŏ still wore a wispy smile. "I've been thinking. . . . This is a fight I have to continue. Not in order to stand up to those people, but for the sake of Yŏndu, Yuri, and Minsu. And for Pada and Hanŭl and Saemi. And for all the babies I saw at the hospital, babies who have just come into the world and were sleeping so peacefully. And for my father—hmm, we've certainly made good use of my father today, haven't we? I want to make it clear that I never felt I was the object of pity because of my father, never felt it was my bad fortune to have the father I did. If you want to talk about poverty—well, in this corrupt world of ours even those who want to put on a good face can get fired, can fail in business, can go bankrupt because they co-signed on a bad loan. Or you can be born poor. Even if my father had preached that we should kiss up to those in authority, that's no guarantee that we wouldn't have ended up poor. And as for losing your father at an early age, that's been the fate of children always and everywhere. Fathers die from torture, from illness, in accidents, or by their own hand. Actually, my father's life and death made me realize why—in spite of the handicap of being poor and having just my mother, which after all is the situation of half the world's people—why I'm someone precious, someone that others can be proud of. Because of my father, I wasn't just some wretched girl raised by a single mother that everyone feels sorry for. And if I ever did feel pitiable or unfortunate, it was during the rare times I wanted to compromise myself, even though I knew I shouldn't."

Kang felt a gentle prickle run down his back. He could sense the many times she must have asked herself such questions, all the inner conflict she had experienced, all the long walks she had taken along the sea wall while coming to this conclusion.

"Hey, Kang, it's going to be hard, but let's give it a try! Let's take it all the way to the end! If the courts don't work, we can take to the streets, and there's always the press. We can't toss the kids back to those dogs. Sergeant Chang said, 'Do you think deaf kids have the same level of human rights as the judge, the prosecutor, the attorney, the family that runs the home?' He said there's no way we can win. How about that? All right, then. The judge and the prosecutor and the attorney may not think so, but as far as you and I are concerned, the rights of the Yi family and the rights of deaf children are the same. Not an ounce of difference. I'll fight for that."

She stuck out her hand. _You too?_

Kang regarded her intently, then reluctantly extended his own hand. Their handshake was firm.

Noticing his indecision, she grinned. "You know, at school you used to say I was always right, and you always felt you lacked confidence. Every once in a while, I really split a gut over that."

Finally, they were able to laugh together.

Kang passed a fitful night—not that he had expected otherwise. Sleep rarely came, and when it did it was accompanied by scraps of nightmares that, however faint, marched through his head before passing on. The next morning as he was shaving, he stopped and looked at himself in the mirror. His cheeks were more hollow, his skin more coarse, and he looked to have aged several years overnight. Again a voice told him, *Don't think about it, just get out of here.* He imagined the looks he would get from his fellow teachers and the students when he arrived at the home, and suddenly he began to feel numb, as if shot with a poisoned arrow.

His phone rang. Yŏndu's mother. Yuri was in a bad way, and it looked like she would need to be taken to the hospital. She herself didn't have a car, so she had gotten the head teacher's approval for Kang to take Yuri in his car. It was the same tone of voice Kang had come to expect from her. He wondered if she had heard about yesterday's hearing. Probably. No greeting, no commiseration about the hearing. Only "Since you're here, sir, our minds are resting easy," spoken in a gentle voice. The next instant Kang realized that this arrangement must have been made out of consideration for himself by Sŏ, Pastor Ch'oe, and the teachers who had signed the petition presented at the news conference.

After picking up Yŏndu's mother, Kang arrived at the dormitory. Yuri came hobbling out. He thought at first that something was wrong with her legs, but it turned out to be her vulva. After the shock she'd experienced in court, Yuri had weakened and fallen ill, and this most sensitive area had become inflamed and itchy. Yuri couldn't resist scratching at it, and eventually a festering sore the size of a small fist had developed, and the area had grown even more inflamed. For several days she had been treated with a cheap ointment at the nurse's station, but that, too, had aggravated her condition.

At the emergency room at the university hospital, Yuri's clothes were removed to reveal that her vulva was swollen and giving off a thick discharge—it was awful to look at. The sore wasn't large but would require surgery. Yuri would have to be admitted.

The procedure was simple and Yuri, crying in pain, was transferred to the recovery ward. She was given a painkiller, and before long it had taken effect and she was yawning. She hadn't slept for days and her eyes were sunken. Kang recalled what Minsu had told him about his brother Yŏngsu walking in discomfort after Pak Pohyŏn had assaulted him.

It must have hurt a lot. But you'll get better now, Kang signed to her.

As Kang tucked Yuri's quilt about her, she looked at him bashfully, tears still pooling in her eyes, and gave him a sheepish smile. In those oblong eyes he could see her grandmother. He quickly looked away, recalling what Sŏ had once said: "Maybe it's fortunate that Yuri's intellectually impaired." And now this girl who didn't know the meaning of "agreement" noticed Kang looking off into the distance and tapped at his sleeve. He turned back to her and she signed to him: _Teacher, don't get sick._

When Yuri saw that he didn't understand, she signed again. _Yŏndu and the other kids were up all night worrying about you. They said you might get real sick and so at a time like this we have to do what our teachers say and study real hard. Teacher, don't get sick. They told me that when I saw you today, I should tell you this._

And then she punctuated this statement by drawing a large heart in the air, over her forehead. The next moment he had gone to Yuri and taken her in his arms. Her tribulations in court and the sleepless nights because of the sore made her feel as light as a butterfly. The moment her body came in contact with his, Kang felt a tingle deep in his heart. He knew then how much he had come to love these children.

↜

Your imagination has a way of taking the fearful and building it into the absolutely terrifying. You know better and yet you end up deceiving yourself. And so when Kang arrived at the school the following morning, contrary to his expectations, no one reacted out of the ordinary.

In the teachers' room Pak Kyŏngch'ŏl and Yun Cha'ae looked at him with hostility, but this was nothing new. And then the teachers who had signed the petition at the press conference came up to him.

"You've been through a lot, Mr. Kang," said one of them. "Don't worry about those other matters. The children have been up all night dealing with the cyberbullying and the online trolls."

Kang checked his email. And sure enough, like a post office box full of letters, his inbox was flooded with emails written the previous night by his students.

10

Once again people thronged the plaza outside the Mujin
District Court. It was like a marketplace. There were television
cameras, reporters, citizens' groups, and a contingent from the
First Church of God's Glory. The weather couldn't have been
finer, a sparkling autumn day that was exactly what people
mean when they talk about autumn in Korea—the deep blue
sky, the merest chill to the breeze, the fresh, oxygen-laden air
ushered in from offshore. The paddies flanking the expressway
were golden with ripened stalks of rice, and deep beneath the
ground in the seaside reed fields, roots interlocked with roots
to keep the ocean at bay.

Inside the courthouse the judge seemed sufficiently aware
of the press presence, for he was trying to look austere but
ended up stiff instead. As he prepared to read the verdict, the
courtroom lapsed into utter silence.

"Considering that the defendants in their capacity as
educators sexually assaulted young students at an educational
facility for the hearing-impaired, the crimes are especially
vicious. Furthermore, the fact that they committed indecencies and sexual abuse, regarding the victims as objects of
sexual desire even though their role in society was to guide

and protect these disabled children, calls for severe punishment. But even while they have been found by this court to have inflicted scars on their students, we also take into consideration their great contribution to the society of this region, the fact that none of them has a criminal history, the fact that some of the guardians of the students who were sexually assaulted have petitioned this court not to punish the defendants in view of their having looked after the children, and finally the pleas of the two defendants, the sons of the Home of Benevolence founder, that it is their duty to keep vigil over their father, whose elderly infirmities have placed him at death's doorstep. And defendant Pak Pohyŏn is found by this court to have committed a series of sexual assaults on children in his capacity as a guidance counselor. I hereby sentence the defendants as follows: Yi Kangsŏk, two years six months' imprisonment—suspended—and three years' probation; Yi Kangbok, eight months' imprisonment—suspended—and two years' probation; Pak Pohyŏn, six months' imprisonment!"

The shouts started as soon as the interpreter had put the numbers into sign language.

"No criminal history?! Ten years of sexual assaults, dozens of victims, and all they get is probation?!"

The police tried to quell the commotion, but the spectators were not to be calmed. A mixture of shouts and hallelujahs filled the air, and before long the courtroom was out of control. The brothers Yi had detained Hwang and were shaking hands with him; both were smiling from ear to ear. Pak Pohyŏn, who alone among the defendants had been jailed while awaiting trial and who now would have to return to prison, stared vacantly into space.

Kang noticed Pak and the film of moisture on his ratlike eyes. Three men had committed crimes; only one was to be punished. Next to Pak, his government-appointed attorney, still looking half asleep and otherwise expressionless, packed his briefcase. As Kang left the courtroom, he heard Yŏndu's mother weeping. Outside, the First Church of God's Glory contingent sang a hymn. The sky was the color of blue steel.

∽

The next day, before he left for school, Kang found on his doorstep a letter informing him that he had been terminated or, more precisely, that his contract as a temporary teacher had been nullified. The grounds for dismissal were conduct detrimental to the good name of the Home of Benevolence Foundation and personal indecencies. Four other teachers who had stood by the students were terminated as well, and the teachers who were guilty of providing moral support received a pay cut. From that day on, the entrance to the school grounds was closed to the public, but outside it parent protests awaited the return of Yi Kangsŏk and Yi Kangbok. A detachment of police was posted there. And every day the fired teachers stood outside the gate. In the distance students could be seen peering through the windows at them.

Several days later, the lunch menu at the Home of Benevolence was to have been seaweed soup and eggs. But when the assistant cook went to the cold locker for the eggs, she found that the ten trays bought that morning had disappeared. At the very moment she was reporting this to the head chef, the drumming of footsteps could be heard from the hallway leading to the principal's office on the first floor. It was the recess after second period, but instead of going outside to the school playfield, some thirty students kicked open the door to the principal's office and entered. Yun Cha'ae happened to be sitting there.

"What are you kids doing here?" she shouted.

We won't accept a filthy person as our principal. Bring our respected teachers in from outside the gate. Apologize, Principal and Administrator, for calling us liars.

With a frosty look Yi Kangsŏk picked up his telephone and summoned the custodian. "Hey! Where the hell are you? These little bastards broke into my office. Either call the teachers or get the police in here—now! On top of everything else, I have to deal with these little shits? I go away for a few days and this school goes to hell."

Before he could speak further, one of the boys pushed the couch against the closed door, barricading it.

The principal blanched. "Cha'ae, get those kids out of here right now!" Fear tinged his voice.

Yun put the principal's words into sign language. The children stayed where they were, glaring at Yi Kangsŏk. Someone pounded on the door. The children advanced on the principal and Yun, one step at a time, their eyes seething with anger and rage. One of the boys signed to Yun. *Is this the table where you did Yuri?*

Yun hesitated, then interpreted for Yi Kangsŏk.

A boy who had witnessed the principal assaulting Yuri the day Yŏndu became involved started signing. *You told us that if we talked about what we saw, you'd make us pay for it.*

That's enough! Yun signed to the children.

One of the boys whipped around toward her. *You made the girls take Yŏndu to the laundry room, didn't you? And you tortured her there, didn't you?*

Another boy signed violently: *You said deaf people are born promiscuous?* And then he drew himself up in front of her.

Yun hesitated, then made a dash for the door, pushing aside the couch just enough to get her hand on the doorknob. The silence in the office was like a taut rope, and now that rope was severed; to the agitated boys, Yun's attempt to flee was the signal to attack. Out came the eggs and the flour. The students had gathered here to chastise Yi Kangsŏk, but the principal had managed to crawl out of harm's way beneath his desk and was temporarily forgotten—which left Yun the target of their egg-and-flour bombardment.

⌇

The thirty students were charged with assault. When a photo of egg-splattered Yun Cha'ae appeared in the *Mujin Daily,* public opinion, which until then had been sympathetic toward the children and the Action Committee, cooled drastically.

"What Next for Home of Benevolence?"
"Young Female Teacher with No Ties to
Incident Assaulted by Students"
"Citizens Lament: How Could They!"

The photo of the despoiled female teacher with her long disheveled hair was both shocking and provocative. That day the police had broken in the door to the principal's office, at which point Yun had run screaming to the shower room. After showering to clean herself, she went to the police station and calmly drafted a statement. The following day, for reasons unknown, she had herself admitted to the university hospital, where after an examination she was advised to remain for four weeks of treatment. In the words of the conservative press, "As a result of the attack by boys who were larger than she, her fragile body bore various contusions, there was a laceration near one of her eyes, and she has developed a phobia toward people—a lengthy recuperation is anticipated." The newspapers went on to report that "after the incident the students submitted a self-reflection statement, but the school authorities have stated that they will continue to investigate until it is known who is instigating the students, and from an educational standpoint they will show no leniency in an effort to restore the moral fiber of the Home of Benevolence."

The situation at the home entered a whirlwind phase. Parents pulled their children from the dormitory and would not allow them to attend the school. Those who could afford it transferred their son or daughter to a school in a different city. The four teachers who had been fired, together with students and their parents, put up a tent across from the Bureau of Education and demonstrated.

ESTABLISH A PUBLIC SCHOOL FOR THE DISABLED
REINSTATE TEACHERS FIRED WITHOUT CAUSE
WE CANNOT RETURN TO A SCHOOL THAT TAKES
BACK TEACHERS WHO SEXUALLY
ASSAULT THE STUDENTS

Predictably, the Bureau of Education refused to meet with them. In spite of everything, students gathered at the tent every morning. Those students whose homes were distant were for the time being fed and boarded at the church that Pastor Ch'oe had established.

A blackboard was put up inside the tent and classes were begun. Sex education was taught in first period, democracy in second period, and so on. The wind grew colder, but inside the tent, heated by the ardor of the teachers and students, it was cozy. The children smiled and laughed more than they had in the dormitory, and they shared their food down to the last instant noodle. Kang taught the children the poetry of Éluard, Prévert, and Paek Sŏk.

⌒

The afternoon that Kang's wife arrived, the mercury was forecast to plummet that night, with freezing temperatures at the higher elevations for the first time this season. Two months had passed since the day she had called him in hysterics, and since then she had avoided contact except for mundane matters such as figuring out where she had put her official seal—she had to get an impression of it certified—and reporting that for her father's seventieth birthday she was sending him on a trip instead of preparing a banquet.

Saemi was exhausted from the long ride, and Kang loaded her onto his back before climbing the steps to his apartment.

The girl was noticeably heavier. After a moment's hesitation, his wife brought up the rear.

And finally, they were sitting across from each other.

"It's been a while, dear. It looks like you don't stay here very often. It feels cold."

In fact Kang had been spending nights in the tent. Someone had to stay overnight, and often this task fell to him because he lived alone.

"I'm sorry, dear . . ." His voice trailed off as he prepared to light a cigarette. But then he remembered sleeping Saemi and put the cigarette back in his pocket.

"Are you really?" she asked.

He considered her question. "Yes, I'm sorry, dear. And to Saemi too . . . you must have had a hard time with all those rumors."

She didn't immediately reply. Their silence was like that of a couple who had divorced long ago.

"I have a distant relative—a third cousin or something, older than me, on my mother's side—and we've been close ever since we were young. He went to the US right after his military service, and it looks like he's made a big success of himself. He's back here for the first time in ten years, and I just saw him. He's opening a suitcase factory in China, and he'll need to incorporate it here in Korea."

She checked his reaction before speaking again, this time in the quiet but forceful tone of someone who has chosen her words carefully.

"In other words he needs a manager here in Korea. Someone with experience in China . . . He'd like to meet you. He's going back to the US in three days, and he has to make a decision by then. That doesn't give us much time, so I thought I would come down."

Kang looked down without replying.

While they were lying next to each other in bed, his phone vibrated. On the display was Sŏ's name. He sensed his wife had seen the name and had tensed up. He pushed the call-reject button. He was about to turn toward his wife when the phone buzzed again. And again it was Sŏ. In his irritation he wondered if there was an emergency, but then his wife's hand reached out and covered the phone. Her eyes pleaded with him, testing him, warning him that greater difficulties awaited them unless he accepted her plea. The phone buzzed yet again, and this time he turned it off. Only then did he sense a release of tension from her shoulders.

He turned on his side and cautiously rested a hand on her chest. To his surprise she didn't push it away. Her body was familiar and warm. As he mounted her he realized how much his own still youthful body had longed for her, and he sensed she felt the same. Afterward, they managed to wipe the perspiration from their foreheads and at the same time hold hands beneath the quilt.

"Let's go back to Seoul tomorrow. I heard about your firing and was wondering when you'd return. How come you haven't?"

She said this in a sleepy voice, as if this one act of lovemaking had returned them to the way they used to be.

He didn't answer. In the dark he could see, blinking on and off like the lamp of a lighthouse, the clear faces of Sŏ and Yŏndu and Yuri and Minsu.

"Promise me, hmm? In the name of Saemi, promise me, Inho, dear."

With a nasal moan she draped her bare arm around his neck. The fleshy arm passed across the stubble on his face, leaving the soporific scent of baby powder.

"All right. Let's get some sleep and tomorrow we'll revisit."

"No, promise me now. Or I won't go to sleep."

Her pouting reminded him of the way she was when they were dating. He felt like they had gone back in time, before his departure for Mujin. She released his neck, and to his surprise she laughed.

"I never dreamed you'd join the ranks of the activists. You never thought much of them—you said they were irresponsible toward their children."

"You must be tired. Why don't you get some sleep. I'm going to have a smoke." Giving her a peck on the forehead, he took his phone and went out on the balcony, her voice trailing behind him.

"You should quit smoking too. I know an herb doctor who uses acupuncture to help people quit."

He slid the balcony door shut and her high-pitched voice could no longer be heard. He lit a cigarette, and before he knew it he was looking out at Sǒ's apartment. The lights were off—where could she be? He drew deeply on his cigarette and turned on the phone. With a shudder it began vibrating, one message after another, the names coming up on the display— Sǒ, Pastor Ch'oe, the teachers they were working with. There was also a text message: _they're tearing down the tent school first thing in the morning. everybody gather. let's keep our tent school. please help._

He called Sǒ.

⤶

I always talked anxiously, said that a pipe dream is poison
And the world is like a book: once you know the ending you can't go back and change it.
That's right—I have a dream, I do, a dream I believe in. . . .

Listening to the song on her answer tone, he thought back to that night—to the young hooker, the mad hag, the grab-and-dash guy . . .

"Hey, Kang. Sorry to bother you when you're with your wife after all this time. But tomorrow's the twenty-eighth anniversary of the Mujin Democratic Uprising, and it looks like the tent's being taken down at daybreak, before the festivities get under way. And it's not the police that are doing it; they're using a demolition company. You know how mean those guys are, right? Everybody's coming back from home. And even though the teachers told the kids to stay away, they're saying they'll be here too, to help keep watch. But we're short on men. Kang, you ought to be here. And I have to confess, this is the first time for me. . . ."

In the background Kang heard the tent flapping in the wind. And the chattering of Sŏ's teeth. Through the balcony's glass door, he saw the faces of Saemi and his wife inside. Warm in there, cold where he was; bright there, dark here—two clearly divided worlds.

"I can't go just now, but I'll be there before daybreak. How come you're shivering like that? Don't be afraid. You're . . . brave, remember?"

"Oh? I didn't realize I was shivering," she said cheerfully. "That's strange, I've *always* been afraid. But the truth is, it's a cold night. Anyway, be sure to come."

"I will. I might be a little late. But count on me."

"That's right," she said with a short laugh. "He may be a little late but he always shows up—that's our Kang Inho!"

ϛ

My dear love,

I think this is the first letter I've ever written to you except that time I was in China on business when we were dating. Where to begin? Let's start with Mujin and the fog and a certain hope and another me that I discovered in the fog of Mujin.

When I arrived here I felt like a defeated beast—all the capital in that massive metropolis couldn't digest me, and I got thrown up by it. I was wandering around like a dog with its tail between its legs looking for scraps of food. But when these things happened to the children I was supposed to teach, I felt something awaken inside me. Call it a thirst for justice, or maybe divinity, or anything more noble. I discovered for the first time that I was making an effort for something that didn't involve money or pleasure, that actually involved pain. And in the process I tasted quite unexpectedly the joy of my entire being awakening to the fact that I was a human being, a person with dignity. This was a feeling I had never experienced, something unfamiliar and lofty, but there was more—I also learned that I as a human being had always had this within me, and I learned that I loved myself the most when I was fighting for my neighbors, fighting to be with them. And as a human being with dignity, I wanted to fight those who trampled on others with dignity who couldn't defend themselves. In the context of my life, there was nothing the least bit insignificant about this. And so I want to finish what I've started, not so much for someone else but for me. I think that if I could see the children studying in an environment where they would never again be abused, I could walk away with a lovely recollection of my ordeal.

My dear, I regret not telling you at the outset that this path I chose turned out to be the right one, not only for myself but for the three of us. I wonder if you would believe me if I said that I am doing this for Saemi's sake. I appreciate knowing about the opportunity involving China, but please tell your cousin I'm sorry.

If I left here now, I'd be just a disgusting creature that sexually assaulted his student, someone who washed up in Mujin, earned a few coppers, and managed to get himself fired without cause, another defeated beast slinking around looking for its next meal. Maybe I'd become someone who was defeated by capital that couldn't digest me and now by savagery. I think you'll understand this, but if I went back now, I would be forever miserable—even if I ended up making a fortune.

My dear, they're coming to take down the tent where the children had classes tonight. These children are barely healing from the abuse and the scars. By now they feel as dear to me as Saemi. Some of the teachers are there too. Those colleagues of mine suffered because they spoke up and said that what's not right is not right. And by now they feel as dear to me as you.

I might be gone when you wake up. When you and Saemi get back to Seoul, please be patient with me a little while longer. I won't be that long—I promise. I'll return to you and Saemi, a dad and a husband who can walk tall with gusto.

My dear, I was never a flag-bearing hero. Nor am I scum that just watches while dogs have their way with young, powerless children. Mujin has taught me that. I'm trusting in you to help me keep what's left of my pride. And I pray that you will trust in me.

Your loving husband

He folded the letter and placed it near his wife's pillow. He looked at Saemi's face, faintly illuminated by a streetlight beyond the balcony. When she was younger he'd thought she resembled him, but now there was no mistaking that she was starting to take on her mom's appearance.

"Aren't you coming to bed?" came his wife's sleepy voice.

"Yeah, but I have something to do first. Don't worry about me, and get yourself some sleep."

"Hold me, will you? I had a strange dream."

This was the way she had been before he had left for Mujin. He felt sorry for her, lifted the quilt, and lay down beside her. She buried herself in his chest and looped her arms around his neck. As he patted her back, the letter came into view, looming before him in the dark.

The wind was rattling the windows. It made him feel that the flapping of the tent he had heard while talking with Sŏ was coming instead from the letter. The wind picked up, and it felt colder as daybreak approached. _Do you really have to?_ a voice asked him. _Yes, I really have to,_ he answered. _Really? In spite of everything? Are you sure?_ came the voice again. _Yes, in spite of everything, I'm sure, I really have to_—this he could not answer. He closed his eyes.

↶

Dawn was like a dusky cape settling almost imperceptibly over the window. It looked cold.

His wife had just returned from the bathroom.

"What are they doing, calling through the night—don't they ever sleep? And who are they, anyway? Is this what they do in Mujin?"

She had good reason to sound vexed—the buzzing of the phone had wreaked havoc with her sleep.

Kang picked up the phone and checked the display—one "Sŏ Yujin" after another, her last call arriving at 5:15 a.m. He couldn't imagine what had happened there after that. The sky was clouded over, and the wind was still blowing fiercely, buffeting anything not solidly fixed in place. Autumn leaves not yet in full color had been stripped from the trees and were whirling aimlessly through the air. Kang heard a sign clatter to the ground. He retrieved the letter he had written, got up, and went out on the balcony. The wind was cold and blustery and, combined with the dampness, chilled him to the bone.

He managed to light a cigarette, then reread the letter. Finally, he ripped it up and threw it over the side of the balcony, the scraps of paper flying off into the void.

↶

The tent had been ripped apart, the blackboard smashed. The children had never seen a demolition team at work before. They were brushed aside by the club-wielding men, and five of them were taken into custody. Ch'oe Suhŭi, chief inspector of the Mujin Bureau of Education, was on her way to work when she passed by the site and saw the huge dump truck. She shook her head.

"Oh, I am so sick of those filthy, crude, low-class creatures."

↫

The twenty-eighth anniversary celebration of the Mujin Democratic Uprising was scheduled for 10 a.m. in the plaza outside City Hall. Sergeant Chang was anxious—he had received a report that the deaf, the parents of children at the Home of Benevolence, and various citizens' groups would assemble in the plaza at that time. The media would gather as well, television crews and all, and the prime minister was expected. It promised to be a large-scale event, and if something went wrong, Chang could bet that his next promotion wouldn't be to his advantage—and he certainly didn't want to end up on the new chief's shit list. The new chief was already ramming home his determination to clip every last link to corruption. Six months from now all of his pronouncements would be forgotten, but in the meantime Chang would have to step lightly.

↫

When it came time to pack his belongings, Kang was amazed at how much he had accumulated in the name of daily necessities. Into the trunk of his car went the quilt and the notebook computer, and while he was taking one last look around, he discovered a pink ribbon beneath his desk/dining table. It was the ribbon Yŏndu had tied around the envelope containing the letter she'd written him—the letter that began *To our teacher Kang Inho*—and Kang could almost hear coming from it the giggling of girls. The pair of tiny golden bells were still attached to it. He picked it up and took it to the wastebasket, but ended up putting it in his pocket. And there he stood.

❧

"Shall I drive?" asked his wife. "You don't look well."

Without a word he got into the passenger seat. His wife settled Saemi in the back seat, then climbed in and started the car.

"I guess you didn't get any sleep last night—no wonder you look tired. I'll be okay with the GPS, so no worries—why don't you take a nap? You must be feeling sorry you didn't say goodbye, but you can always come back sometime, right?"

"Sure," he said. And he closed his eyes.

❧

"Next, the prime minister will read a congratulatory message from the president. The president was hoping to attend, but he left yesterday for a tour of the US and cannot be with us. But he wants it known that words alone cannot do justice to the contribution that Mujin has made to democracy and the expansion of human rights in this land of ours. Ladies and gentlemen, please give a warm round of applause to the prime minister."

As the prime minister approached the podium, a gust of wind blew over one of the wreath stands nearby. Crimson petals flew off on the wind. In no time a second stand had collapsed. You might have heard murmurs spread through the crowd gathered in the plaza and the next moment, from a distance, the beat of drums. The drumbeats drew nearer. From the podium the prime minister gazed about his audience, who wouldn't have noticed the cold-induced goose bumps sprouting on his face.

"It is a great honor for me to be here in Mujin, our nation's mecca of democracy and cradle of human rights."

❧

The demonstrators advanced, beating on their drums. The majority were deaf, so there were few to take up the call when one of them chanted a slogan. It was a strangely quiet demonstration.

WE WANT TO GO BACK TO OUR SCHOOL! read a placard.

A PRINCIPAL GUILTY OF SEXUAL ASSAULT CANNOT BE ENTRUSTED WITH CHILDREN! read another.

From a hill that commanded a view of the streets, Sergeant Chang, radio in hand, barked out instructions to the policemen posted on the sidewalks.

"Don't let them near the plaza. Drive them toward the Bureau of Education intersection instead. Make sure you do that, and if a few of them get banged up, then too bad! If they get within range of the TV cameras, we're done for."

It was more blustery now. The drumbeat continued. Chang's gaze went back to the demonstrators, and he searched for Sŏ. It was difficult to make her out because of her short stature, but sure enough there she was in the front row of marchers, at the far end, coming toward him. She kept looking about, trying to find someone. And every once in a while, she seemed to be looking behind her as well. *Don't tell me another bunch are on the way,* Chang muttered to himself, tsk-tsking. Then he felt the sting of icy raindrops on his head and cheeks. *Hallelujah, heaven's on our side.* Chang smiled. He saw Sŏ stumble. He could visualize her facial features, the tight lips and the impenetrable expression. He hoped she wouldn't be among the "banged-up" ones. With this thought he put the radio to his lips again.

"All right, ready with the water cannon. Three . . . two . . . one . . . fire!"

⌒

The rain started as they were heading up into the hills outside Mujin, and when they arrived at the pass, it was coming down so hard they couldn't see in front of them. Kang looked back down along the winding road and saw clouds covering the city.

The day he arrived here, he had seen a milky sea of fog. Today it was a dark gray sea of clouds.

"Oh my gosh, look at this rain!" said his wife.

The windshield wipers were on high. Kang's head rested limply in the crook of his elbow, which was wedged against the rain-streaked passenger window. A sign appeared indistinctly through the rain. The lettering on the navy-blue background was whiter than fog: "You Are Now Leaving Mujin—Have a Safe Journey." Kang put his hands over his face and kept them there.

↫

Dear Inho,

How have you been? I just realized it's been six months since you left. When I went to look for you later on, the auntie next door told me you had left in a hurry that morning. Afterwards I called several times but never got through, and finally I got a message saying your number was no longer in service. So I thought I'd try email. I hope you're doing well.

Yesterday I went to Yŏndu's father's funeral. He went peacefully, holding hands with Yŏndu and her mother. He was comforting them, saying he had no worries, that they were surrounded by good people. He was a really fine man. His burial mound looks out onto the water from Mujin, and you should have seen all the people there. Afterwards we all had a meal, and Yŏndu started talking about you. Yuri still cries whenever your name comes up. Actually all of us there, and not just the girls, were thinking about you—the only one who was absent. None of us can understand why you left Mujin that morning without saying anything, but we know it must have been very difficult for you. Whether you had to leave because you were getting threats or whether it was something else unavoidable, you must have had it tougher than we did. For someone with your character to say you'd come and then not come must have been really difficult.

In case you're wondering, here's what's going on with us. That day I was arrested for obstruction of traffic and illegal encampment. But I ended up with a good judge, not a dyed-in-the-wool conservative. I was guilty as charged, but since I didn't stand to benefit personally from what I'd done, I only had to pay a million-and-a-half-won fine. I guess I got a stiffer sentence than the Yi brothers—they didn't have to pay a copper. Anyway, I got to thinking that all the judges in Mujin were lenient, but then the children's appeal was turned down—and the agreements signed by Yuri's and Minsu's families were a key point. As for the charges against the thirty students who attacked Yun Cha'ae—that's still dragging on. She says she'll never forgive them—she absolutely won't. So I guess our battle still hasn't ended.

The children don't go to the school anymore. For one thing, Pak Pohyŏn got his job back, if you can believe that. The parents and Pastor Ch'oe thought long and hard and finally asked Yŏndu's mother to take in six of the girls. So they've transferred to a nearby school. One piece of good news—that repulsive Ch'oe Suhŭi has been transferred, and the new chief inspector has approved a special-education classroom for one of the mainstream middle schools. So Yŏndu's home is now a dormitory for the girls—we call it the Holdŏ.

Holdŏ—it's not an English word. It's short for "alone we stand, together we live" in Korean. Those are the two hopes that Pastor Ch'oe has for the children there. Yŏndu's mother was hard put to make ends meet after her husband came down sick, and now she says she likes raising those poor girls and feeding them and earning some money in the process. As for the boys, do you remember the interpreter? Well, he's in charge of them now. Some benefactors stepped forward, and now there's a Holdŏ for the boys too—eight of them live there, including Minsu. We worried so much about housing for the children, but because of what happened to them at the home, all the good people of Mujin have become their supporters. It looks like there are a lot more good people in the world than I thought.

Yuri is a lot better now. She's being treated by a psychologist. And not just Yuri. There's Minsu—now hold on to your hat when you hear this—Minsu has grown _six_ inches in the past six months. A good dinner every night can do that. And it's amazing how the children's minds and hearts have grown too. They now realize how precious they are, and now they can say no to violence. I had dinner with them once, and I asked them what they felt was their biggest change since those things happened. Here's what Minsu had to say:

We know now that we're as important as anyone else.

I want to tell you, I almost cried when I heard that. When I see the children growing up so proudly I get to thinking, did we really lose out at the trial?

This evening in Mujin the fog is coming in as I write. The fog—it's never going to end—making all the lights hazy, making people shut their doors and lower their curtains. I wonder what else will happen within that milky cloud when it gets between people and cuts them off from each other. There's only one thing that penetrates the fog—sound. Pastor Ch'oe is always asking the children to pray for people who have ears but can't hear. Our ears long to hear from you. You're not feeling sorry for us, are you? We only had a short time together, but we remember the devotion and love you showed us then. Even if you've forgotten us, we'll always miss you. Take care, and I wish you happiness from the bottom of my heart.

↩

Kang looked out the window. Between this building and the next was a park filled with office workers taking advantage of the lunch hour. The sun shone strong, the tree leaves drew solar energy, and a fountain continuously shot out a fat stream of water. The brilliant May sunshine symbolized to Kang all the fervent desires of this city. The people were in groups and already were looking for shady spots. A mass of lonely people all by themselves and yet lonely together. Until the end, they'd never be alone and yet never be together.

Most had removed their jackets in the heat, and a sea of white dress shirts stood out against the emerald-green grass. *You're not feeling sorry for us, are you?* He could almost hear Sŏ's voice. *Our ears long to hear from you.* The mass of white shirts on the grass became a hazy, swelling, mottled blur.

Almost like fog.

Afterword

In the autumn of 2019, we enjoyed a forty-five-day residency
at the T'oji Cultural Center, just outside the city of Wŏnju,
Kangwŏn Province. One day during lunch with the other
writers, we saw on display in the cafeteria a copy of a Korean
magazine devoted to artistic production by the disabled. We
were struck by this discovery, for in present-day Korea, disability
tends to carry no less of a stigma than elsewhere in the world.

This discovery served to remind us of Gong Ji-young's
Togani, a novel we had translated almost a decade earlier in
which hearing-impaired children figure prominently. We were
attracted to this novel for a variety of reasons. First, we had
been introduced to this author's works in the 1990s when we
translated one of her most accomplished short stories, "Ingan
e taehan yeŭi," under the title "Human Decency." Moreover,
we have a long-standing interest in translating trauma literature, and in *Togani* we saw trauma as an agent of death among
a particularly vulnerable population—disabled children. We
also had personal connections to the subject matter. Ju-Chan
Fulton holds a graduate degree in special education and
worked for a time with the disabled, and Bruce Fulton taught
at a Korean middle school in Chŏlla Province, where the novel

is set, as a US Peace Corps volunteer in 1978. And as a university professor, he has worked with disabled students.

Togani is notable for showcasing the author's growth as a writer. Early in her career, she focused on student activism and the labor movement, both of which were suppressed by the dictatorial Chun Doo Hwan regime of the 1980s. In subsequent decades she broadened her vision to include gender equality and human rights. As she mentioned in a 2011 interview with us, "I think about ways in which my writing could have more meaning in society."[1] In the case of *Togani,* she was drawn to media reports of investigations launched in 2005 focusing on the Inhwa School, a facility for hearing-impaired students established in 1961 in the city of Kwangju, South Chŏlla Province. The investigations uncovered a history of abuse of the children dating back to the 1960s.[2] Gong skillfully embedded this outrage in a novel of manners in which the upper crust of a provincial city comes together to deflect attention from the perpetrators of the abuse. Virtually unprecedented in contemporary Korean literary fiction are the lengthy courtroom scenes in which the guilt of the perpetrators is established through sign-language testimony by the hearing-impaired victims of the abuse—notably, that of teenager Kim Yŏndu. The narrative also contains a strong epistolary element that strengthens Yŏndu's emergence as the true hero of the novel: she is first responder to her classmates who have been sexually assaulted and a medium between the hearing-impaired children and a society that by and large regards them as an alien presence.

We have retained *Togani,* the title of Gong Ji-young's novel, as the title of the translation. The primary meaning of *togani*

---

1. Bruce and Ju-Chan Fulton and Soohyun Chang, "Interview with Gong Jiyoung," in "Writer in Focus: Gong Jiyoung," *Azalea* 4 (2011): 71.

2. See "Gwangju Inhwa School," Wikipedia, accessed January 2, 2022, https://en.wikipedia.org/wiki/Gwangju_Inhwa_School.

is "melting pot" or "crucible," and the author has acknowledged Arthur Miller's 1953 play *The Crucible,* which involves
the trials of purported witches in Massachusetts Bay Colony in
the 1690s. A related though more colloquial meaning of *togani*
is "feverish excitement," and it is in this sense that the term is
mentioned several times in the novel.

We gratefully acknowledge a generous translation grant
from the Korea Literature Translation Institute (now known
as the Literature Translation Institute, Korea). Bruce Fulton
wishes to thank the students in his Modern Korean Novel
seminar course in fall 2020 at the University of British
Columbia for their responses to the translation, which we
incorporated in our proposal to the University of Hawaiʻi
Press. Finally, at a time when publishing houses both small and
commercial have adopted a "maybe they'll go away if we don't
answer them" approach to writers and translators not represented by an agent, we wish to thank our editor, Stephanie
Chun, for helping to secure acceptance from the UH Press
Editorial Board of a translation that languished on the desks
of the author's two agents for a decade. We wish to emphasize
that as always it is we who brought our proposal for the translation to the publisher.

About the Author and Translators

Gong Ji-young *is a household name in Korea and in communities abroad, respected for her dedication to gender equality and human rights. Born in Seoul, she graduated from Yonsei University with a degree in English literature. Her first published works were poems, but she has since published numerous novels and story collections as well as a collection of essays.*

Bruce *and* **Ju-Chan Fulton** *are the translators of numerous volumes of modern Korean fiction. Their translations of Korean short fiction have appeared in journals such as the* Massachusetts Review, Granta, Ploughshares, *and* Asymptote. *Bruce Fulton is the inaugural occupant of the Young-Bin Min Chair in Korean Literature and Literary Translation, Department of Asian Studies, University of British Columbia; the recipient of a 2018 Manhae Grand Prize in Literature; and the editor of* The Penguin Book of Korean Short Stories.

Printed in the United States
by Baker & Taylor Publisher Services